PENDRAGON CYCLE, BOOK ONE

PENDRAGON'S HEIR

LORI BOND

CBAY Books
Dallas, Texas

Pendragon's Heir
Pendragon Cycle #1

Copyright © 2019 by Madeline Smoot

Book Cover Design : www.KimG-Design.com
Stock images : Bigstock.com
Individual Image Credits:
Coin: mirzamlk/Bigstock.com
Dragon: dean zangirolami/Bigstock.com
Frame: valex113/Bigstock.com
Effect 1: sakkmesterke/Bigstock.com
Effect 2: art_of_sun/Bigstock.com

For more information, write:
CBAY Books
PO Box 670296
Dallas, TX 75367

Children's Brains are Yummy Books
Dallas, Texas
www.cbaybooks.blog

Paperback ISBN: 978-1-944821-60-9
ebook ISBN: 978-1-944821-61-6

Printed in the United States of America

For CPSIA information, go to cbaybooks.blog/cpsia

For Tricia and Jessica, who always believed in this book.

CONTENTS

WHERE I'M PLAGUED BY VISIONS OF A GLORIOUS PAST

THE FIRST IMAGE POPPED INTO MY HEAD IN THE MIDDLE OF SECOND PERIOD trig. One minute I was staring at the sine wave I'd just graphed on my tablet, and the next minute I was staring at a coat of arms painted onto the breastplate of a medieval knight.

I blinked twice, but the image stayed in my mind's eye, superimposed over my graph. It was like trying to focus on two things at once. Ms. Terrie droned on about the various trig functions and the graphs they produce in relation to a unit circle. At the same time, I just as clearly saw an intricate green shield topped with a gold crown and emblazoned with three gold dragons. The two dragons at the top faced each other as if about to fight while the third dragon on the bottom wrapped around a tower. It wasn't like any coat of arms I'd ever seen before, but then again, I wasn't exactly an expert on heraldry.

I took a deep breath. This wasn't the first time a picture had popped into my head and refused to go away. For three years now—ever since I was thirteen—random images would appear, rattling around in my mind, sometimes for days. Before now, the image had always sort of grown in clarity over time, but today, the image appeared complete and vibrant, overlaying the everyday world.

I reached down and snuck out my sketchbook and a pencil. For the rest of class, I alternated between graphing the various functions on my tablet and sketching out the knight and his coat of arms. My drawings didn't make the picture in my head go away, but it made the knight seem less urgent, less immediate. I tried to be discrete, but I sat in the second row. It wasn't a huge shock I got caught. It also might have had something to do with the colored pencils I pulled out ten minutes before class ended.

"Miss Taylor, a word," said Ms. Terrie at the end of class.

I didn't sigh because I had learned last month when Ms. Terrie had caught me texting that sighing only made things much, much worse. Instead, I colored in the last golden dragon then paused for a moment to compose myself. I grabbed my tablet, notebook, and backpack and headed for the front of the room. A couple of girls sent me sympathetic grins, but none of them were close enough friends to wait for me.

The next few minutes passed with me taking an impromptu, verbal quiz on the lesson for the day. Ms. Terrie's next class meandered in, taking their seats, but no one interrupted my little trigonometric moment of doom. When the bell buzzed for third period, Ms. Terrie finally stopped.

"Well, you appear to have learned the material despite your distraction." She waved a hand at my sketchbook still open to my completed drawing. "Next time though, promise me you'll save your little artistic endeavors for a more suitable time and place."

I nodded, but I didn't promise. If I'd learned anything in the past three years, it was that pictures would grow in my mind whether or not I wanted them.

I took the late pass Ms. Terrie handed me and scurried out of the room to my next class. At least in junior AP English, I sat in the back. My teacher barely nodded as I slunk into the room holding up the late pass. Last week we had finished reading *Pygmalion*, and now we were watching *My Fair Lady* in honor of the original play.

I crammed my sketchbook and colored pencils in my bag, glad to be done with today's intrusive image. Already it had started to fade from my mind's eye. I never got more than one image a month, and I figured if I was lucky I might even go six weeks or more before the next. I slid down in my seat, trying to find a comfortable position to watch Eliza and the Professor sing about the rain in Spain. Then another image slammed into my head blocking out the entire classroom.

I shot up in my seat, kicking the chair in front of me. This picture was even more vibrant than the last one. After a second, my vision cleared enough that I noticed the kids on either side of me were giving me weird looks.

"Elaine, you okay?" asked Jared. He half turned and glanced at me out of the corner of his eye. Then he turned all the way around and stared.

"Yeah," I muttered, reaching down to pull my sketchbook

back out. I'd never seen an image so well-defined before. It wasn't just like I was looking at a still from a movie. Instead, it was almost like I was standing in a frozen scene.

"Seriously, if you're about to projectile vomit or something, I don't want it to be on me."

I rolled my eyes. "I'm fine."

"You don't look it. What's with your eyes?"

I didn't know what he meant, but I didn't get to ask.

"Ms. Taylor, Mr. Alexandrov, do you have something you would like to share?" called the teacher from the front of the room. Apparently, he'd stopped staring at his phone long enough to notice we weren't fully engaged in the movie.

I shook my head and ducked down over my notebook. Jared turned back to the front. Once our teacher had gone back to his phone, I started drawing the latest image. I drew the same medieval knight; only this time, he stood in a more majestic pose with his arms straight out in front of him as if he planned on holding back an entire army with the strength of his arms alone. There was something odd about his armor now that I was paying proper attention to more than just the coat of arms on his chest. There were little ridges up and down his arms that I was sure weren't part of a normal suit of armor. It was like little things were sticking up out of the suit.

It wasn't just the bumps that were a little odd. His silver armor almost sparkled in the sun in places instead of being a dullish gray. The cut was also almost modern somehow, like someone had decided to wear medieval armor but make it out of high-tech material instead of iron or steel. However, just as I was no expert on coats of arms, I was also no expert on suits of armor. The guy's helmet looked properly medieval with its little slits on the face and feather plumes on the top. I also couldn't picture a modern knight wearing a big purple cape that streamed in the wind behind him. In fact, there was only one modern knight I even knew of, the eccentric gazillionaire superhero Pendragon in New York. That guy had built a half dozen robot knights or something and ran around saving people from rogue robots and stopping train derailments. I wasn't drawing Pendragon though. In the video that trended all over the Internet last year when he fought the Horned Menace, Pendragon's armor looked nothing like my picture. His armor was gold and bulkier with a clunky crown perched atop the helmet.

Behind the first knight, I drew two more knights. Their armor was made from the same material as the first knight, but they didn't have the coat of arms or the silly cape. The two other knights had drawn the strangest looking longswords. Even though the static image in my head was silent, I could almost hear the energy sizzling off the swords' sharp edges. The swords glowed too as if made from a cross between a piece of metal and some kind of energy weapon. My imagination was so weird. I did a rough sketch, and just as suddenly as it had appeared, the image faded from my mind.

Class ended, and I grabbed my stuff. I'd almost made it to the door, when the classroom flat out disappeared. One minute I was walking past desks and students, and the next I was about to slam into the knight with the stupid cape and the outstretched arms. Behind him three knights guarded some kind of tower with a girl standing behind a crenellation at the top. I froze, shocked at how real all of it looked, like I had stepped into a photograph. For the first time I understood how Alice felt when she fell down the rabbit hole. I tried to back away from the knight, but I only managed to trip on my own feet. I stumbled into someone behind me.

"God, Elaine," Jared muttered behind my back. He grabbed my elbow, saving me from falling flat on my butt. "What is with you today?"

Maybe it was the fall or Jared catching me, but I sort of snapped back into the classroom. I still saw the knights, and the tower, and the medieval damsel in distress, but I could also see Jared peering at my eyes.

"Thanks," I said. It sounded more like a squeak than my actual voice. Normally, I wasn't this awkward, but not being able to see the real world was messing with more than my mind.

Jared shook his head, but he let me go when he realized I wasn't going to drop to the floor in front of him. "You should think about going to the nurse," he said, passing me to get to the door. He glanced at me one last time. "At least have someone look at your eyes."

I didn't bother to answer since I was losing the classroom again to the image in my mind. I tried to go to my locker, but I slammed into someone else on the way.

"Watch it," the person said, but I couldn't tell who was speaking. I saw a kid with a knight's helm instead of a face.

"Sorry," I mumbled. I ducked out a side door and made my way, almost by touch, to my car.

As soon as I'd gotten in the front seat, the picture faded down to a more manageable level. The knights, tower, and girl still beckoned to be drawn, but I also saw the parking lot through my windshield. I waited a few more minutes, but the image didn't flare up again. It seemed to have settled down into an annoying, but more familiar, level of strange.

I fished my phone back out of my bag and called home.

My mom picked up her phone after the first ring. "Hi, kiddo. What's going on?"

"I'm skipping chemistry lab," I said, not bothering to mess with polite conversation.

"Sorry?" said Mom in that no-nonsense voice that meant she wasn't going to like the next thing I had to say.

"I'm not going to my next class," I said again. I shuddered just imagining the chaos that might happen if I lost the real world while mixing chemicals during an experiment. Although I was pretty sure they didn't let us work with combustibles, I'd seen too many movies where kids blew up their schools on accident because of a stupid mistake

"I think of myself as a tolerant parent," said Mom.

"I think I'm tolerant too," said Dad in the background. Clearly, I was on speakerphone.

"But there had better be an excellent reason your butt isn't in class."

"You know how I get those pictures in my head?"

"Ah, yes, your artistic inspiration?"

I snorted.

"Did the muse strike?" Dad asked.

"Like a tractor-trailer." I rubbed my forehead as if the movement would erase the picture from my head. It didn't work. "Only this was more than just an idea for a drawing or even like those normal times where a picture kind of resolves in my head. One minute I was in class, and then, bam, the whole place disappears, and I'm in a photograph. I couldn't see school at all."

"That does sound weird," Mom said. "Do you need one of us to come pick you up? Only we're both in the middle of important projects." Mom's voice trailed off.

I stared out at the parked cars in front of me as if one of them understood my mother's obsession with scrapbooking. Her photo albums were works of art, but it was never-ending annoying when they took precedence over everything else, including me. "Yes, well, it would be a tragedy if you had to leave while the glue was still wet."

"The glue," Mom said as if she was already half-distracted by whatever project she was working on. "Can't let the glue dry."

"The audit I'm working on is fascinating," Dad called from his side of the room. Dad was an accountant who worked from home. Our house wasn't big enough for my parents to have separate spaces, so my Mom had set up her elaborate scrapbooking station on the other side of his office. "You can help me with this audit if you're up to it when you get home," Dad added. "I can come pick you up, and then we can tabulate the debits."

8

"I will never be up to helping with an audit." Math was just fine, but I did not see the beauty of a balance sheet the way my dad did.

"Do you think you'll be able to draw it out?" Mom asked.

I nodded, glad one of my parents had remembered why I called. Then I realized she couldn't see me over the phone. "I'll try."

"It can't hurt." Mom was a firm believer in using art to expunge the images. It had been her idea three years ago for me to start art classes. "I'll see if your father has any ideas about this," she added.

I waited for Dad to say something, seeing as he was sitting right there and all, but the silence stretched out until it became uncomfortable. I realized this would be one of those talk-about-Elaine-and-tell-her-later-what-we-discussed kind of conversations.

"Okay, then," I said. "I'll sketch this picture out and see what happens."

"You know you can call us anytime if you need us," Dad said.

"I know."

"If you're lucky," Mom added, "you'll be able to get back into school by your next class."

I tried not to snort. Today was feeling anything but lucky.

WHERE I FIND MYSELF ILL PREPARED FOR REAL LIFE

"ELAINE? ELAINE TAYLOR?"

I turned around, wondering who would yell out my name in the school parking lot in the middle of the day. A cute guy a couple of years older than me dressed in an impeccable gray suit walked toward me across the parking lot. Even though the guy looked like someone had brought to life a Renaissance masterpiece of some pagan deity, "stranger danger" ran through my head. How did this guy know my name? I kind of wished I was still sitting in my car where I'd have a nice steel door and some shatter resistant glass between us, but the car had gotten hotter than the latest designer after having a new look trot down the red carpet. I had abandoned it a half hour ago to sit on a curb a couple of spots down.

This guy looked okay—well, better than okay—like an underwear model had stepped off a billboard and into real life. Still, I'd seen enough reruns of every police TV show every network ever made for me to know that a sociopath could have the face of an angel.

The guy saw me, and he was headed my way. "You're Elaine Taylor, right?" he asked.

I stood up, but I didn't answer. I hadn't decided if I would talk to him or run for the school or what, when he screamed, "Get down!" He pulled out a gun.

I froze. I'd never in my entire life had a gun pointed at me. Other than my dad's hunting rifle, I wasn't even sure I'd ever seen a gun in real life before.

"Elaine, get down," the guy yelled again.

I realized the guy wasn't pointing the gun at me, but something behind me. I started to turn my head to look, but before my head turned even a quarter, something slammed into my back, knocking me face first into the ground. For a second, I thought I'd been shot, but it didn't hurt the way I had always imagined a gunshot would. In fact, it felt like something big, and maybe metallic, had shoved me from behind. I gasped until I caught my breath, and then I rolled over. I instantly wished I had stayed on my face.

My initial instinct was that I must have hit my head, and hit it hard, when I fell to the ground. There was no way the chaos around me was anything other than a massive hallucination. My boring innocuous school's parking lot had erupted into a war zone. Huge metal knights in actual shining armor fought with some sort of advanced tactical SWAT team. These weren't medieval knights though. These were technological robotic marvels shooting lasers from tiny guns in their arms and using rockets and bullets along with their swords.

I smiled at my amazing imagination when one of the robot

hallucinations landed in front of me, blocking a SWAT guy headed my way. This had to be a dream because the knight wore a purple cape very similar to the one I had been drawing on my knight all morning. The cape looked silly in my drawing, but it looked ridiculous in real life. When I woke up from this weird concussion-induced dream, I'd have to ditch the cape from my drawing.

A robot hand slammed into the window of the car to my right, raining glass all over the ground and me. It was that weird safety glass, so I didn't get hurt, but the glass falling on my face acted like a jump start for the dead battery that was my brain. For the first time since I'd fallen, my shock-addled mind finally decided to process the battle raging around me. I realized that this wasn't a dream, a hallucination, or some other trick of my overactive imagination. There were actual bullets flying and real rockets exploding all around me. That robot knight being forced back by the advancing SWAT guys would step on me and crush me any minute now if I didn't move.

I hurled myself back onto my stomach and scrambled under the nearest car. It was a tall off-road pickup with oversized tires. I crouched behind the nearest tire and hoped the rubber would shield me from the bullets being sprayed all over the entire area by the SWAT team.

Curling into a little ball with my eyes tightly closed, I kind of half-hoped everything would go away, but of course it didn't. I needed to formulate a plan, one that hopefully ended up with me unhurt. Something heavy slammed into the truck, rocking it back and forth. I shrieked and shut my eyes even tighter. Unhurt seemed unrealistic; I settled on alive. I needed to figure out how to get out of this alive.

Shutting my eyes hadn't shut out the battle. Bullets hitting cars, concrete, and metal knights make a lot of noise, and every few seconds there would be another explosion as each side blew stuff up. There was a louder explosion from somewhere off to the right. The car rocked again, and I squeezed myself into a tighter ball with my arms up over my head and around my ears. The smell of rubber burning and something like burnt bacon filled my nose, and I gagged. There were no pigs at my school. The only meat within miles of this parking lot was human.

I couldn't focus with robot knights and SWAT teams doing their best to kill each other. I told myself over and over to think, to focus on getting away. Unfortunately, I had nothing. Much to my surprise, I was not all that great under pressure when that pressure threatened my life. Apparently, high stakes academic testing had not prepared me for this kind of situation. Neither had reading two or three biographies of superheroes or the passages in history textbooks describing famous battles between good and evil. Now, when despite all odds I somehow found myself in the middle of the kind of epic battle that the networks would broadcast about for weeks, all I wanted was to crawl away using the cars as shields. It was a fine, if cowardly, plan—except for the part where not a single voluntary muscle in my body moved. For the first time, I understood what people meant when they talked about being paralyzed by fear.

"Elaine!" a voice called again. It hit me that someone had

been screaming my name over the din of battle for some time. I cracked one eye open a micrometer. The cute guy in the suit had crawled under the car with me. His impeccable clothes were covered in dirt, and the guy's dark curls were disheveled in a manner I would have found irresistible had I not been about to die.

"Are you okay? Are you hurt?" the guy asked me.

I shook my head although I wasn't sure which question I answered. Maybe I wasn't hurt yet, but I was not even sort of okay.

"I need backup now!" the guy yelled into thin air. "Ten minutes isn't good enough. We're pinned under an attack with a firefight all around us."

I didn't know who the guy was trying to talk to, but even with my half-paralyzed brain, I assumed he was some kind of agent. He looked kind of young for FBI, but most of what I knew about them came from streaming old *X-Files* episodes.

"We have to get her out of here," the guy yelled.

I hoped he meant me, but I didn't get a chance to ask. The huge pickup above us seemed to lift into the air. The knight with the cape held it for just a moment before tossing it at an armored vehicle trying to pull into our row of the parking lot. The vehicle didn't explode, but it swerved and plowed into six or seven cars before knocking over a light pole.

"I'll be seeing to her safety," said the knight. He reached down and picked me up as if I was a rag doll.

"No!" cute guy yelled, but the knight ignored him. "Sir Kai, protect," he said, and then the knight tossed me up into the air.

For the first time since the guy in the gray suit had pulled out his gun, I started to scream, long and loud. The knight had tossed me higher than I would have thought a metal robot could throw an average-sized girl. I seemed to soar above the battle with the entire scene spread out before me. The battle was concentrated on our section of the parking lot, but smaller battles raged all over campus. Even the ducks were not spared when a knight tossed a SWAT guy into their pond.

I reached the apex of the throw and hurtled back down to Earth. I had not appreciated just how high the thing had thrown me until I started plummeting to the ground. In any other situation, one that didn't end with me splatting like a cracked egg on the pavement, I would have swooned at the panoramic view. The artist in me loved how at this height the details seemed to fill in as I fell. Unfortunately, it didn't seem like I was going to live long enough to ever draw again.

I had just enough time to find it ironic that I was going to die from falling onto the top of a burning SUV and not from the firefight raging below me when bits of metal flew at me from every angle encasing my entire body in a thick metal covering. Once again I'd been wrong. Being wrapped in a thick pitch-dark coffin while plummeting to the ground was the thing that really scared me. For a second I wondered if I had passed out, the darkness and fear were so complete.

Even though I couldn't see a thing, I felt myself falling. I tried to ball my fists up and bang on the walls, but I wasn't in a box like I had thought. Instead, I'd been encased in a metal suit with individual arms, legs, even fingers. None of my muscles worked.

Before I disintegrated into a ball of hopeless panic, a digitized voice said into the void, "Initializing." Screens appeared around my head, covered in readouts that, although in English, meant nothing to me. Somehow, I had gotten encased in one of the suits of armor. An image appeared like a window in the armor's helmet. I could see and, when the audio came online, hear the chaos. I watched the ground race toward my face at an alarming rate.

"Ground proximity warning," said the electronic voice. "Initializing flight now."

Rockets I hadn't realized were on my back ignited. The suit banked and avoided slamming me face first into the concrete parking lot. We took off to the left until my suit and I landed next to the knight with the cape.

"Percival," popped a new voice into my helmet. It was clearer than the rest of the other noises, so I guessed that it was being broadcast direct to my helmet and not being filtered in from outside. "You and Kai get her out of here," said the new voice. It was vaguely familiar but not someone I could place. "I'm sending Red Knight and G1 and G2 as escorts."

"Yes, my lord," said the electronic voice, Percival. With no action on my part, my right arm popped up to the side and shot a laser beam at a SWAT guy, slicing his gun in half. This didn't bother the guy, but it freaked me out. The guy reached into a holster, pulled out a pistol, and shot bullets at my armor I didn't feel.

"Right away, my lord," continued Percival. The rockets on my back ignited again, and I shot into the air. Three other knights flew off in a tight circle around me. As things exploded in the air beside us, the three knights dropped back to use their various weapons against the people shooting at us. My suit, though, shot straight up until the battle raging below was nothing more than a distant pinprick. Even my school looked like a small square on a suburban checkerboard.

I had thought we would stop once we were clear, but my suit banked and zoomed away from the battle, my school, my neighborhood, my parents, and my home.

"Uh, Percival, right?" I asked the suit.

"Yes, miss."

"Um, where are we going?"

"Home," said Percival.

After all that had happened, I didn't quite have the courage to ask whose home.

WHERE I'M KIDNAPPED
FOR MY"OWN GOOD"

A FLIGHT THAT WOULD HAVE TAKEN FOUR TO SIX HOURS ON A COMMERCIAL jet only took forty-five minutes when strapped into a knight-shaped tin can. Forty-five minutes, though, is a long time when you're freaked out and your mind is working overtime. It turned out I didn't have the chatty kind of semi-autonomous flying battle armor. Percival ignored me and my questions for the entire flight.

Once the threat of imminent death disappeared, my brain re-booted, and I had a pretty good idea whose medieval armor I was wearing and where we might be headed. There was only one guy weird, rich, and brilliant enough to have built himself a battalion of medieval robot knights.

As we flew over Manhattan and our destination loomed into sight, I realized I had guessed right. Although technically named Keep Tower, the tabloids and most people called it the Rook since it looked like an eighty-five story chess piece. Built by bazillionaire Arthur Keep, it was rumored to be the base of his superhero alter ego, Pendragon, and his army of knights.

Percival flew me down toward a giant parapet that ran around the building about fifteen stories from the top. Unlike a normal skyscraper with its never-ending panes of glass, the Rook had been faced with stone rumored to be two feet thick. Last year some magazine had named Keep Tower number one on its list of the "7 Wonders of the Modern World." I'd never seen the building in person before, but it was living up to the hype.

We landed on the parapet, which was decked out like the ultimate roof-top garden. A swimming pool that resembled a moat ran along the inner wall, and I had to wait for a drawbridge, an actual drawbridge, to lower. I tried to hang back, to make my armor turn around and fly me back home, but I had no more effect here on the knight than I had back at school. Like some sort of puppet, the Percival armor marched me over the drawbridge, under a portcullis I assumed was for show, and into a medieval great hall.

My armor stopped in the center and stuck my arms out to my side. The armor once again disintegrated and reformed in front of me. Without a word, a wave, or any kind of acknowledgment, it marched off through a door to the left. It actually marched.

"Thanks, Percival," I called out just as it passed through the Gothic arch. I wanted to sound sarcastic since Percival had ignored my begging pleas to take me home, but the armor had saved my life. I sounded grateful. Tired and on the border of hysterics, but grateful. "Thanks, Percival," I said again in a quieter voice, more for me than for the knight that had already left the room.

"Kai," said a voice from my right.

I jumped and whirled around. A lovely woman in an evening

gown stood in another Gothic doorway I hadn't even noticed. My hand grabbed at my heart, but it wasn't like I could reach in my chest to slow it down. "What?" was all I got out.

"Kai," said the woman. "That particular knight was Sir Kai."

"But, someone—Pendragon?—he talked to a Percival, and Percival talked back."

The woman nodded and walked over. "Percival is my baby, my holy grail. I built him from scratch when Arthur first got the idea for his knights, but Percival is only the AI that controls all the knights. You were riding in Sir Kai."

"Okay," I said, not sure how to respond.

"I'm Ginny," said the woman. She moved as if to hug me, but then in the middle of the hug seemed to change her mind. She extended her hand.

I took it and shook. Ginny looked unimpressed with my weak grip, but I had just escaped a firefight, flown halfway across the country, and now stood in front of one of the three smartest people in the world. I felt I'd earned the right to be overwhelmed. "Ginny," I repeated. "You're Ginny, the model turned tech mogul, CEO of Keep Consolidated, Arthur Keep's ..." Here I trailed off. There were so many different accounts online on what Ginny was. My mind jumped around trying to figure out how to finish the sentence.

"Wife," Ginny said for me. "But most people don't realize we're married." She gave me an odd look though, like I should have been one of those few.

My eyes shot open, but I managed to keep my jaw from dropping on the floor. None of the rumors ever had them married.

Clearly, they were in some kind of relationship since they lived together, but they were so private, no one had suspected they'd gotten married at some point. "Do you have any idea why I'm here?" I asked instead of commenting on what had to be the biggest gossip of the decade.

"No, Pendragon dashed out of here with no explanation, but I'm sure Arthur will tell us when he gets back." She waved her hand, and a screen appeared out of nowhere in the middle of the air. A little dot flew over midtown headed straight toward the big circle labeled "Rook."

"Can I call my parents then?" Or a news crew or the police, I added in my head.

"I'm not sure that's a good idea, all things considered," Ginny began, but I interrupted her.

"Have I been kidnapped or something?" I asked. "Because it's not like my parents can pay any kind of ransom."

Ginny turned to me, confusion etched in every line of her face.

"Not kidnapped," said a voice behind us. "Rescued."

I whirled around in time to catch Pendragon's landing. It was the one he always did for the TV cameras where he slammed into the ground his giant sword brandished as if he was about to slay a dragon. Behind him two more knights landed just as hard holding spears and shields like some sort of royal honor guard.

"Arthur!" shrieked Ginny from behind me. "How many times do I have to tell you not to ruin the floor?"

The Pendragon armor slunk off Arthur Keep in a myriad of

different large chunks, the chain mail dragging on the floor, and I got my first real look at my rescuer. Pendragon didn't have a secret identity like a lot of superheroes like the Red Ranger and the Defender. Everyone knew Arthur Keep controlled the armored knight even if most people weren't sure if he physically rode in him or not. It was kind of hard to miss the knights flying out of his various homes. Arthur Keep, though, was almost as much of a recluse as the people who hid behind masks. He did go to some Society and charity events with Ginny, and he sometimes showed his face at his family company, Keep Consolidated, where he had some sort of position besides owning most of it.

But nearly every picture I'd ever seen of the man was of him on the red carpet standing in the background while the paparazzi took pictures of Ginny and asked her questions about her clothes. Ginny might have built and sold Face-to-Face, the pivotal software that brought video conferencing to the twenty-first century, and she might have been headhunted from Face-to-Face to now run Keep Consolidated, a huge multi-national, but at those events she was still the supermodel so famous that even now that she was a big executive, people called her by a single name. I had no idea what her last name even was.

Whenever I had looked at those pictures online, I'd been too busy drooling over Ginny's designer fashions to pay much attention to her bored bland-looking husband in the understated suit holding her purse in the background. Now Arthur seemed to fill the room with a presence he didn't possess in public. It wasn't kingly exactly, but there was something noble about him despite his clothes. I had expected Arthur Keep to be well-dressed. I didn't think he'd wear a suit while flying around in armor, but I had at least expected him to be stylish, not look like a beach tourist had wandered from the pool and somehow gotten lost in a Manhattan medieval castle.

Arthur was a head taller than Ginny even though she was model statuesque, and that meant his Hawaiian shirt seemed to go on for acres. Turtles twining around pineapples are never a good look, but they did nothing for his cargo pants with the half-closed pockets and tools sticking out every opening. Arthur didn't even wear normal cargo pants, which I might have been able to get over, but the kind that had zippers at the knees so the pants could be turned into shorts. Arthur was one of the richest men in the world, but apparently, he couldn't afford separate pants *and* shorts.

I was disappointed despite the way Arthur's smile at me seemed to brighten the room. Superheroes were supposed to be larger than life, not real people with gray hairs and some wrinkles—and not just in his clothes—and eyes exactly the same boring color as mine. Maybe it was from having watched too many unrealistic TV shows, but I felt like the hero that had saved me from a firefight at my school shouldn't have been squinting at me like he might need glasses.

A piece of armor knocked against the floor, drawing my attention away from staring at Arthur Keep's face. The armor flew itself out the door Sir Kai had marched through. I wouldn't have thought it possible for flying disassembled robotic pieces of armor to appear abashed, but somehow this group did as if it could feel the glare Ginny directed at it. The honor guard stayed behind in the hall, turning as if guarding the front door we'd all flown in through.

"I apologize for the rough landing, my lady," said Percival from speakers that had to be hidden in the walls. Other than the floating computer screens, nothing in the great hall would have looked out of place in a British stronghold during the ninth century. "We took the final banking turn too steep."

"Oh, I'm aware this isn't your fault," Ginny said. She marched right past me and stuck a finger into Arthur's sheepish face. "You were showing off for Elaine."

Arthur kissed her finger and then dodged around her accusing hand to kiss her cheek. Pulling her arm into his, he steered her away from the fractured marble floor now crisscrossed with a virtual spider web of fissures. "It's barely cracked," said Arthur. He grabbed my arm and pulled me with them. "Has Ginny given you the tour yet?" he asked me. He bounced on his toes, his clear enthusiasm almost catching. If I hadn't still been shell-shocked from being flown half-way across the country, I might have started getting excited too.

When I shook my head, he said, "Well, come along." He propelled me through the door, but I stopped in shock at the threshold. The room had huge cathedral ceilings at least three stories high and a giant illuminated stained glass rose window on what I was sure was an interior wall. The furnishings were modern and comfortable and yet somehow matched the medieval architecture.

Ahead of me, Arthur interrupted Ginny's continued scolding

to ask why she was so dressed up.

"My cousin's wedding reception," said Ginny. "We need to leave in an hour."

"Didn't we go to her wedding last year? In India?"

"Yes, of course, but tonight is the New York reception for all their friends in town. Remember they decided to have one after all?" Ginny's eyes narrowed. "Do not tell me you forgot. I have it marked on every calendar, and Percival has been reminding you every day for the past week."

"Oh, sweets," said Arthur in a miserable tone that did not match the ecstatic expression on his face. "I can't go anymore." He waved his hand and more of the mid-air screens appeared in front of him. "I have to stay home and try to figure out why the Dreki and LANCE are so interested in Elaine. Such a shame. You know how much I love going out."

Ginny ignored Arthur's blatant lie and turned to me. "The timing is terrible. I am sorry." She made a weak wave with both her hands like she was trying to craft an apology out of thin air. "Normally, we wouldn't abandon you the second you arrive, but Arthur hasn't been seen in public in three months, and he's been scheduled to attend this event nearly as long."

Arthur gave an offended grunt. "I have no idea what you're talking about. Everyone just saw me today. There were at least two helicopter news crews covering the battle at Elaine's school."

Ginny let out a deep breath as if she was suppressing a sigh. "Everyone saw Pendragon today, not Arthur Keep, President of Keep Consolidated's Board of Trustees. The markets get nervous when you don't show your face for months on end. The stock dipped today." Ginny turned back to me. "Otherwise, we would never leave you alone after dealing with LANCE and a traumatic Dreki attack."

"Who?" I asked.

"LANCE and the Dreki. Keep up, Princess," Arthur said. He snapped his fingers at me.

I hurried over to them not sure if he was referring to the conversation or the tour.

"They're the people I rescued you from," said Arthur.

"She didn't need rescuing from me."

We all turned to face the new voice. Another knight stood in the doorway from the great hall. The visor on the knight's helmet flew up, revealing the hot guy from my school parking lot. "I'm grateful for the help though," he said. "I'm not sure how much longer I would have made it out there on my own with no backup."

"Oh, you survived," said Arthur in a flat voice. He turned back to his screens. "Percival, get my armor off the Baby LANCE before he somehow steals some of my tech for Stormfield. LANCE has been trying to steal my knights since the day I got the first prototype working," Arthur said to me.

The guy frowned as his armored spit him out the front with a small stumble.

"Lance? Baby Lance?" I asked since I still didn't understand what was going on.

"L-A-N-C-E," said the guy, righting himself. "It stands for Limited All Nations Cooperative Exchange. I'm an agent in the

26

organization. My name is Will Redding, but Arthur over there is, sadly, nearly fifty, and he can't remember my name even though we've met once before."

"I remember people's names," said Arthur. "It's minor underlings I can't be bothered with. I remember Stormfield's name just fine."

"He's the head of LANCE."

"Not a minor underling," said Arthur. "Why are you here?"

Ginny tapped the elegant diamond watch on her wrist. "Forty-five minutes until we leave," she reminded him. "And I assume Will is here because he somehow stowed away in one of your suits of armor during the firefight."

Arthur shook his head. "It's impossible to stow away. I had Pellinor pick him up before a stray Dreki bullet found a new home in his head. But, Pellinor should have dropped Baby LANCE off at the nearest LANCE depot, not bring him home like a lost puppy. Percival, explain."

"Master Redding is persuasive," Percival said.

Ginny and Arthur shared a bemused glance.

"He must be to convince an AI to countermand a direct instruction," murmured Ginny. She pulled up her own mid-air screen and began fiddling with some lines of code. "I don't have time to run a full diagnostic."

"Why were you being so persuasive?" Arthur asked Will.

"Because she's here," said Will, pointing at me. "LANCE ordered me to bring her in."

"Bring me in? Where? Why?" I asked. "I don't want to go with

27

you." I took a step back away from the whole ridiculous group. "I don't want to be here at all." Superheroes and secret organizations were all fine and good on *TMZ*, but they were a little much to handle in real life. "I want to be home with my nice normal parents."

Arthur snorted, but he didn't tell me he'd take me home.

"It's for your protection," said Will instead. He tried to move toward me, but for every step forward he took, I moved another step back.

"Protection from what?" I asked.

"The Dreki," said Will. "You saw what they can do. We're lucky no one at your school got hurt."

"The Dreki?" I repeated. My voice seemed to sink into itself. "The terrorist group? The one with your arch, archnemesis?" I asked Arthur, stumbling on the last couple of words. I had never been in the company of people important enough to have an actual archnemesis. I sank down onto the sofa I had backed up against.

"Yes," said Arthur. Turning to Will he added, "What do Vortigern and the Dreki want with Elaine?"

"Arthur," said Ginny, "Your tux is on our bed. Figure this out now. If you don't want the stock to tank, the company to go under, and your ability to afford expensive knights to disappear, I suggest you wrap this up."

All of us ignored her.

"This morning, we received a tip that Elaine might be a clairvoyant," said Will. He sat down next to me on the couch, close enough that our knees almost touched. My heart began to race again from the proximity of a hot guy, and I focused on it as a way to delay processing what I'd just heard.

Arthur's eyebrows shot up his head. "Clairvoyant? Impressive. But, I'm a little unclear on why you would think that."

"Clairvoyant?" I asked. "You think I'm a psychic?" I slid down the couch away from Will now convinced that his delicious outer shell hid a crunchy center chock full of delusions.

"More like a Seer or Prophet," said Will.

"If it helps, I don't think you're psychic," said Arthur to me.

"That does not help." I turned to Will. "Why on Earth would you think something like that?"

"LANCE systems flagged a text from one of Elaine's classmates commenting on her eyes," Will said, not looking at me or anyone else in the room. "After accessing the camera on her tablet, LANCE obtained an image of Elaine confirming that her eyes appeared to show the telltale fogged over aspect of a clairvoyant. LANCE sent me to evaluate Elaine for potential recruitment to the Institute."

Arthur's frown had grown during this explanation.

"My eyes?" I asked, but no one explained.

"He's telling the truth," said Ginny. She made a swiping motion and the mid-air screen flew in front of Arthur. "I've found the internal paper trail. All of this mess started with a text from a teen named Jared Alexandrov."

"You're hacked into LANCE?" The disbelief in Will's voice made Ginny smile.

"Everyone needs a hobby," she said.

"There has to be some kind of mistake," I said. Jared had kept mentioning something about my eyes, but there was no way I was a Seer. Psychic powers ran in families, everyone knew that. It was one of the first things studied back when scientists discovered genetics. My family was so boring it made normal seem exciting. My dad was an accountant, and my mom was a stay at home scrapbooking obsessed mom. There were no psychic powers hanging out in our family tree. "There's no way I'm a Seer."

Everyone ignored me.

"Fine. Your creepy surveillance told you Elaine might be clairvoyant, but that doesn't explain why the Dreki showed up. How did they find out she's a Seer if you only suspected it this morning? They almost beat you to her."

"We must have a leak," said Will, with a frown. "I have already notified Controller Stormfield of the possibility."

"Well, you had to do something during your ride here," said Arthur.

I started to laugh even though not a single minute since I'd met Will had been remotely funny. "Hate to tell you this, but you are so wrong about the Seer thing. I didn't see any of this coming." I waved my hands frantically at Will, Arthur, Ginny, and the ridiculous modern medieval castle towering over the midtown Manhattan skyline.

"That's not entirely true," said Will. "I think you left something behind this afternoon." He reached into his jacket's pocket and pulled out a page from my sketch pad. He sat it on the coffee table where Ginny and Arthur who hovered on the other side could see. Someone had stepped on my drawing with a dirty boot print, but the sketch was still visible. It was the drawing I'd been working on in the parking lot, the image that had blinded me walking out of class.

"Did you draw yourself guarded by Pendragon and the knights, Elaine?" asked Ginny in a quiet voice.

My eyes opened wide, and my body sagged. Will reached over to give my arm a comforting pat. Normally, a brief touch from a guy that good looking would have sent me into a fit of giggles, but nothing about this situation was normal.

The princess in my picture might have been me although I hadn't thought it was when I drew the image. The castle though, most definitely looked like the drawbridge to the Rook, and the first knight guarding it wore the armor, distinctive cape, plume, and dragon coat of arms that Pendragon had worn today. The two knights behind him looked similar to the knights now standing guard in the other room. It was eerie.

"That doesn't mean anything," I said, but even to my ears, I didn't sound convincing. "I'm sure I saw something about Pendragon online or something. It's just my subconscious messing with my imagination."

Ginny shook her head. "You couldn't have seen this online." She pointed to the knight with the coat of arms. "Today was the first time Pendragon has ever worn that ensemble. We only finished the armor yesterday."

"I'd lose the cape," I muttered, staring at the drawing.

31

"That settles it then," said Arthur, ignoring me. He dropped onto the sofa between Will and me. He rubbed at his eyes like he was getting a headache. I knew how he felt. When he pulled his hand down, he smiled. "Elaine stays here under the protection of Pendragon and the Knights of the Round Table. She's a powerful Seer that predicted it."

I stared at Arthur and Will in horror. Will stared at my picture for another moment before nodding. "Considering this and the possible leak at LANCE, that's probably for the best for now. I must clear it with Controller Stormfield though, and if she is a Seer, Stormfield will want her at the Institute."

"Over my dead body," said Arthur. "She stays here with us. Now, Princess," Arthur said turning to me as if Will had ceased to exist for him, "where should we put you?"

"But, but, but, my parents, my home ..." I tried to say. I didn't manage to do much more than sputter incoherent nonsense. I turned to Ginny hoping for some support or at least a voice of reason. Surely, she didn't want a perfect stranger staying in her home.

Instead, she gave me a wry grin and cocked an eyebrow. "Welcome home," she said. "Arthur," her eyes narrowed. "Go change. We leave for my cousin's wedding reception in thirty minutes."

WHERE I MAKE A POOR ATTEMPT TO ESCAPE MY IVORY TOWER

"**WHY AM I STILL A PRISONER HERE?**" I STORMED INTO THE BREAKFAST room and threw myself down in my seat.

Arthur pretended not to hear. He could do that because the table in the "small" breakfast room seated sixteen.

"It's been two full days since you kidnapped me," I said. I waved away the robot servant trying to serve me a heaping bowl of cereal. "Why am I still here?"

Arthur looked up from his three tablets. "Because the Dreki is still trying to kill you or capture you. I'm not sure which."

"Lovely." I glared at my spoon. "I still don't see why I'm here with you. Why can't I be in witness protection or whatever with Mom and Dad?"

"We've been through this before. Every day in fact," said Arthur. "Your mom and dad are safe, and they think you'll be safest here," he reminded me.

I wanted to argue, to point out that this still didn't explain why Arthur wouldn't let me call home. Instead, I didn't answer. I had decided to go for sullen teen this morning. It beat rehashing the same old argument.

"But I have a new theory."

I looked up at that.

"I think Vortigern is less interested in your psychic capabilities and instead is enamored with you. Clearly he must have met you at some point, and your winsome manners and subtle charm dazzled him."

"Bite me," I said.

"Ah, there's that dazzling wit now," said Arthur with his most beguiling smile.

It took all of my self-control not to throw my glass of orange juice in his face.

"And what are your plans today, Princess?" asked Arthur.

"What do you think?" With my fork, I traced a rough outline of a flying fortress onto the tablecloth. The image had been plaguing me since yesterday morning. I had around a dozen drawings taped up in my room showing the thing from every angle. Ginny and I agreed it was probably some sort of vision, but we didn't know what it meant.

"I think you'll be staying here," said Arthur with a smile. "Do you want to join me in the explosives lab this morning? I'm trying out a new trigger mechanism for my smart bomblets."

"I hope it blows up in your face," I muttered.

"What?"

"I hope your time isn't a waste," I said louder. "I think I'll pass."

"Prefer to sulk in your room?"

"Something like that." Actually, there wasn't much to do except sulk in my room. I hadn't been able to get on the Internet, not even to stream movies. The Keeps didn't have normal things like TVs or even something as old-fashioned as an MP3 player. Everything was holographic screens run by Percival. And Percival had very strict instructions about keeping me offline.

"Well, whatever you do, just be careful this afternoon. I have to attend a meeting over at LANCE with the Red Ranger, and Ginny won't be back from LA until dinner. Do you think you'll be fine?"

"I'm sixteen, not six. I don't need a babysitter." I glanced up, but the expression on Arthur's face kept me from saying anything else snarky. He looked genuinely concerned. He wasn't doing his big puppy dog innocent face I had learned to distrust. His forehead was wrinkled into deep grooves, and for once, he acted like a guy nearing fifty instead of the thirty-something he pretended to be.

"I'll be fine," I said, looking down at the tablecloth. I couldn't meet his gaze anymore.

"Good," said Arthur. "I'll leave most of the Knights here. Percival will watch the defenses, so you should be safe."

I glanced back up, but Arthur had gone back to the usual carefree part he always seemed to be playing—even in his own home where there wasn't an audience to appreciate the effect.

HE WAS STILL IN THE SAME MOOD WHEN HE CAME TO SAY GOODBYE just after lunch.

"Elaine?" he said.

35

I looked up from the drawing I had been working on. "What?"

Arthur looked amused. "I've been calling your name for at least ten minutes. That must be some picture."

"I think it's a vision, but I'm not sure." Waving at all the pictures I had taped to the wall, I added, "I can't seem to get this out of my head."

Arthur frowned and stared at my eyes for a moment, something he and Ginny had been doing a lot these last couple of days. I wasn't sure what they were looking for, but as far as I could tell my eyes had done nothing interesting. Whatever Jared had seen in class hadn't happened again. With a small shake of his head, Arthur moved closer to get a better look at my drawings.

I realized that Arthur had never been in my room. The Keeps might be keeping me a prisoner for my protection, but they hadn't been obtrusive about it. For the first time, it occurred to me how much worse this all could be.

"Do you mind if I take a few of these with me to LANCE?" Arthur pointed to a few of the pictures, the ones that showed the flying fortress thing from a couple of different angles.

I shrugged. "Sure." I handed him the drawing I had been working on. This one showed a control room of sorts with lots of buttons and gadgets and stuff I couldn't name. "Maybe this one will help too."

"Interesting." Arthur already seemed to have forgotten about me. He wandered from the room studying the pictures in his hand. At the last moment, he stuck his head back through the door. "I should get home before Ginny, but have Percival call me if anything happens."

"Okay, 'Dad,'" I said in my most sarcastic tone, but the sad smile Arthur gave me stopped me from saying more. For the first time I wondered why Arthur and Ginny didn't have any little Keeps running around the Rook. Arthur would probably make a good, if somewhat over-protective, father.

After Arthur left my room, I waited ten minutes. They were the longest ten minutes of my life.

"Percival," I asked the air, "where is Arthur?"

"Lord Arthur is one minute from the LANCE New York branch office. Shall I phone him for you, Lady Elaine?"

"No!" I took a deep breath. "No, that won't be necessary, Percival. Thank you."

The first thing I did was head for the elevator. The fact was I didn't know how to get out of the Rook. This was my only chance to break out of here and try to get home, and I had no idea how to do it. Instead of sitting in my room sulking and drawing for the last two days, I should have been planning my escape. I felt like a fool, but there was nothing to do about it now. With only a few hours to escape, I shouldn't waste them on should-have-dones.

Like I had since this nightmare began, I refused to think about home and my parents. I tried not to imagine what they had been going through. Arthur swore he had talked to Mom, but for all I knew, they thought I was dead. My hand shook as I fumbled around the elevator's door, looking for the normal buttons. I took a deep breath and banished the image of my parents from my mind. First, I had to get out of this ivory tower. Then, I would

37

figure out a way home.

I couldn't find a button for the elevator. I also couldn't find a stairway, an escalator, even a fireman's pole. There didn't seem to be any way off the floor we were on.

"This is ridiculous," I said out loud. "Ginny doesn't fly out of here in armor, and Arthur wanders off to labs on other floors all the time. Percival, how am I supposed to get out of here if there's a fire?"

"In the event of a fire, my lady, a knight would fly you to safety."

"Awesome," I said. I tapped my fingers on my teeth for a moment before flicking my hand up, summoning one of Percival's never-ending mid-room screens. "Percival, show me a floor plan for the Rook."

It appeared. The great room was easy to find on the map, seeing as it took up most of the floor. There was a stairway from Ginny's study that led to the master bedroom, and I found my hall with my room and the other seven guest bedrooms. I still did not see a way down to street level. Finally, I gave up. Even though I suspected he would report it to Arthur, I asked Percival how a person got out of this place.

"Besides the elevator I control in the great room," said Percival, "there is a stairway at the end of the residential hallway." A blue dot appeared at the end of the hall my room was on. I had studied that wall. There was no sign of a door there. It figured that Arthur had one of the best secret doors I'd ever seen, not that I'd seen many in real life.

"Good," I said. I flicked my hand again, and the screen disappeared. "Let's go open it up."

"As you wish, my lady," said Percival. "However, I must warn you that Sirs Gareth and Gawain guard the door on the other side. They will not harm you, but they also will not permit you to pass."

"Awesome," I said again. "Then how exactly am I supposed to get out of here, Percival?"

"I believe Lord Arthur desires you to stay in the main living quarters of the Rook, my lady."

"Which is your polite way of saying I'm not going anywhere anytime soon." My dreams of running away from here were fading fast. I threw myself down on a sofa with my arm across my face. "Is there any place I can go?"

"Lord Arthur did not leave any direct instructions about the terrace."

I pulled my arm down from over my eyes. "Why Percival, I believe you're trying to help."

If a computer had the ability to turn its nose up, Percival would have right then. "I am doing nothing of the sort," said the AI, his computer-generated voice somehow managing to drip with contempt. He all but sniffed at me in disdain. "I have merely answered your question."

Bouncing off the couch, I headed for the door leading outside. "Let's see this terrace."

I barely controlled my impatience while I waited for Percival to raise the portcullis and lower the drawbridge. Sometimes—pretty much all the time—I felt that Arthur took the whole medieval theme a little too far. Arthur's home dripped with defensive weaponry, but I seriously doubted that the drawbridge, portcullis, or moat had any defensive value. I said as much to Percival.

"The moat is ornamental," said Percival.

I wandered the entire terrace. As I had suspected, being out there didn't bring me any closer to freedom. I was still seventy stories above the street. Even if I had a death wish and wanted to climb down the side of the building, the terrace stuck out from the sides—just like on a real rook chess piece. I would have to somehow climb over the side of the battlements, down a buttress and then inch sixty-eight stories down the sheer side of a building. I wanted to go home, but I didn't want to go home in a body bag.

In the end, I contented myself with sitting on the drawbridge and dangling my feet above the moat. I should have been depressed about my foiled escape attempt, but with the sun shining down on me, I had a hard time maintaining my anger. After all, it was my fault I hadn't been able to escape this time. I would plan better for the next time the Keeps left me alone.

"Lady Elaine," said Percival later. I had no idea how much time had passed while I sat soaking in the sun. "Will Redding is ascending in the elevator."

"Who?"

"Will Redding of LANCE."

"Oh." The calm warmth drained out of me. I pulled my feet onto the drawbridge and stood. "Tell him he can meet me out here." My righteous anger flared up again. How dare Arthur send a babysitter to look after me. What did he think I would do? Escape?

40

"I will notify …" Percival's voice began to trail off.

"Percival?" I asked, but there was no response.

The drawbridge I had been pacing on began to rise—and rise quickly. I was almost pitched off into the moat, but I kept my feet and ran back inside before the door shut.

The entire penthouse was going into some kind of lockdown. Huge metal shutters were flying down over all the exterior windows, and the normal electric power seemed to have shut off. The great room was now lit with creepy emergency lights.

"Percival," I yelled again. "Percival!"

The AI didn't respond. Adrenaline flooded my body, but I didn't know if I should freeze or flee, or even where I should run. I had no idea until that moment just how much I relied on the disembodied computer voice to help me through most moments of my day.

Behind me, the door to the elevator began to push open, as if someone from inside was dragging at it. Somehow I managed to keep from screaming. Instead, I ducked behind the sofa. I was in one of the most heavily fortified and well-armed homes in America, and I had no way to defend myself against whatever was coming out of the elevator.

A pair of hands pulled the elevator doors open. A second later, Will stepped out around the door, just like a cop on a TV show, with his gun out and ready. "Elaine," he hissed. The room was so silent with no Percival and no background computer noise that even though Will whispered, it seemed as though he had shouted.

"Will?" I stuck my head up above the couch.

41

"Thank goodness you're still here. LANCE says there's a Dreki assault force in the building." He ran over and ducked behind the couch with me. "Where is the safe room?"

"What?" I was having trouble processing his words. "Dreki? Here?"

"The safe room," said Will. "Surely Arthur has a half dozen of them built into this place. The room where you go if anything happens," he added when I still stared back at him, completely dazed.

"My room," I said. "I'm supposed to go to my room and Percival is supposed to seal me in and send knights. But something's wrong with Percival and maybe the knights too."

Will had already stood and was pulling me up with him. "Come on, let's get to your room. We can probably seal it ourselves, and even if we can't, it'll be safer than this huge open space."

I nodded and turned for my hallway. We had almost reached my room when something that sounded like shots came from the other side of the hidden door at the end. I didn't stop to wonder or worry about whether the knights there could defend me. I pulled Will into my room and slammed the door shut.

Will fiddled with a keypad by the door that I had never even noticed. For two full days, I had sat here staring at the walls and ceiling of the room, and I had never once realized that the door had a keypad. How on Earth had I seriously thought I could either escape Keep Tower or stay alive once I was out? Had my entire plan been to trust in chance and luck?

No, there hadn't been a plan. The Dreki would have been able to grab me off the street before I'd made it even a block. The realization of just how stunningly ill-equipped I was for the new realities of my life was more devastating and more frightening than the gun battle that seemed to be happening on the other side of my door.

"Got it," said Will. Another metal shutter, like the ones in front of the windows, slammed shut over my door. My room had no windows, so we were now in a bunker-like space, completely cut off. Even the noise from the hallway disappeared. Will pulled over my metal desk, scattering pencils, papers, and my drawings all over the floor. He set it on its side and ducked behind it. "Get over here," he said. "This will give us some cover."

My desk wasn't big. It was meant for a single person, and it was one of the old-fashioned kind that had drawers to the floor on either side. For both of us to fit in the space behind the table top, I had to duck down behind Will, as close as possible. He crouched in front of me, his gun aimed at the door.

Without warning, something exploded outside the room. Will turned and dove over me, using his body to form a cocoon around mine. The building shook, and drywall rained down on us from the ceiling.

"You okay?" asked Will.

Dust covered me, and his chest crushed down on my back, but I wasn't hurt. "Yeah," I choked out.

Carefully, Will pulled himself and then me up.

"The door held," he said.

For a long while nothing else seemed to happen. I helped Will pull the desk all the way over to the far wall. We both got behind it again, but this time, Will didn't aim at the door. Whatever would come through wouldn't be stopped by the six bullets in his revolver.

For both of us to fit between the wall and the desk, I had to sit on Will's lap. In any other situation, I would have found it awkward to sit on the lap of a super-hot guy I'd only met once before. Will had one arm around me. I was curled into as tight a ball as possible with my head burrowed into his chest. In the past when I watched movies, helpless heroines always disgusted me. I wanted the woman to jump up and kick both the hero's and the villain's sorry rear ends.

It turns out in real life and death situations, I was more than happy to cede all control over to the person in the room with combat training. The feminist in me didn't care at all that the person willing to sacrifice his life for mine was male. I thanked every god and goddess in every pantheon that there was someone else in the room willing to defend sorry, helpless, useless me.

"Reboot complete," said Percival into the silent room. "Initializing."

Will and I both tensed, but nothing happened.

"Elaine? Princess?" Arthur's voice came over the speakers into my room. The explosion must have damaged the speakers because his voice kept cutting in and out. "Elaine, it's okay. I'm here with an entire squad of LANCE paratroopers. The Red Ranger has rounded up the last of the Dreki and is taking them back to a LANCE detention center. You can come out now."

I looked at Will. "Do you trust that? Do you think it's Arthur?" Will shook his head.

"Elaine, come on, sweetheart. I know you're scared, but it's safe."

"Sweetheart?" I muttered. "Now, I'm really not coming out. That doesn't sound like Arthur at all."

"Elaine, I'm going to come in since you don't seem to want to come out. Try not to hurt yourself attempting to stab me with a pencil. The pen may be mightier than the sword, but I'm wearing engineered carbon fiber titanium armor."

Will and I looked at each other. "That sounds like Arthur," we both said at the same time. Will gave me a small smile.

The metal shutter over my door retracted, and my door began to open. Will took careful aim, and I peeked over the edge of my desk. Through the dust motes that still clouded my room, Pendragon stepped inside.

The visor on his helmet snapped up, revealing Arthur's enraged face. I'd never seen him look anything less than impishly cheerful. That his clear fury was directed at us shocked my already shell-shocked system.

"Isn't this cozy," Arthur all but raged. He pointed the laser cannon mounted on his right arm at Will's head. "Get your hands off her."

Will raised his hands above his head, proving without a doubt that he was not manhandling me.

"Elaine, get away from Baby LANCE, right this moment."

Although I didn't appreciate either the tone or the command,

I stood up. Arthur was still pointing a cannon at us.

A voice squawked from the earpiece Will wore. I was going to need to do some serious work on my observation skills. I hadn't noticed that before now either.

After taking a deep breath and looking as though he were about to do the bravest thing of his life, Will stood with me and took hold of my arm.

"I'm afraid she can't leave me, sir," he said to Arthur. "Controller Stormfield just ordered me to bring her in to the Institute."

WHERE EVERYTHING AND NOTHING IS EXPLAINED

ARTHUR'S VISOR SLAMMED DOWN, AND HE AIMED THE PULSE CANNON on his other arm at the LANCE paratrooper standing in the doorway. Missiles sprouted up and down his arms and legs.

"Whoa!" I yelled, blocking Will's body with mine. "Percival, get Ginny on the phone now!"

"Under no circumstances is Elaine leaving this building with you," said Pendragon.

"No one said I'm going anywhere," I said. "Percival, where's Ginny?"

"Dialing now," said Percival.

"But Controller," started Will.

"Shut up!" I hissed at him. "I'm trying to save your life. Do you really think you and your men can win against Pendragon? And I'm not even talking about his other ninety-two knights and whatever else he and Percival have cooked up."

"Hello," said Ginny. She crackled over my damaged speakers.

"Hi, Ginny? It's Elaine and Will Redding here. Arthur and

LANCE are at a standoff over whether I should go into LANCE custody. It looks like I might get killed in the crossfire."

"Arthur," snapped Ginny. "Under no circumstances are you to start a firefight in the middle of the house. I am not living through another round of renovations."

"Too late, my sweet," said Arthur. "The Dreki set off a bomb outside Elaine's room an hour ago."

"I swear, if you don't wipe Vortigern off the face of the Earth, I'll do it for you. That's the third residence they've ruined this year." Ginny's voice sputtered and hissed. I couldn't tell if it was the busted speaker or her indignation.

"Firefight?" I said.

"Yes, Elaine, I remember. Will, I'm less than a half hour out from Keep Tower. Can you see if Controller Stormfield can meet me there, and we can all discuss this in a diplomatic fashion? I agree with Elaine that a firefight would defeat your purpose of taking her in alive."

I glared at the speaker. I didn't like sounding so disposable.

Will had nodded and received some kind of instructions through his earpiece. "Yes, ma'am," he said. "Controller Stormfield says he would be happy to meet in person to discuss the situation. He too can reach Keep Tower in thirty minutes."

"Excellent. Arthur, I expect to find Elaine, Will, and all the LANCE agents alive when I get home. Do you understand?"

"Fine." Pendragon sounded like a sulky child denied the chance to burn ants with a magnifying glass. "But they aren't taking her without a fight."

"No one is going anywhere in the next half hour." Ginny hung up.

"Can we at least get out of this room?" I asked Will and Pendragon. "It's dusty, and I suspect no one will accidentally blow off my head in a larger space."

"May I suggest the great room?" asked Percival. "I will begin repairs in this room and the hallway once you vacate them."

"Excellent idea, Percival." I pulled my arm out of Will's hand and joined Pendragon. "Thank you for coming to save me again," I told him.

Arthur's visor popped open. He gave me a small smile. He reached around and patted my neck. Something on his armor caught at my skin and stabbed me. I flinched and reached behind me, but I only wiped off a tiny dot of blood. Whatever had caught at me hadn't been big.

"Don't worry about all this." He waved at the LANCE troopers and Will. "No matter where you go, I will always be able to find you."

For some reason, I found this rather über-creepy statement comforting. For the last couple days, I had been nothing but a selfish spoiled brat. I had been behaving like a child, throwing tantrums and sulking instead of helping with my situation. If I had been Arthur, I would have been more than willing to hand me over to LANCE and let me be their problem. I didn't understand why he was being so protective of me, and I didn't care. Right then, I was happy he kept rescuing me.

We made it to the great room without anyone discharging a

weapon. The paratroopers arranged themselves around the room as if they thought I would hurl myself out of a seventy-story window to evade them. Arthur stomped around in full armor, glaring at everyone in turn.

I pulled Will over to the couch with me. "Sit," I told him, throwing myself down. We left huge dust streaks all over the thing, but I didn't care. "Tell me why Arthur is so upset about you taking me in to LANCE."

"It's because they want to lock you away in the Tool Shed," yelled Arthur.

"I'm talking to Will, not you," I yelled back. "Is that true?" I asked Will.

Will shrugged. "Controller Stormfield thinks you'll be safest at the Institute."

I waited for a moment, but neither Arthur nor Will seemed inclined to elaborate. "And what is this Institute or Tool Shed or whatever?" I prompted.

"It's a secure location for top assets," said Will. "Our most progressive scientific research and intelligence gathering forces are there, along with some of our more unorthodox agents."

"It's a bunker hundreds of miles underground filled with misfit geniuses and people with paranormal powers," threw in Arthur.

"Then I'm surprised you're not there," I snapped back. "We're trying to have a private conversation."

"It's also like being in underground jail. I hope you don't like the sun, Elaine, because if you go there, you're never going to see it again."

"I'm sure that's an exaggeration," I said, turning to Will. "Right?"

Will said nothing. He looked down at the revolver in his hand but didn't answer. That did not seem like a good sign.

I looked around the room. It hadn't been as affected by the blast, but lamps had been knocked over, and there was a crack arching up through some of the panes of the rose window. Keep Tower wasn't feeling as secure as it had earlier when I couldn't find a way out.

"Will," I leaned over until our heads were almost touching. I looked deep into his eyes, like maybe I could pull a vision up out of them—something that would tell me what I should do. "Be honest. Should I go with LANCE to the Tool Shed?"

Will chewed on the inside of his lip for a moment. "I think you would be safer at the Tool Shed," he finally said.

I sighed and leaned back, unsure about what I had expected him to say. He was a company man, and he would toe the company line. He also might honestly believe the Tool Shed was the best choice.

"But I think you would be happier here with Arthur and Ginny," Will added.

I raised my eyebrows, but I didn't respond.

We didn't speak for a few more moments. I was just about to ask Will why he was in LANCE when the bell for the elevator rang. Everyone, including Pendragon, aimed their weapons at the elevator door. I couldn't figure out why. It seemed unlikely the Dreki were going to start announcing themselves or enter buildings in the normal way.

The doors opened, and Ginny and an older man dressed in a crisply pressed gray suit stepped out of the elevator. The man looked more like a prosperous businessman than Arthur ever did.

"Ginny," I said with a sigh.

"Controller Stormfield," said Will at almost the same moment. He looked as relieved as I felt.

"Maybe now we can have some sanity around here," I said.

Will grinned.

We stood up to join the little knot of people in the center of the room.

Arthur and the controller had started arguing the moment they laid eyes on one another. Arthur was still refusing point blank to turn me over, and Stormfield was throwing a very British, well-bred, frigid tantrum over Arthur having aimed his weapons at the LANCE troops.

Much to my dismay, Ginny ignored both of them. She stood over to the side fiddling with a screen filled with lines of code. She shook her head at me when I came up.

"I've never seen a virus even remotely like this. I'll need to bring in Tori to consult. If she's even getting the dead-drop emails I'm leaving all over the Internet." Ginny made a face and then pulled her email up on her tablet, scribbling away with a stylus.

"Uh, Ginny," I said, "I'm worried about Percival too and all, but I kind of think Arthur and Stormfield are about to come to blows."

Ginny glanced at the two yelling men for a moment and rolled her eyes. "I'm letting them yell themselves out, and then I'll settle all of this. Don't worry." She gave me a smile before patting me on my arm. "I've been expecting something like this."

"You thought the Dreki would blow up your house?"

Ginny shook her head. "No, that I didn't expect." Her upper lip curled up in dislike. "No, I've been expecting Stormfield. Remember that Will was talking about bringing you in the day you got here?"

I nodded. There wasn't much from that day I had forgotten.

"Arthur and I contacted your mother that night. We made the legal adjustments necessary the next day before your parents went into hiding. A judge ratified the new custody arrangement this morning before I left for LA."

"Wait, my parents are hiding?" Somehow I couldn't picture my boring mom and dad using fake IDs and living assumed lives.

"Yes," said Ginny. She gave me an odd look. "The Dreki are looking for your parents even now. It's not as though they ever stopped. Also, they clearly want you badly if they are willing to try to breach the Rook. Kidnapping your parents to force you into their hands seems a natural move. It's why we couldn't risk letting you contact them before they created themselves a secure location. I'm sure the moment your mother can, she'll contact you. I've been trying to reach her, but she's severed all her former aliases. It's why I'm having to leave dead-drops."

Ginny's words made no sense. I felt light-headed. I reached back to grab onto a table or something to help me stay upright, but the only thing there was Will. He sort of wrapped his arm around my waist and helped me stay standing.

"Your parents are gone, and they're good," said Will. "That's why I came over today. I wanted to tell you they've vanished and seem safe. LANCE can't find any trace, and we believe the Dreki don't have them because they are still looking for them too."

I was in a state of complete shock, but Ginny didn't seem surprised.

"Your mother is very good at what she does," said Ginny.

I wanted to laugh hysterically. My mother was very good at getting dinner and scrapbooking and driving me to dance lessons back before I had a car. These weren't the kind of skills that hid you from terrorist and secret government organizations. I started to ask Ginny what she meant, but she had turned away from me. Arthur and Stormfield had worn themselves down. Stormfield stared coldly up his nose at Arthur, and Arthur had wound down to merely vile mutterings.

"Ah, gentlemen," said Ginny, "I believe you wanted to discuss Elaine's living arrangements." She reached into her portfolio and pulled out a file folder. She handed the file to Stormfield. He opened it and flipped through the pages.

"As you can see," said Ginny. "The custody agreement has been revised granting Arthur full and permanent custody of Elaine. A judge signed off this morning. One of the conditions of custody is that she remain in one of Arthur's residences until either she comes of age into her primary trust or leaves for college."

"Trust?" I asked, but I'm not sure anyone but Will heard me. They would have ignored me anyway.

Stormfield looked put out. I couldn't tell what annoyed him more, Pendragon getting into a shootout with his men if he tried physically removing me or the possibility of a protracted legal battle with the Keeps' legion of lawyers. Arthur and Ginny were literally the richest couple in the nation. They would have the best lawyers.

Stormfield snapped the file closed. "This is lovely that Arthur has been named guardian of the child, but I'm not sure how this changes matters. LANCE has the authority to take into custody and relocate to a safe location any individual either in danger or with intelligence-providing capabilities. A Dreki contingent just attacked your home to seize a powerful clairvoyant. I'm sorry, but Elaine qualifies under both provisions. She's coming with us."

Arthur made a horrible noise.

Stormfield looked at him in concern. "It was kind of you to save her and take her in before we found the leak at LANCE last night, but she's not your responsibility anymore. Let us take this ticking time bomb off your hands. My God, man, why do you care so much?"

"I don't think you read that file carefully enough," said Ginny. "Take a closer look at her birth certificate."

While Stormfield flipped the folder back open again, I stared at red-faced Arthur and unflustered Ginny. "Not that I'm not grateful and all, but why are you so determined that I stay?"

"I told you she didn't remember," Arthur said to Ginny.

"Oh God, those are her parents?" said Stormfield.

Ginny shot me a look I found hard to read, but it seemed

part horrified, part embarrassed. "But Tori swore ..." Her voice trailed off.

"I know, but I told you last night that twelve years is a long time." Arthur looked positively sheepish. I didn't trust him at all.

"This makes a difference," said Stormfield, "but I'm not sure how much of one."

"What difference?" I asked. I turned to Arthur. "What should I remember?"

"Well, Princess ..." Arthur scratched at his nose and looked every place in the room except at me. "You're my biological daughter."

WHERE I FINALLY TAKE CONTROL OF MY UNCONTROLLABLE LIFE

FOR A MOMENT THE WORLD STOOD STILL. **G**INNY AND **A**RTHUR LOOKED embarrassed; Stormfield seemed to be calculating new variables into an equation; and Will took a big step back. It was a good thing I was back to standing on my own, or I would have toppled over.

"Oh, please, that's the most ridiculous thing I've ever heard," I finally said. "When would you two have even met? My parents have been together since high school, and my mother didn't cheat on Dad with you."

Ginny turned away like this horrifying conversation was making her ill. I knew how she felt.

"There's a lot about your mother you don't seem to remember," said Arthur.

"Like what?"

"Let's start with her real name."

"Elsbet Gertrude Taylor," I said. I'd seen it a million times on her driver's license and credit cards.

Arthur shook his head. "No that's just the name she's been living under for the past twelve years. Her real name is Victoria Castile although she went by Tori."

"Tori Castile?" hissed Will. "Your mother is Tori Castile?"

I turned to him. "Does that name mean something to you? Because it means nothing to me."

Will nodded. "But she's been dead …"

"Twelve years," finished Arthur.

"Tori Castile is the Viral Vixen."

"Who?" I asked.

"It's a little before your time," said Will. "She was this huge hacker about twenty years ago."

"Hacktivist not hacker, and she was before your time, too," said Arthur. "You're what? Twenty?"

"Seventeen," said Will.

"You're only seventeen?" I asked. Certain possibilities formed in my brain. I shook my head. I couldn't get distracted. Now was not the time to cope with the impossible by drifting off into a dream world. "You're saying my mom, my boring stay-at-home mom that needed me to set up her new Keep smart phone, is a super hacker?"

"She had twelve or thirteen aliases and phones," said Ginny. "I was friends with most of them. Perhaps she had you help as a bonding exercise."

I stared at Ginny, calm, collected, and until now, normal Ginny. She had always been the eye of the Keep household hurricane, but even she seemed to have fallen off the deep end.

"You know my mom," I said. The disbelief still poured from my voice.

"Of course," said Ginny. She shot a fond smile in Arthur's direction. "She introduced me to Arthur."

I felt like my mind and not my bedroom ceiling had blown apart in the Dreki explosion.

"This is all touching," Stormfield said, "but I'm sure we can continue this family reunion back at LANCE."

Arthur's face turned from a bright red to a purple that almost matched the cape still hanging from his armor. He had not taken my fashion advice. "If one of your LANCErs comes within an inch of my daughter, he will leave here in a million pieces," he yelled in Stormfield's face.

Will took another step away from me.

"You do not want to make an enemy of LANCE," said Stormfield in his clipped manner. "You wouldn't survive multiple attacks from both the Dreki and LANCE."

"Watch me," Arthur screamed back.

Ginny shoved herself between Arthur and Stormfield. In her calm, measured way, she began talking at the LANCE leader. The man wasn't listening because he and Arthur continued to bellow at one another meaningless, posturing phrases.

I felt a little dizzy, like my life spiraling out of control was manifesting itself in physical symptoms. I turned toward the LANCE troopers spread out around the edge of the room. They were there both to guard against the Dreki and to prevent me from fleeing.

"Will." I spoke just loud enough he would hear me, but the

bickering adults wouldn't. I needn't have bothered. Those three were so engrossed in their argument that another Dreki bomb could have gone off without disturbing them.

Will stepped back over and leaned his head near mine.

"This Tool Shed Institute you and Arthur were talking about, it's a lock her up and throw away the key kind of place, isn't it?"

"That's not how I would describe it," Will started.

"Yes or no, Will."

Will shrugged and then slightly, but firmly, nodded his head up and down.

So, the LANCE option was out. I turned back to Arthur and Ginny both in their own way fighting tooth and nail to keep me with them. But current life at the Keep household was also confining even if I could still see the sun. There had to be a third option. Ever since the Dreki had attacked my school, I had been drifting around, letting others make choices for me. No more. There had to be a way for me to regain control of this situation.

And then I realized there was. I remembered they thought I was a powerful Seer with a front-row seat for the future. So, I would give them the future I wanted.

I grabbed Will's arm and sort of stumbled into him.

"Are you okay?" he asked.

I shook my head. "Dizzy," I murmured. It wasn't quite a lie, but I wasn't anywhere near as faint as I tried to appear.

"Here." Will helped me sit down on the floor, concerned etched on his gorgeous face. "Keep your head down so you don't pass out." He stayed kneeling next to me, holding my hand. It was kind of sweet.

"Uh, Sir," he said. "Ma'am." He tried again several times, louder and louder each time, before yelling at the top of his lungs, "Controller, Mr. Keep and Ms. Ginny."

The sound seemed to cut out of the three combatants. As one, they turned toward Will, ready to rip out his throat for interrupting their passionate discussion.

"I think there's something wrong with Elaine," he said before they unleashed their fury on him.

Will wasn't lying. At that point I was no longer faking anything. I had the worst case of stage fright I had ever experienced in my whole life. This was worse than the dance team tryouts in ninth grade. This was worse than starting the PSAT. This was worse than telling my mom about my fender-bender in the school parking lot. So much unspent adrenaline coursed through my body, I shook several inches back and forth. I probably looked like I was having a seizure although I wasn't. Although goose bumps covered my arms, sweat ran from my face as if I had finished running a mile. I was about to try lying to a master of lies, an unstable armed genius, and my stepmother. My body seemed to be pretty put out by the whole idea.

Arthur and Ginny rushed over. Arthur all but shoved Will out of the way in the process, but Will kept hold of my hand. Ginny put her hand on my head as if checking for a fever. Arthur did the same for my back.

"Her vitals are out of whack," said Arthur, getting some sort of readout from a sensor on his suit's glove. "I didn't realize a person's heart could beat that fast."

"I'm, I'm having a vision," I got out between my chattering teeth. "It's of me and Arthur and Ginny."

Weirdly, at the moment, an image popped into my mind. It wasn't like before with Arthur's tower or the flying fortress. Instead of staring at a single snapshot style image I could draw, it was like I watched a scene from a silent movie.

The LANCE troopers and Stormfield had disappeared. Instead, of the disheveled room, Will and I sat on the couch watching TV. We looked as if we were at least good friends—if not something more. We weren't snuggling on the couch or anything, but my knees were partly in his lap with one of his arms across them. Behind us where we couldn't see him, Arthur glared at us, while Ginny rolled her eyes at him and tried to pull him away. It was a calm, almost sweet, intimate family scene. It was also so far-fetched and unlikely to happen, I assumed I had chosen a weirdly inappropriate time to hallucinate. However, I got an idea of how to make my fake vision more appealing to all sides.

"And LANCE," I added. "I'm seeing a future with me, Arthur, Ginny, and LANCE." I didn't want there to be any mistake about what we were talking about. My eyesight snapped back from the weird silent movie to the scene in front of me.

Stormfield, who had been staring intently at my eyes, raised a single eyebrow at me. He didn't appear to be buying my "vision." I would have to do a better job selling it.

"We're here," I said, trying to shake the cozy home-life scene back out of my mind so I could concentrate on the future I wanted to see. "I mean, that I still live here with Arthur and Ginny."

"Ha," said Arthur.

"I'm not done," I said, glaring at him. "LANCE is here too though. I mean, that there's a member of LANCE living here too, training me on all the basics I need." I didn't want to be more specific than that since I had no idea what kind of training I might need. "And I'm not in here all the time," I added with a pointed glare at Arthur and Ginny. "I go out and see the city and do stuff, but I always have my LANCE person or one of you with me." Besides being a huge compromise, I figured this last little bit was prudent. After today, it was clear I was in no shape to go roaming around outside by myself. I wasn't even sure it was safe to leave me in the Rook by myself.

"Absolutely not," shouted Arthur. "I will not have LANCE scum skulking around my house trying to worm their way into my technology."

"It would be a compromise, dear," murmured Ginny. "And we would get to keep her."

Arthur looked mutinous, like a kid who's been told to do his homework instead of getting to play video games, but he didn't respond.

Stormfield frowned, clearly displeased. "I suppose it's a possibility," he said with some distaste as if the words sullied his mouth. "But I will pick the agent to remain."

"Oh, I know who that is," I said. Alarm bells rang in my head. I hadn't gotten the greatest impression of Stormfield, and I did not want him picking my LANCE babysitter. Really, though my options were limited. I only knew one LANCE agent's name. "You pick Will."

Will looked surprised but also pleased.

Stormfield shot me a look liked I'd just waved a dead skunk in front of his nose. "I highly doubt that. Will is still young even if he did graduate out of the LANCE Conservatory early. He's only had four years in the field. I would not entrust such a long-term high-ranking asset to him."

I wanted to kick Stormfield. Without changing his expression, Will somehow gave the impression of being crestfallen. I squeezed his hand.

"Oh, but you pick Will," I said. "Because Will is the person you sent to evaluate me at school. Because Will is the person who saved my life from the Dreki today while the rest of LANCE was monitoring people's text messages or whatever it is you do." At the last minute I realized that I had no idea what LANCE did, so that kind of weakened my argument. "And because Will is the only person from LANCE Arthur won't spend the entire time following around glowering at," I finished.

"I wouldn't count on that," said Arthur with a rather pointed look at Will's hand holding mine. Will dropped my hand faster than a live grenade.

"Besides," I said as sweetly and as piously as a person shaking from the effects of full on adrenaline poisoning can manage, "you do assign him here. I Saw it." I smiled and fluttered my eyelashes at him demurely.

Stormfield ground his teeth. I'd caught him, and he knew it.

If he agreed to my vision, then I stayed here with the Keeps and Will. If he denied my vision, then he would be denying me as a Seer. If I wasn't a Seer, then he couldn't take me to the Tool Shed. The only thing to do was to agree. Besides, Ginny was right. It was a decent compromise for everyone except Will. I hadn't asked Will if he wanted to move into the Rook for an indefinite amount of time.

Arthur rubbed his hands over his face as if the stress was getting at him too, but when he pulled his hands back down, he wore a triumphant grin like he knew I had won.

"Fine," Stormfield said. "But there will be some serious contingency plans put into place."

"Of course," said Ginny, standing. She took Stormfield by the arm and led him over to the couch. "We have many, many details to work out. But Elaine appears to be suffering from shock. She has been the focus of a Dreki attack and nearly forcibly removed from her home for the second time this week. Perhaps, we should let her rest?"

Stormfield waved me away as if shooing at an obnoxious gnat. Considering this entire fuss had been entirely about me, it felt anticlimactic.

"Percival," yelled Arthur.

"At once, my lord," said Percival. The door to the entry flew open and eight of Arthur's knights marched in the room. The LANCE team shifted uneasily. I couldn't blame them. The robots were intimidating in their matching armor.

"Sir Dinidan and Sir Gareth will escort Lady Elaine to her

new room," said Percival. "I have taken the liberty to select the beige room as it is the least damaged of the guest suites."

"Fine," said Arthur. "And have the couple dozen knights outside continue circling the building in Grail Defensive Pattern four. If there's a Dreki within ten miles of this building I want it exterminated like the vermin it is."

"Of course, my lord," said Percival.

One of the knights gently picked me up and carried me like a child, a twitching, adrenaline fueled, scared out of her mind child, toward my new room. Will tried to follow me, but Arthur called him back.

"Your guard duty hasn't started yet," he growled. "I don't know how I feel about this," he said to Ginny.

"You'll get used to it," she said.

Once in my new room, Dinidan or Gareth—unlike Ginny and Arthur, I couldn't tell the knights apart—left me on my bed. For a moment, I tried meditating to calm myself down. It didn't work. What I needed was to go for a run or to take up karate. Basically, I needed to put my flight or fight response into action. In the end, I did about a thousand jumping jacks to bleed off my adrenaline. When I had stopped twitching, I threw myself back on the bed.

"Oh, sweetie," said a voice out of thin air.

"Mom?" I rolled over onto my stomach. One of Arthur's ubiquitous mid-room screens had appeared a few feet from the bed. On the screen sat my mother, biting on her lower lip.

"Ginny has been trying to get us to call for the last few days, and when we saw the Dreki attack, we decided we'd better check in. I am so, so sorry about all of this," she said. "We watched that horrifying little scene in the living room. I never dreamed you'd forgotten about Arthur. We saw him so often before we had to go into hiding when you were four."

"You mean it's true?" Until now I hadn't accepted this whole Father/Daughter situation with Arthur. Half of me found it too far-fetched to be real, and the other half of me thought this was some kind of clever dodge Ginny had made up to keep me with them.

"We had already broken up before I even realized I was pregnant," said my mother. "We had some," she paused for a moment, chewing on her lip while she thought out her words, "ethical disagreements on my methods."

"What does that even mean?"

"Well, Arthur supports my goal of helping the poor. He does not support my methods."

"You mean hacking?" I couldn't believe everything I'd heard was turning out to be true.

Mom waved that away. "Oh no, dear. He has no issue with that. He and Ginny hack into things all the time. They've probably decrypted the entire LANCE computer system for fun. I know I have."

I stared at this stranger wearing my mother's face.

"No, for example, he wouldn't have liked how I published all those emails from those bank executives. You know, the emails that brought all those embezzlement indictments last year."

"That was you?"

"Of course, dear. You didn't really believe a rogue third world country with no online infrastructure that's lost even its single IP access point because of sanctions could have hacked a complex banking system, did you?" She didn't wait for me to answer. That was wise. It would have been a long wait.

"No, and your father would have objected when I redistributed a good deal of those banks' and the bankers' wealth back to the masses. He would have preferred presenting the evidence to the police or just rounding them all up himself. You know."

"No, I really don't," I said. "I've known the man three days. Three days, Mom. I don't even know what to say."

"I'm sorry, sweetie. We never realized you'd forgotten him. I mean, who did you think I was talking about all of those times I mentioned your father?" My mother sounded sincere, but she was making too much eye contact, like she realized looking away would give away the lie. Considering this was a trick she'd taught me for getting out of trouble, I couldn't believe she was trying to use it on me now.

"Oh, I don't know. Maybe when you mentioned my father I assumed you were talking about Dad?"

"Hi, Pumpkin." Dad popped onto the screen like he'd been waiting off camera for the right moment to appear. My mouth fell open. Sometime in the last two days, my dad's hair had turned snow white, and he'd grown a full matching beard like some sort of hipster Santa. Even his eyes had changed color from blue to brown. "What do you think of the new look?" he asked.

I thought there was a one hundred percent chance I was about to throw up on my new bed. "You really are master criminals skilled at disappearing."

"Hacktivists, Pumpkin. Your mom and I have taken down many corrupt people and institutions, all for a tidy profit. I'm not the world's best forensic accountant for nothing."

Mom gave Dad a squeeze around the waist. "He finds me all of our targets. We're so glad you know now. It's been so hard pretending to be normal parents all these years."

I rubbed my face like Arthur had earlier in the great room. I wondered if the stress with LANCE had given him the same tension headache my parents were giving me. "Why didn't you tell me about any of this—Arthur, the hacking, that we were hiding?"

My mother looked at me like I was the one that had been hiding a secret life this whole time. "There never was a good opportunity." She turned to Dad. "I mean when do you tell the kids you're wanted by everyone from INTERPOL on down? When they turn eighteen?"

"You know what would have been a good time? Before Arthur blurted it out in front of a room of LANCE troopers. Like any time, say, my entire life."

Mom nodded. "Well, hindsight being 20/20 and all. But I have every faith in you, dear. You can trust Arthur and Ginny. They're good people even if they are too law-abiding and obsessed with ethics and morals for our taste. Civil disobedience never hurt anyone."

"I'm not sure stealing billions is civil disobedience," I said.

"We only kept twenty percent," said Mom.

My mouth fell open. "And I got a used car for my birthday?" In my rather shell-shocked state, I was clearly latching on to the important details of the conversation.

An alarm beeped on Mom's end. Her fingers clicked keys and swiped at things.

"I have to go, sweetie. Someone has noticed my little patch into Ginny's system. It's probably just Ginny, but I better go in case it's someone else. We'll arrange a visit as soon as this little fuss dies down."

Little fuss? I didn't get to object though. My parents' faces disappeared before I could even tell them I loved them. I burrowed my face into the cover on my bed. I badly wished I could go to sleep and wake up from this nightmare back into my real life. Except, apparently, that life had never been real either.

WHERE I LEARN THAT MAYBE THIS ISN'T ALL ARTHUR'S FAULT

NOBODY BOTHERED ME FOR THE REST OF THE NIGHT. I'M SURE THAT Arthur and Ginny monitored me through whatever sensors they had hidden in the room, but no one, not even some LANCE operative, invaded. I was immeasurably grateful.

After a sleepless night of tossing and turning and the occasional light nap, I dragged myself out of bed. I couldn't put it off forever, so I trudged down the hall in my pajamas to the breakfast room. To my surprise, the room appeared empty—at least empty of humans. Several of Arthur's silent robot servants milled around. One of them brought me over a bowl of cereal as soon as I sat down.

"There it is." Ginny's head popped up from under the table holding a ball-point pen.

I screamed, spraying milk and cereal all over the place as my spoon went flying.

Ginny spun around, looking concerned, and four knights ran into the room.

"Sorry," I choked out, hacking up the marshmallow that had gotten stuck in my throat when I screamed. "I thought I was alone. I must be kind of jumpy."

"Understandable," said Ginny. She sat at the table and fiddled with some papers next to her plate. I really needed to pay attention when I entered a room. I hadn't even noticed the other place setting on the otherwise empty table.

One of the robots handed me another spoon, and I went back to shoveling cereal in my mouth. I wasn't hungry, but eating gave me something to do.

With a sigh, Ginny stopped rearranging her papers. "I am so sorry about all of yesterday, Elaine."

I stopped mid-chew, unsure what to say.

"We should have done a better job of protecting you from the Dreki attack. They never should have been able to breach the building, much less access this floor."

I swallowed, but I still didn't know what to say. Yesterday had sucked, and I probably would be in a Dreki jail cell now if it hadn't been for Will, but I didn't blame the Keeps. It wasn't like they had known they would be hacked and attacked.

Ginny must have misread some look on my face. "Don't worry." She reached over and patted the sleeve of my pajamas. "We've taken every precaution. Arthur and I were up all night reprogramming and retooling the defenses. The next Dreki attack won't be anywhere near as close."

"The next one?" I sputtered out, my voice rising at least an octave and a half. I rubbed my hands across my face. Of course, there would be a next one. The Dreki had already tried twice to grab me. They wouldn't give up now when they'd been so close.

"Don't worry," she said again with another gentle pat. "We'll battle that dragon when it comes to us."

Awesome.

"But I am so very sorry about the way you found out about …" Ginny paused, struggling for the right words. There weren't any, so I broke in with the wrong ones.

"About how my parents have been lying my entire life? How my dad is my step-dad and my biological father is, well, Arthur?"

"That sums it up," said Ginny with a smile. "I must tell you though that I genuinely had no idea you didn't remember Arthur. From the familial way you two have sparred since the moment of your arrival, I assumed you were picking up where your relationship had left off. I didn't realize that for you the first time you two had ever come face to face was when he slammed into the foyer's floor." She frowned for a moment and scribbled in a notebook. "I have got to find a better material for that floor before he ruins it again."

Ginny looked back up at me. "I apologize. I sometimes get distracted by random thoughts, and I must write them down before I forget them."

"Mom says that's the calling card of a highly creative mind," I said, the doubt creeping into my voice. Could I trust anything my mother ever said, even something as innocuous as that?

"Well, your mother would know. She has one of the most creative minds I've ever seen."

"You really are friends with my mom?" Even though I now knew my mother had been leading a double life, I still had trouble picturing her as BFFs with someone as glamorous and brilliant and amazing as Ginny.

"We were roommates in college sophomore year and the only girls our year in the computer engineering program at FTSU. We've stayed in touch ever since. You're a lot like her."

"That's what Dad always said. My dad, you know, I mean." I stumbled on my words not sure how to avoid insulting either Arthur or Dad.

"Not Arthur," said Ginny. She smiled at me. "You mean your dad, not the sperm donor. That's what your mother used to call Arthur when he annoyed her."

I snorted. That sounded like Mom.

Ginny's smile faded. "But I've never agreed with your other parents' insistence on cutting all contact between you and Arthur. If I could chat with you mother, I saw no reason why Arthur couldn't stay in touch with you."

"What happened? Why does everyone think I should remember Arthur? Even Mom acted shocked when she realized I had no idea she didn't mean Dad when she referred to my father."

Ginny waved her hand to summon one of the mid-air screens. She did something with her tablet, and the window she had opened there appeared on the screen. She pulled up a folder with the uninspiring name "Untitled-4." Inside was a list of .jpg files with eight-digit numbers for names.

Ginny ran her finger down the list until she came to the one she was looking for. I realized with a small start that the file names were dates without the dashes and that she had just picked a picture of my fourth birthday.

The file opened showing a picture from my actual birthday, not the birthday party we'd had the week before. I remembered that party because it was bigger than any of the other parties I've ever had since. There had been pony rides for my friends and a bouncy castle.

This picture though, I didn't remember this scene at all. The cake had four lit candles, and I was leaning down to blow them out. Arthur held me in his arms while my arms hugged his neck. Arthur. He held me, pure joy radiating from his face. Ginny and Mom stood in the background, so Dad must have been taking the picture. I didn't look uncomfortable or like I was being held by a stranger. I didn't have that tense expression kids get when they're having to put up with hugs from distant relatives. My face was intent on the candles, not half worried about the man holding me. The scene was easy, a picture of laughter and a great deal of love.

I pulled the screen toward me so I could see the small details of the image even better. "Why don't I remember this?" I turned to Ginny. "How can I not remember any of this?"

Ginny looked sad and embarrassed, and I realized with horror that I had forgotten her, too. She was standing in the picture, so she and Arthur must have been together even back then. I knew if my parents had forgotten me, I'd be mortified. It was one thing to not recognize a stranger, but this was my father and step-mother, and I appeared to have known them well enough to be comfortable around them. And I was four years old in the picture, old enough to remember things. It's not like they disappeared when I was four months old.

"Memory is a tricky thing," said Arthur. He passed Ginny and dropped an absent-minded kiss on the top of her head before sitting down on the other side of me. "No one knows how or why some things fade away. Although how you forgot my astounding genius?" Arthur pointed at his head. "That's beyond me." He grinned, but even I realized Arthur wasn't as okay as he pretended.

Silence filled the room, and I looked down at my forgotten cereal, unable to look anyone in the eye. I knew it wasn't my fault I'd lost Arthur and Ginny from my life, but I felt as guilty as if I'd chosen to exile them forever.

In his most chipper tone, Arthur broke the silence. "But that's neither here nor there." He slid a box in front of me. "I've come bearing gifts." When I didn't move, he prodded the box, so it wiggled a tiny bit.

I sighed and opened the box. Inside a next generation Keep smart phone sat on a little square of velvet. It was thinner than the last generation phone I'd had and lost when the Dreki attacked my school. My family had always exclusively used Keep Consolidated computers, tablets, and phones instead of some generic PC, and now I had a good idea why.

I turned the phone on, and my old cover picture popped up. It was my parents on their fifteenth wedding anniversary. They looked so happy and in love, and now I wasn't even sure they were married.

"What is this?" I asked Arthur.

Arthur leaned over to glance at my screen. "Tori and Raul, I'm assuming."

I shook my head. "Not the picture." I was only distracted for a second by Arthur using what had to be my parents' real names. It only beat home how little I knew. I would have said the picture on my phone was of Elsbet and Peter. "I mean the phone. What's this for? I thought you wanted me to stay off the Internet."

Arthur's eyes narrowed like he was annoyed although I got the impression he wasn't annoyed with me. "This is to avoid repeating past mistakes." He tapped the phone twice, and it unlocked to the home screen. He tapped on another icon that looked like the normal phone icon except it was red with a black handset instead of blue and white.

"This phone is a special prototype that Keep Consolidated will never put into production. I've been working on it since you got here. This phone doesn't use commercial cellular or data networks. Instead, it uses the proprietary network I set up for the knights. Once we get your parents the other prototypes, you'll be able to stay in touch."

I couldn't help it. My eyes watered up although I managed not to ruin the phone by bawling all over it.

Arthur cleared his throat and fidgeted with a cup of coffee the robots had brought, but Ginny handed me a napkin.

"Yes, well, I wasn't happy when Tori disappeared with you, and then when we finally found you again after six years, she still wouldn't let me talk with you." Arthur crossed his arms and stared at the far wall instead of looking at me. "I mean, I understood the running, sort of. She had incurred the wrath of the entire Illuminati, and they aren't a group of people you anger lightly. The governments had to form LANCE just to deal with them. I still can't imagine what your mother was thinking trying to hack them."

"She thought they were a typical terrorist group like she and Raul had hacked before," Ginny reminded Arthur. "And she thought she was helping."

"Wait. What are you talking about?" I stopped catching up on my email and looked between Arthur and Ginny. "The Illuminati isn't real. It's a conspiracy theory people use when they don't understand what's going on."

Arthur snorted. He rubbed his hands across his eyes and then down the rest of his face. "That's just what they want you to think. What's that quote about the smartest thing the devil did was to convince you to forget he existed?"

Ginny tapped away on one of her tablets. "That isn't even remotely close to the Baudelaire quote." She turned to me. "What Arthur is trying to say is that the Illuminati is very real. To pretend otherwise would be foolish, not to mention dangerous. They've already tried to grab you twice."

"And that was before they realized you were linked to Tori or me," said Arthur. "If they've figured it out … I don't trust that LANCE caught their leak." His voice trailed off, and I didn't ask for any more information. Arthur provided some anyway. "Well, let's just say that Tori and Raul put a dent in the Illuminati's coffers before the Illuminati caught on and sent their Dreki assassins after them."

"Wait," I said again, putting the pieces together. "You're not saying the Dreki are the same thing as the Illuminati, are you?"

"Ding, ding, ding," Arthur said. "Close enough. The Dreki was the Illuminati's army of assassins, at least until the Dreki took over the entire group a couple of years before you were born. Princess, you've won yourself a prize." Arthur yelled up at the ceiling, "Percival, bring in Dame Morgause."

A knight walked in the room. It was smaller than all the other ones I had seen so far and clearly meant for a female figure. I turned for Ginny's reaction, but she looked as shocked as me.

"I said I came bearing gifts." Arthur's satisfaction was palatable. "Plural, with an 'S.' One phone cannot be gifts. So, Elaine, meet Dame Morgause."

All my questions about the Dreki and the Illuminati and how my mom had angered them flew out of my mind. My mouth moved a few times before I got out any words.

"Arthur," I asked, "did I just get knighted?"

WHERE I FINALLY SEE WHAT ALL THE FUSS IS ABOUT

Ginny didn't seem pleased about the knight. She began grilling Arthur about the thing's various technical specifications and safety settings, but her questions meant nothing to me. Meanwhile, I circled the armor, round and round, trying to decide how I felt.

Arthur had just explained to Ginny that no, most of my ammunitions were not live when I decided that there was no way on Earth or any other planet that I would be seen out in public in that thing.

"No," I said to Arthur, returning to my chair. "Just no."

For the first time since entering the room, Arthur looked put out. "What do you mean no? You can't have live ammunition the first time you put your armor on. That would be ridiculous."

"That's what you consider ridiculous?" I wanted to bury my face in my hands. "Arthur, why does my armor have boobs? Weird pointy boobs?"

Arthur's eyebrows shot up his forehead. "Well, I kind of

thought your mom would have discussed this with you, but here it goes." He stared at the ceiling for a moment as if the answers to my questions were written up there. "When a young girl flowers into a young woman, her body goes through many changes," he started.

"Are you saying my man-made robot suit of armor went through puberty?" I interrupted.

Ginny choked on her tea but then became very interested in the lines of code on one of her tablets. Clearly she wasn't going to enter this minefield. I didn't blame her. I'd never been in a more mortifying conversation in my life.

"No, your suit didn't go through puberty." Arthur gave me a look like I was the one being dense. "But Princess, it's designed to your exact physical dimensions. I had Percival scan you the night you got here while you were asleep."

I chose to skip that super-creepy statement so we could stay focused on the important issues. "My body looks nothing like that." I pointed at the cones jutting out from the armor's breast-plate. "I don't care what Percival told you, but you shouldn't be able to put someone's eye out with your chest."

Arthur shrugged. "I thought it might be useful. Besides, it's not exactly the same size from the outside, of course, but inside you should be snug and safe."

"I don't care. That armor looks ridiculous. I will not wear it."

"She has a point," said Ginny, breaking in.

"Two of them," I muttered with a glare at the robot armor's two chest funnels.

"The thing looks like a Valkyrie from a bad performance of Wagner. You just need a horned Viking helmet with golden braids on the top of the helm to complete the look." Ginny shot me a sympathetic smirk, but it was still a smirk.

Arthur didn't get to make whatever snide comment brewed on the tip of his tongue. Instead, Will walked in at that moment.

"I've moved most of my things into the room next to Elaine's," he said. He might have been planning to say more, but his voice petered out when he caught sight of my overly endowed armor. "Is Controller Stormfield aware you plan to, um, arm Elaine?"

"I'm sure you'll tell him in your little daily check-in with LANCE," said Arthur with a sour frown at Will. His brows lowered as Will kept staring at the armor, especially the breastplate. "I'm beginning to see your problems with the aesthetic design," said Arthur to me.

"You think?" I asked.

With a glare, Arthur turned back to Will. "Do you think you can keep your eyes off my daughter's robot's chest?"

"They are impossible to avoid," I said, sparing Will the burden of responding. The poor guy flushed and looked like he might have trouble sputtering out an answer. Will glanced over at me and flushed even darker before glaring at the safety of the floor.

"Seriously, Arthur, what made you think I'd be okay with pointy boobs?" I continued.

"Percival, redesign the breastplate of the Dame Morgause to be less," Arthur paused, looking for the right word, "revealing."

"Percival," I cut in, "redesign the breastplate to look like all the other knights from the exterior. I'm fine with having it perfectly contoured from the inside."

"Yes, my lady," said Percival. "I shall begin construction now."

"Thank you," I said. "I trust your judgment."

"I was programmed by the best," said Percival.

Arthur huffed and glared at all of us, especially Ginny and me.

The Dame More Goes or whatever ridiculous name Arthur had given the armor, turned and flew out of the room back toward Arthur's workshops and the armory.

"Oh, I get to fly?" I gave Arthur a smile, the first one since he'd marched the atrocious looking armor into the room.

"Of course," said Arthur. "It won't be much use if you can't jump off buildings."

"You have a skewed view of the world." I glanced at Will. He stared at the carpet, but his face had turned back to its usual color, and he had a faint smile as if he enjoyed Arthur's discomfort. "So, you're moving in next door?" I tried to sound like the idea didn't leave me wanting to run screaming in terror at having to live so close to such a hot guy.

Will smiled, and his eyes met mine. "Percival and I determined that the room next to yours had the most strategic value."

"I bet you two did." The way Arthur stared at Will made me glad Arthur wasn't wearing his Pendragon armor. Arthur might have put a small rocket in Will's chest if he'd been armed. "Percival, a word." He turned and stormed out of the room yelling something at the AI about his "precious little girl" and "hormone crazed Baby LANCEs."

Will studied the floor again, but I rolled my eyes. Sadly, I was probably safe from those kinds of dangers. If I had learned anything from TV, it was that hot secret agents like Will tended to be into even hotter super spies with the ability to take down an entire legion of Dreki with nothing more than a pair of high-heeled shoes. So far, I had managed to turn into a quivering ball of goo when put in mortal danger. It had not been attractive.

Part of me was glad that Will would be next door. He had a habit of saving my life, and the close proximity would just make that even more convenient. On the other hand, I kind of wanted to get in the habit of saving my own life. Having Will always within shouting range might make me lazy and dependent on him. On the other, other hand, having Will living in the room next door might mean I'd get to see him without his shirt. While cowering up against him in abject fear last night, I had still noticed the guy had rock-hard abs. For a second, I imagined what a shirtless Will would look like. I had an overwhelming desire to draw him, even though I rarely drew people from real life. Arthur might be worried about the wrong teen.

"Are you sure next door to me has the most strategic value?" I only sounded slightly uncomfortable.

Ginny raised her eyebrows at me in question, but she didn't ask me anything.

"I would have thought a security center or something would make more sense," I plowed on. "Do we even have one of those?" I asked Ginny.

"No." She shook her head at me. "And no, Percival and Will

are right. Rooming next to you would be the safest place. I've been considering moving Arthur and myself down to your wing, but with Will here, I'll be able to stay in my bed."

"How splendid for you." I turned to Will and stuck out my hand for him to shake in what I hoped was a friendly, yet professional, kind of greeting. "Welcome home."

Will gave me a tentative smile and reached out to take my hand. The second our palms touched, the room around me vanished.

I sat in a restaurant or café. On the table in front of me sat two coffee mugs. One of them seemed to be mine since hot chocolate and marshmallows filled the cup. I hated coffee. Across from me, an older gentleman with what should have been a kind face gave me the most chilling smile I've ever seen. It was as if the Devil had somehow co-opted God's features for his own use. For the first time, I understood how a rat felt when mesmerized by a snake.

"So what do you say, my dear?" asked the man.

"She has nothing to say to you," said Will from behind me. I turned, surprised. I hadn't realized he was there.

Will placed his hand on my shoulder. "Come on, Elaine. Let's get you home."

"She goes nowhere with you." The man raised a gun and shot Will in the center of the forehead. The coffee shop around us erupted in chaos as customers threw themselves on the ground. I barely noticed. All I could focus on was the red hole in Will's head and the sightless gaze in his eyes as he slid to the floor.

I started to scream and scream and scream.

I was still screaming when something slapped me across the face. I was on the floor of the small breakfast room. Will had his arms around me half supporting me into a sitting position. Ginny had both hands on my face and stared deep into my eyes.

"I think she's coming back," she said to Will. "Her eyes are clearing."

Arthur came tearing into the room, a half dozen knights fanning out behind him. The knights were armed and scanned the room for probable targets.

"Unhand my daughter," Arthur yelled. He carried his giant Pendragon sword Excalibur and brandished it at Will's head.

"Unhand me? What is this? A bad movie?" My voice sounded weak and raspy, like I'd been to a rock concert where you had to yell at the top of your lungs all night.

"She's back." Ginny took her burning hands from my face and sat back on her heels. She shut her eyes for a moment before taking a few deep breaths. When she opened her eyes again, she had returned to cool, calm Ginny, not the frantic woman who must have slapped me a moment ago.

"What is going on?" Arthur asked at the same moment I said, "What was that?"

"I think Elaine just had her first fully realized vision," said Will.

"That was like nothing I've ever Seen before," I said. "This wasn't just a picture like I normally draw or even a silent film." My mind flitted back to that moment last night when I had Seen Will and I all cozy on the couch. That still seemed like such an unlikely future that I couldn't bring myself to believe it had been a real vision. "Just now, I was there, one hundred percent, all the way there. I smelled my hot chocolate. I felt a draft from the door blowing across my face. I could have touched the blood." I trailed off and turned away so I wouldn't have to look at Will's face.

Will's arms around me stiffened. Arthur dropped to his knees and tossed his sword behind him. It clattered on the floor, rocking back and forth until a knight retrieved it. Arthur picked up one of my hands and patted it gently, the way my mom used to pat my hands after a bad nightmare.

"Blood?" he said, his voice surprisingly gentle. "Whose blood, Elaine? Did someone hurt you?" He tightened his grip on my hand for a moment, but then he regained control. He started patting my hand again.

I shook my head. "It wasn't my blood. I was sitting at a table in a coffee shop with a scary guy. He kind of looked like Controller Stormfield, but this guy was oppressively evil."

"And Stormfield is only subtly so," Arthur said with a faint grin.

I glanced at Will to see how he was taking the veiled slander directed at his boss. That was a mistake. The Will sitting next to me holding me up might be very much alive, but all I saw was the entry wound on vision Will's forehead. I shivered and turned back to Arthur and Ginny.

"Elaine, Princess, you still haven't told us about the blood."

I bit my lip, and I started to shake just the tiniest bit. Will's arms around me tightened as if he thought he could hold me together. He couldn't stop the vision though. For the first time, I had truly Seen the future. I had Seen him die.

"Someone, someone tried to save me from the bad guy. Someone always has to save me, doesn't he? I really have to do something about that," I rambled.

Ginny took my other hand in hers. "Did something happen to the person trying to save you?"

I nodded, and my eyes filled with tears. "The man, the bad man, shot him at point blank range. I didn't see it coming. Neither of us did."

Arthur and Ginny exchanged a loaded glance. "Did you recognize the person who was shot?" Arthur asked.

"It was Will," I whispered.

Behind me, Will went still. He even stopped breathing as if my words alone had already killed him. I had trouble catching my breath with Will's dead arms around me. I snatched my hands out of Arthur's and Ginny's grasps and scrabbled at the floor, trying to stand up.

"Air," I said. "I need air." The entire Rook, all eighty-five floors, seemed to press at me from all sides. Will's arms let go of me, and I crawled to my feet. I ran for the drawbridge that led to outside.

"Percival, let Elaine out on the terrace," Ginny ordered from behind me. By the time I reached the entrance hall, the portcullis had already risen, and the drawbridge had lowered. I ran around the outside of the moat as fast as I could, but I couldn't outrun the vision in my head. I also wasn't any freer out here than I had been inside the small breakfast room. By the time I started my second lap, Arthur, Ginny, and Will stood on the drawbridge watching me, concern etched on their faces. I couldn't take their stares.

Slowing down, panting, I came to a stop next to one of the crenellations. I climbed up on my knees to get a better look at the panoramic view in front of me. Manhattan bustled about beneath me, the cars and taxis inching along in the traffic. Down there was freedom from eccentric superhero fathers and secret organizations. Down there, people didn't watch their new friends get killed in visions. Down there, life was normal.

I stood up on the edge of the crenellation, holding on with one hand.

"No!" yelled Will. All three screamed my name. They were running for me, but the terrace was large, and they were too far away.

"Percival."

"Yes, my lady?" the AI said from some speaker hidden on the terrace.

"You had better have a knight catch me." I turned and jumped off the building toward freedom.

WHERE I LEARN THAT YOU CAN CHANGE THE FUTURE, BUT YOU CAN'T OUTRUN FATE

IN RETROSPECT, JUMPING OFF A BALCONY SEVENTY STORIES ABOVE New York City was not one of my better decisions. However, as I plummeted to the Earth, I couldn't second-guess myself. I would have been more frightened if I hadn't noticed a knight peel away from his defensive position and dart down for me. It broke into small pieces and reformed around my free-falling body. Just like at my school, the knight initialized and pulled me out of my dive long before I smacked into the sidewalk below. It turned to take me back up to the terrace.

"Percival, halt this tin can," I shouted.

Percival and the knight halted in mid-air, hovering some-where around the fiftieth floor.

"Elaine, get back up here this minute. You are grounded for life," Arthur screamed over the knight's internal speakers. "If you ever pull a stunt like that again, I will personally see you locked in LANCE's Tool Shed."

"Oh, bite me, Arthur." I had never heard an emptier threat.

His every move since he'd rescued me had been designed to keep me out of LANCE's clutches. I didn't see him turning me over to them now because he'd had a little scare.

"Young lady, don't you use that tone of voice with me. You get back up here, or I'll …" Arthur's voice cut out like someone, probably Ginny, had cut his feed.

After a moment of silence, I asked Percival to show me how the knight worked. The AI explained all the different screens and told me what commands to say to move in the armor. I practiced moving back and forth and turning somersaults in the air while Arthur maintained radio silence. Percival had just shown me how to use the targeting system for the rockets when Arthur came back on the comms set.

"Elaine." He basically spit out the word, like he was trying to talk in a civil tone but horribly failing. "It has come to my attention that I may not be appreciating the trauma your vision caused."

"Can't argue that," I muttered. I had Percival calculate a flight plan for any mid-sized town in upstate New York that he liked. I didn't care where we headed as long as I wasn't in New York City.

"So, Ginny and I, and oh yeah, Baby LANCE, would like it if you would come up here and talk to us about how you're feeling."

"You want to talk about my feelings?" I didn't know about Will or Ginny, but Arthur had not struck me as someone in tune with his inner emotions. Or someone interested in others' inner emotions.

"Princess, we're just worried." Arthur's tone lost its biting quality, and for a moment, he sounded sincere.

"I'm worried, too. I'm worried about that future happening. I'm worried about you or Ginny or Will getting hurt because you all keep protecting me. Please don't come looking for me. I'll send the knight back as soon as I'm somewhere safe. Percival, execute your flight plan."

The knight banked and shot north, away from the Keeps and their tower. I had my viewscreen pan back to the Rook's terrace. Arthur and Ginny stood by the edge of the moat having a passionate argument while Will stood off to the side frantically typing on his phone. I sighed. It had been too much to hope that LANCE would just let me go. Arthur rubbed at his face and waved his arms, but he didn't climb into Pendragon or send any of the knights after me.

"Percival, is there some kind of stealth mode for this thing? I don't want LANCE or Arthur or the Dreki tracking me."

"We are impenetrable to ground radar and sonar, my lady," said Percival, "and I have taken the liberty of removing this knight from Lord Arthur's inventory. He cannot track it."

"Thanks."

It only took about ten minutes to get to the town Percival had chosen. We landed in a small wooded area on the outskirts, near a little used gas station. I stepped out of the knight, and for the first time, noticed my bare feet and pajamas.

"Brilliant." I frowned down at my toes wiggling in the dirt. "I need to buy shoes and clothes." That's when I noticed the next big hitch in my plan. "I don't have money. I don't suppose the knights come with credit cards."

"Not exactly," said Percival. "If you'll follow me." The knight, with Percival in control, turned and headed for the gas station. It walked up to the ATM and placed a hand on the side. The ATM's screen blurred for a moment and then went blank. "How much money do want?" asked Percival. "I would estimate needing at least one thousand dollars."

"Don't these things have withdrawal limits?"

"Not for me." If a disembodied AI could sound smug, Percival oozed self-satisfaction.

I glanced around, but no one was there to notice an armored knight hacking the ATM. "Okay. Give me a thousand dollars, but wait. I don't want to steal from someone. I'm not my mom."

"Perhaps you would prefer funds from one of Lord Arthur's personal discretionary accounts?"

I shrugged. "That's okay, then. We'll call it twelve years of missed birthdays." I also didn't complain when the ATM spit out fifty twenties. Stuffing most of them in my bra, I placed two hundred dollars in my front pajama pocket so I could buy shoes. "I don't suppose you could drop me someplace a little closer to a shoe store."

"Of course, my lady." Percival opened up the front of the knight, and I climbed back in. After being covertly dropped off behind a big box store, I bought a cheap pair of sneakers, a small duffel, and two changes of clothes. I kind of expected my bare feet and pajamas to get some strange looks, but no one seemed to think anything of a barefoot teen buying travel supplies.

A polite stranger pointed me to the bus station, and I bought a four hundred dollar ticket to Butte, Montana. I couldn't think of any place more remote than that. If I was the Dreki or LANCE, I would look for me in interesting large cities. I hoped that Butte wouldn't even cross their minds.

Since I had two hours to kill before my bus left, I headed next door to the café. I ordered a small grilled cheese and water. When I sat down to wait for my food, an overwhelming sense of déjà vu hit me. I couldn't place why the restaurant looked so familiar. I had never been in upstate New York before, much less in this town. The place didn't appear to be part of a chain, so it was unlikely I had visited a similar one somewhere else. I was still staring around me with a frown when a woman slid into the space across from me.

"Hello, Elaine," said the woman.

I froze, instantly trying to figure out the best way out of the building. The front door sat behind me, and I didn't see any other obvious exits. Why had I not figured this out before? "How do you know my name?" I asked to buy time.

"You'll tell me in a minute," the woman said. Her eyes clouded over for a moment as if she had developed an instant case of cataracts. Almost as quickly they cleared back to their normal color. "Well, now you won't tell me. That's the problem with meddling with the future. It changes things."

"Wait, did you See? What happened to your eyes? Who are you?" The woman wasn't in tactical gear, brandishing an assault weapon, so I didn't peg her as a Dreki. She also wasn't wearing the gray suits favored by Will, Stormfield, and the other LANCE agents I'd seen. Her simple green sweater complimented her eyes, but it didn't tell me anything about who she was.

"You can call me Cassie." She offered me her hand to shake, but I didn't take it.

"As in Cassandra?"

"You read Greek myths?" Cassie gave me a skeptical glance like she had trouble believing I read anything at all.

"Some, but I read two or three superhero biographies when I was a kid. Don't you work with the Defender? I thought you were a lot older." The woman across from me wasn't young, probably around thirty-five, but the great Seer, Cassandra, had been helping the Defender for at least twenty years.

"We started young," Cassie said with a smile. "Like you, I hear."

I frowned. "How did you hear about me? Is there a subversive news channel dedicated to knowing LANCE's secrets? You know about me, the Dreki know about me, I'm surprised most of America doesn't know about me."

"The Dreki's knowledge is troublesome, but I know about you because Pendragon told the Defender. They thought news of a new powerful clairvoyant might interest me. Have you discovered your trigger?"

"My what?" Unsure what she meant, I glanced around as if I expected triggers to be lying around the café.

"The person or sensory input that helps you channel a vision. Ahmet, the main clairvoyant that works for LANCE, can only access his visions from a deep trance state. It's not useful in the field, but he provides great tactical intelligence.

"Smells bring my visions. Yesterday, I smelled a cup of coffee and Saw myself talking with you today. It took me nearly three hours to figure out what town you were in. Why ever did you leave Manhattan? I had assumed I would find you there."

Taking a deep breath, I launched into the story of all my visions from the one of me at the Rook to the bad one I'd had earlier in the day. I even told her about the possible vision where Will and I hung out on the couch.

Cassie nodded throughout. "You're going to be very powerful someday. You've already had a number of unaided visions, but I think for you the strongest will always be channeled through touch. Let's try." She held out her hand palm up as if she wished me to read her fortune. "What do you See?"

I grazed her palm with the tip of my index finger. This time I Saw the vision, but I didn't become completely immersed. I could still see Cassie sitting across from me, but I also Saw her get home to an apartment somewhere. A moment later, the Defender dropped in through the skylight, he pulled off his mask revealing his secret identity, and the two kissed. It was the kind of familiar kiss that couples of long standing gave one another.

I pulled my finger back, and the vision faded.

"Patrick Jennings is the Defender?" I asked. "The actor from *Danger Road*? I must have binge watched the entire series last month. How can he have time for both the show and being a superhero? Does this mean he does his own stunts?"

"Shh." Cassie glanced around, but no one seemed to pay us

96

any attention. "It's called a secret identity for a reason. You have to keep it secret."

"And you two are like dating or something? I Saw him kiss you."

"Engaged actually. What was I wearing? You need to use clues from your visions to figure out where and when they will happen."

"You're wearing what you have on now."

"Good." Cassie nodded, a pleased expression on her face. "Then I get home safely." A slight cloud passed over her eyes. The hazel part of her iris didn't disappear like last time, instead it was more like a faint mist had obscured Cassie's pupils for a second. I wondered if that was what had happened to my eyes back at school. No wonder everyone kept staring at my eyes and making comments.

"But I get home safe only if I leave now." Cassie stood and slid over a small piece of paper. "Call when you have questions. I should already have the answers. And remember the future is not fixed. What you See can be changed. Try to change for the better." She nodded goodbye and hurried past me for the front door.

I stayed in my seat, tapping my fingers on the table. For a second I wondered why Cassie had to leave so suddenly, but I assumed it was an experienced clairvoyant thing. Someday I might leave other people just as confused as I abruptly ran to some event in the future.

Instead, I focused on what Cassie had said about changing the future. That was what I was trying to do by running away. If I could keep the Keeps, and especially Will, away from me, no one would have to die. I traced my finger along a groove in the table and wondered what was taking my grilled cheese so long. I turned to glance back at the counter and froze.

An older man with a determined look on his kind face came toward me carrying two steaming cups. He sat a cup of hot chocolate with marshmallows in front of me then slid into the seat Cassie had left only five minutes before.

"Ah, Elaine," the man said. His voice chilled me. Little goose bumps popped up on my arms. "I've been trying so hard to arrange a little meeting with you, but you appear to recognize me. Perhaps your father has spoken of me?"

I nodded, but I couldn't speak. An overwhelming feeling of despair tied my tongue into knots. I recognized the man, but not in the way he meant. This was the man from my vision, the man who would shoot Will any second now. I hadn't run from my vision but straight into it. If I had stayed at the tower like Arthur had wanted, I never would have been in this café now. No wonder the place looked so familiar. I turned, searching the room for Will, but no one new came through the door.

"Are you expecting someone?" He glanced around too.

"I sincerely hope not," I said.

This surprised the man. "Good. Allow me to introduce myself. I am Vortigern, Elector of the Dreki." He held out his hand to shake, but I didn't take it. There were some people's futures I didn't need to See.

Vortigern didn't seem bothered. There had to be plenty of people that had refused to shake the terrorist's hand.

"Don't you mean the Illuminati?" I asked him.

Vortigern looked pleased. "I see your father, or perhaps one of your LANCE minders, has been speaking with you after all." He reached forward as if to give my hand a gentle pat in a weird parody of the way Arthur had been comforting me earlier. I jerked my hands into my lap.

"But King of the Illuminati is so outdated now," he continued. "It brings so many crackpot theories to mind. Since taking over, I prefer to see the organization abandon the shadows and use the noble name of our warriors."

"The Dreki."

Vortigern nodded. "I would like to discuss you becoming a part of my organization."

"What?" This so surprised me I quit watching for Will. My head snapped back to Vortigern.

"Yes, dear. What did you think we've been trying to do all week?"

"Kill me" was the first thing that came to mind. Instead I said, "You've been trying to recruit me?"

Vortigern smiled in the way I had always imagined vampires smiled before draining their victims. "My dear, you have no idea how much we want you."

"I have a bit of an idea," I said thinking of the battle at my school and the bomb they'd set off in the Rook.

"You would be one of our most valuable assets. Being able to See the future would be an amazing tactical advantage for us." He stared deep in my eyes, and once again I knew how a rat felt when mesmerized by a snake.

"So what do you say, my dear?" asked the man.

"She has nothing to say to you," said a voice from behind me just like in my vision.

This time though, I didn't turn. I grabbed my untouched cup of hot chocolate and threw it in Vortigern's face. At the same time, I jumped up. "Run, Will!"

I spun around, but Will didn't stand behind me. Instead Arthur grinned. He wore his normal board shorts and hideous Hawaiian shirt except for the knight's glove on his right hand. He had the rocket from that glove aimed at Vortigern's nose.

Vortigern wasn't in any danger of pulling a gun this time. He had jumped back so the hot chocolate had landed on his lap instead of his face. Vortigern stood brushing at his pants in a futile gesture to remove some of the steaming liquid. He glared up at us.

"Pendragon. Your timing is impeccable, as always. I don't know what you plan to do with a single rocket. I have eighteen men surrounding this building."

My stomach dropped to my toes. Vortigern might not have shot Will, but he still might kill Arthur and me.

Arthur gave Vortigern a pitying stare. "I know about your men. I have eighteen knights outside targeting them. There's also twenty-two on the roof with lasers targeted at your head." Arthur turned to me. "Elaine, let's go."

"You're bluffing," said Vortigern. "You would never risk this many innocent people to blow me up." He waved at all the other café patrons. A few had noticed the commotion and had backed away, but most were still oblivious.

"Who said anything about blowing you up?" Arthur rolled his eyes. "I said lasers. The knights have lasers aimed at various parts of your head with pinpoint precision targeting. Just twenty-two little holes and bye-bye higher brain function. The owners of this place won't even realize they have holes in their roof until the next time it rains."

Vortigern paled slightly. He opened and shut his mouth, but he didn't bluster out a retort. He also didn't move.

"Come on, Princess. We're leaving." Arthur grabbed my arm and steered me to the door. Outside three knights stood waiting on the pavement.

"I have never been so happy to see you," I said in a low voice. "I'm so glad Will didn't come."

The helm of the nearest knight flipped open, revealing Will's face. I jumped almost a foot in the air.

"You didn't think you could run away from LANCE that easily, did you?" he said with a small smile.

Arthur huffed. "Yes, Baby LANCE insisted that either he came with me, or he called out LANCE reinforcements. I decided I preferred the devil I knew. However, considering your vision, he agreed to wait out here. Am I correct in assuming that your vision just played out?"

I nodded, and to the guys and my surprise, I hugged both Arthur and Will. "I am so glad no one died today."

"The day's not over yet," said Arthur in a cheerful tone that did not at all match his words. He pointed over at the extra knight.

"Armor up."

I stepped into the spare knight while the rest of the Pendragon armor assembled around Arthur.

"Don't even think about trying to co-opt this knight," Arthur said over the headset. "I've had Percival revoke all of your flight controls for now."

The knights took off. Once we were mid-air, an additional forty joined us.

"You weren't bluffing. You really had all those knights targeting everyone." I shook my head, but that made my knight wobble, so I stopped.

"I don't bluff," said Arthur in his smug tone. "I may outright lie, but I never bluff. And Princess, next time you decide you want to go to Montana, just ask. We own a twenty-thousand acre ranch out there. We can go visit anytime."

I sighed. "Of course, you do, Arthur. Of course, you do."

10

WHERE I LEARN THAT WILL HATES SPILLING HIS GUTS

DINNER THAT NIGHT WAS A SOBER AFFAIR. I WAS NOT, AS **G**INNY pointed out, grounded for life, but I was grounded for the foreseeable future. This seemed kind of a joke since I couldn't leave the residential floors and, until I jumped off the balcony, hadn't been outside for days. I nodded though and accepted my punishment meekly enough. It seemed to make Ginny and Arthur feel better, and I had run away and made a huge mess. Grounding seemed fair.

The rest of dinner concerned my future education. Will would teach me basic LANCE agent stuff, and Arthur would train me to use my knight once her breastplate had been refitted. No one thought I could go to school. There wasn't a school secure enough to protect me from the Dreki, and no one wanted to even think about endangering the other students. Ginny decided she'd find me either a good online program or tutors. No one appreciated my suggestion that I drop out and get a GED.

"Do you think you could pass the GED at this point?" Arthur

asked. Unlike Ginny and Will, he at least took my suggestion seriously. "I mean, I've seen your grades."

I tried to brush past this reminder that I'd been a part of Arthur's life even when he hadn't been in mine. "What about them? I get A's and B's in every class. I had a whole bunch of pre-AP and one AP class this year."

Arthur shoveled another bite of lasagna in his mouth. "That's my point. I don't think you realize how hard the GED is, Princess. I took it two years ago, and even I had trouble. You only get about two minutes to answer each question, and you need to remember everything that might come up in high school. I mean *everything* from stuff you forgot after ninth grade to things you don't even cover until you're a senior."

"You took the GED," I said. The doubt dripped out of my mouth the way the sauce dripped off my fork of lasagna. "I thought I read somewhere you went to a swanky boarding school."

"The swankiest." Arthur made a face like his food had gone bad, but I figured it was the memory of his school. "I took the test to see what I was asking of my employees. Keep Consolidated has lots of jobs, both manufacturing and desk, that don't require a degree. We did used to require a high school diploma or GED though. At least, we did until I almost failed it. Now, you take a job specific test to see if you can do the work. If a coder can pass Ginny's test, for example, they're in, no formal schooling required."

"That's unusual." My entire life, all my teachers had drilled into us how we wouldn't be able to work without a college degree.

Arthur shrugged. "I'm an unusual man," he said through a mouth full of food. "I run an unusual company."

"You run?" Ginny slammed her fork onto her plate with a clank.

Arthur reached over and patted her hand. "Ginny runs an unusual company for me."

"That's better." She looked only the tiniest bit appeased.

After dinner, I went to my room and drew for about an hour. Even though my new style of visions had changed from the ones I'd grown up with, I hoped drawing them would still help purge them from my system. I drew and colored in a picture of Cassie kissing the Defender. The picture made me smile; the two seemed so content with one another. Arthur and Ginny looked like that when they thought no one could see them.

After I finished Cassie's picture, I drew a quick, rough pencil sketch of Vortigern sitting behind his cup of coffee. I gave the coffee mug more detail than I did Vortigern. The second I finished, I wadded up the sketch and threw it in the trash. This wasn't a vision I wanted to remember.

There was one other vision I didn't want to remember, but I couldn't bring myself to draw Will with a bullet in his head. That future might not have come to pass, but the image still disturbed me. I paced my new room back and forth. Like everything in Arthur's home, the room was huge. I walked laps around the room, twenty steps for each side, but I still didn't feel better.

Finally, I decided to just see Will for myself, to see him alive and safe. I stepped into the hallway and realized I had no idea where he might be. He'd mentioned moving in next door to me, but had he meant my current room or my old room? Was he in the room to the right or the left?

I wandered up the hall, wondering which door to knock on. I didn't have to wander long. The door to the right of my current room had a new, hand-written sign taped to the front: *Will's Room. No Keeps Allowed. (This means you, Arthur.)*

I grinned. The sign hinted at a more whimsical side to the serious LANCE agent. Of course, you rarely see the whimsical side of a person during Dreki attacks. The fact was I knew nothing about Will Redding except that he was super-hot and knew how to save my life. He could be a practical joker or a secret bassoon player. He could be anything beneath the Agent Redding persona.

I knocked on the door and cracked it open when there wasn't an answer. I stuck my head in, but Will didn't seem to be home. His room was laid out almost identical to my old room with a queen bed, a small sitting area centered around a sofa, and a one person metal desk along the far wall. This morning, before all the craziness with visions, Will had claimed to move in, but I didn't see any real sign that Will lived here. If it hadn't been for the sign, I would have assumed this to be another empty guest bedroom.

I snuck into the room, but nothing happened. Alarms didn't go off. Traps didn't fall from the ceiling. Nothing. Will hadn't mounted any special LANCE defenses.

The doors to both the walk-in closet and the bathroom were shut, but I didn't feel like opening them. I assumed Will's bathroom looked just like mine, and I assumed his closet was full of his boring gray agent suits. The guy probably didn't even own anything else. Since he looked amazing in his suits, I shouldn't complain.

I plopped down on the couch, intending to wait for Will to get back. I didn't want to hunt him down, but I also didn't want to go to bed without seeing, once again, that he was alive.

Laying my head down on the arm of the couch, I stared at the end table and the silver picture frame siting on it. Slowly, I realized that Will must have brought something with him after all. I sat up and picked up the frame to get a better look.

There were three kids in the picture, probably around thirteen or fourteen years old. Will stood on the right side, his arm around a Japanese girl. On her other side, a Russian boy held the girl's hand. They all wore some sort of school uniform—black slacks and gray jacket for the guys, a black pleated skirt and gray jacket for the girl—with a LANCE crest on their jackets and little flag lapel pins on their collars designating their countries. Will wore a little American flag, and I had guessed the other two kids' nationalities based on their pins.

The three kids had genuine smiles. I had never seen Will that relaxed even in informal moments like tonight's dinner. Although, technically dinner hadn't been all that relaxed with all the repressed tension from my little runaway attempt permeating the atmosphere.

The door to the bathroom opened, and Will stepped out in only a pair of boxer briefs, a towel ruffling his hair. It was a good thing I was already sitting since he was even more stunning in real life than I had imagined. Will had the kind of body and face that could have inspired Michelangelo's David. I knew I was feeling inspired, and usually I only drew my visions, not from real life.

"Oh, hey," Will said, noticing me staring at his half-naked body.

The blood rushed to my face. I'd probably been staring at him all bug-eyed, the way cartoon wolves stared at sheep. I wanted to hide my face behind the picture but with the amount of heat radiating from my cheeks, the thing might have burst into flames. "I thought you weren't here."

"So you were snooping through my room?" Will raised an eyebrow at me and disappeared in his closet.

"What? No," I sputtered. "I was sitting here waiting for you."

"It's okay," he said, reemerging in a T-shirt and a pair of jeans. So, the guy did own normal clothes. "I'm going through your room tomorrow."

"What?"

"Just kidding." He grinned and threw his towel back in the bathroom.

Will sat down on the couch next to me. This was the first time he'd been this close when I wasn't in the middle of a crisis. I was surprised to discover that my heart raced from the proximity even without the threat of imminent death. He tapped the picture with his hand, bringing my focus back from contemplating the nearness of his thigh. "This was a great day."

"What?" I had returned to the tongue-tied inability to form words in front of cute guys, an MO that had been such a hallmark of my social success at school.

Will took the picture from my hand, so he could look at it closer. Our fingers brushed, and I got a little electric shock. It wasn't the magical kind of shock true love delivers in a novel. It was the normal kind of static electricity that hurts.

Will didn't seem to notice. He had probably been trained to ignore any kind of physical discomfort. "This was a great day," he repeated, staring at the picture. His mouth smiled, but his eyes looked sad. The day in the picture might have been great, but it didn't take a genius like Ginny or Arthur to tell that things hadn't stayed that way.

"Were those your friends at school?" I asked.

"Something like that," said Will, but he didn't elaborate. I didn't feel like I knew him well enough to push so we sat there in silence while Will lived in his memory. Shifting so that my back was now to the arm of the couch, I faced Will's profile. I found it easier to breathe with the extra inch between us.

Will sat the picture face down on the sofa cushion next to him. He turned so he sat sideways too, facing me. "So, what did you need me for?"

"Uh." The blood flooded back into my face.

"Did you want to talk about your training?" he prompted.

"Training?" With a monumental effort, I pulled my mind back into the room.

"I'm going to give you a sort of modified version of basic agent training. We'll start tomorrow."

That got me interested. "Like code-breaking and tailing?"

Will laughed. "You've seen too many movies. More like self-defense. You can't always be in armor. Besides, I suspect that Ginny is a better code-breaker than all of LANCE put together."

"True." I gave Will an evil grin. "Ginny told me at dinner she's teaching me to hack. We'll see who can keep secrets then."

Will raised his eyebrows. "I don't remember her saying that. I'm pretty sure I would have noticed if she'd mentioned hacking."

I waved away his doubt. "She said code, but this is Ginny, tech genius, best friend of the Viral Vixen, and wife to eccentric gazillionaire Arthur Keep. She totally meant hack."

Will smiled for a second, but then he narrowed his eyes. "Why are you here, Elaine? It's not to talk about training."

I looked away, unable to meet his eyes.

"It's about the vision, isn't it? The one where I died?"

I didn't answer. I picked at the hem of my tank top.

"It's hard to see someone die, especially the first time." Will's voice dropped until he spoke so softly, I barely caught his words. "Especially when it's someone you know."

I glanced over, but now Will was the one not looking at me. He stared off into space. I wondered who he'd seen die. I wondered how many he'd seen die. I didn't ask.

"Where did Vortigern shoot me?" Will turned back. He wasn't mad like I would have been. He didn't seem sad or resigned or anything other than a little curious.

I shook my head, unwilling to say, even though an imaginary bullet hole seemed to sit in the middle of Will's forehead.

"Was it the heart?" Will picked up my right arm by the wrist

110

and placed my hand on his chest over his heart. His other hand covered mine, pressing it firmly into place. "Feel it? Mine's still here, still beating. Vortigern didn't get me. Arthur and I saw to it."

Beneath my hand I felt Will's warmth radiating up through his T-shirt. I couldn't feel his heart beating through all the rock-hard muscle, but it was a nice, dramatic gesture. Logically, I knew an alive Will had a beating heart. I didn't need to feel a pulse to prove it. I left my hand there though. There was something comforting about Will's solid warmth.

When I glanced back up, Will still stared at me intently. "It wasn't the heart, was it?" Will glared at me. I tried to pull back, but Will still held my hand against his chest. "Vortigern shot me in the gut, didn't he? That snake-skinned, dragon-loving jerk."

"What? No," I said, surprised by Will's sudden vehemence. "It was in the forehead."

Will shrugged, a relieved look on his face. "Oh, well, that's fine then."

This time when I pulled back, he let my hand go. "What do you mean, 'that's fine?' You were freaking dead. Stone-cold-lifeless-eyed-dead." I hugged my legs up to my chest as tight as possible and crushed my eyes against my knees. "So-long-and-thanks-for-all-the-laughs dead."

"But a forehead shot, that's a good way to go, Elaine." Will scooted closer, wrapping his arms around my defensive cocoon. "It's a clean, fast kill. No pain, no suffering. Did you know it can take up to twenty minutes to bleed out from a stomach wound?

You're just lying there writhing around in excruciating pain for twenty minutes."

I turned my head until my cheek rested on my knee so I could glare at Will. "Is this supposed to make me feel better? That you died in a preferable way? You were still dead! Why does that not bother you?"

Will wrinkled his nose for a moment, thinking. "It's my job."

"Your job is to die?"

With his arms still around me, Will shrugged. "Kind of. Do you know what the life expectancy is for a Conservatory kid like me? For a kid raised by LANCE, sent to their school, trained since the age of six?"

"The age of six?" I whispered, but Will didn't hear me.

"Twenty-five. That's the oldest most of us see. Twenty-five. If we don't die in the field before then, LANCE retires the rest when we outlive our usefulness, and it's not the sort of retirement where you live out your golden years in Florida. It's not the kind of retirement where you live."

I sat up, horrified. "But I thought LANCE was the good guys."

"They are. We are." Will's arms dropped from around me. He was now too upset in his own right to comfort me. "But sometimes good guys do bad things for the greater good. So, yeah, when the time comes, it'll be my job to die for the greater good."

I grabbed Will in a bear hug—as if physically restraining him from that death. "Your job sucks." I buried my face in his neck.

Will sighed. His arms crept back around me in a gentle hug back. "Yeah. I know."

We sat there, me squeezing the life out of Will, Will hugging me.

It was an awesome moment, so Arthur had to ruin it.

"Unhand my daughter," he yelled from the doorway.

"I should have locked the door when I came in." I reluctantly pulled myself off of Will's shoulder. Turning, I rolled my eyes at my livid parent. "You have got to get a new line."

"What are you doing in here? You are supposed to be grounded." Arthur stood there with his arms crossed, tapping his foot while he waited for me to walk over to him.

"I can't talk to Will?"

"I'm pretty sure being grounded means no boys, doesn't it?" For a second Arthur looked uncertain. After all, he'd only actively been playing father for twenty-four hours. "You still haven't told me what you were doing in here."

"I came to see if Will kisses as good as he looks," I said, filling my voice with as much sarcasm as I could manage.

Behind me, Will made a choking sound. Arthur turned an interesting four shades of purple before all the blood drained from his face leaving it ghostly pale.

"Oh, good grief. That was a joke. Why do you think I'm in here? I wanted to remind myself that Will was alive."

"Oh," said Arthur. For a second he looked a little guilty, but it was only for a second. "Next time use the security feed to check. The sensors track his biometric data, so you can see he's alive."

"I will." I decided not to be mad that the rooms were all being monitored, not when I would find this security feed useful.

"I'll check them every day. Did you know that for the next eight years, LANCE will keep sending Will on suicide missions, and if he doesn't die, they'll just kill him off themselves when he turns twenty-five?"

"What?" Even Arthur looked taken aback, and nothing phased Arthur.

"That's not exactly what I meant," said Will.

Arthur's eyes narrowed into little slits. "I have never trusted Stormfield or that nest of vipers. Young man, I may not trust you, I may not even like you, but I will not allow you to die while living under my roof." Arthur stormed from the room yelling for Percival to get Ginny to hack into LANCE's systems.

Will and I raised our eyebrows at each other.

"That took a surprising twist," I said.

Arthur stuck his head back through the doorway. "And there's no casually kissing my daughter while you live under my roof either." He disappeared back into the hall.

I flushed, but Will gave me a mischievous grin. "Then, I guess we'll just have to content ourselves to a serious relationship with no casual, only passionate kissing, right Elaine?" he said with a shrug.

As soon as I peeled my jaw off the floor, I fled the room.

WHERE I LEARN HOW MUCH I NEED TO LEARN

THE NEXT MORNING, I WAS DRAGGED OUT OF A DEEP SLEEP BY A banging on my door. Since this was the first decent night's sleep I'd had since moving into the Rook, I groaned and tried burrowing my way deeper under my covers. Nothing made the horrible thudding at my door go away—not ignoring it or cursing at it.

Finally, I asked Percival if we were under attack, and if so, to tell the Dreki to come back at a reasonable hour.

"The Dreki have not penetrated our defenses, my lady," Percival sounded insulted that I would think the Dreki would circumvent him. I didn't point out they'd done it only two days before. "Master Will wishes you to join him for a healthy constitutional."

That got my attention. I even pulled the blanket off my face. "He said that? Healthy constitutional?" What was this? The eighteenth century?

Percival sniffed. I hadn't realized he could do that. "Master Will may have called it an early morning run around the outer terrace."

"Yeah, not happening." I rolled over and pulled the blanket back over my head. "Tell him to go away."

Percival must have relayed my message because the banging stopped. I snuggled deeper into my blankets. I enjoyed the peace for about six seconds.

The lights in my room started flashing on and off with the kind of strobe effect that can give people seizures. "Morning, sunshine," Will's chipper voice boomed from over the loudspeakers in my room. "Time to get the blood pumping. We're going for a run around the terrace. No jumping off it though."

I didn't appreciate the joke. "You traitor, Percival!" I yelled. "You're supposed to be on my side letting me sleep." I tried cramming my pillow over my head, but Will had Percival add klaxon alarms. "You win," I screamed at them both. I threw my pillow at the door, but my room was so big, it landed in the middle of the floor. "I'm up."

The lights went back to a normal illumination, and the alarms stopped.

"Can I come in?" Will asked.

I wore a sports bra and leggings. The answer was an emphatic no. "Give me a second," I said. I pulled on a T-shirt while trying to brush my teeth at the same time. I couldn't do anything about the pink crease running down the side of my face from having slept at a weird angle on my pillow. At least, I could scrub the line of dried drool off my other cheek. My hair was a loss, so it got thrown in a ponytail while I sprinted back across the room to my door. I threw it open.

Will leaned against the opposite wall. He looked amazing in a close-fitting tank top that showed every defined muscle on his chest. I kind of felt the need to drool again. Instead, part of me was shriveling up and dying from mortification that Will was seeing me all rumpled and half asleep. Had I remembered to check for eye boogers? I reached up and rubbed both my eyes like Arthur did every time he was stressed.

I flushed when I realized Will was checking me out from head to toe. I'd just seen myself in the mirror. It wasn't a pretty sight.

"You forgot your shoes," he said. "You don't want to run four miles barefoot."

My flush deepened to a throbbing red when I realized he'd only been looking to see if I'd dressed for training.

I turned and headed back to my closet. Will followed me into my room.

"Four miles? This is inhumane," I muttered.

"It's time to train. Didn't you get the new schedule Arthur and Ginny sent an hour ago?"

"Don't you people sleep?"

Will shrugged. "At the Conservatory, we got up at four. You got to sleep in an extra hour."

"It's five in the morning?" Will didn't see my look of horror since I was rummaging through the boxes of brand-new shoes stocked in my closet, hoping there would be something I could use for running. I pulled out a gorgeous pair of designer heels only to put them away again. Not appropriate training wear.

"I get you for three hours every morning for self-defense."

Awesome. I would get to look this good for Will every day. "Yay?" I managed.

At last I found a pair of running shoes at the back of my closet. When I first got here and Ginny had asked me what kind of clothes I wanted, it hadn't even occurred to me I would need stuff like running shoes. I only had the leggings and sports bra because I liked to sleep in them. I said as much to Will.

"You don't use them for working out?" he asked while I pulled on a pair of socks and the shoes.

"I hate working out. All that sweating. Even dance team is more than I'd do if I didn't have to have some kind of PE credit."

"Wow." Will nodded his head up and down in wonder. He gestured to the door, and I followed him out. "That's a new level of lazy. You're gonna loooooooove self-defense."

I slammed the door behind me.

He was right though. I hated self-defense. I hated how I didn't seem to possess a coordinated bone in my body. The little skill I had when dancing didn't transfer over into hand to hand combat. I hated that no matter what I did, I ended up flat on my back with Will on top of me—and not in a hot look-deep-in-each-other's-eyes kind of way. More like a knee-in-my-stomach or an arm-in-my-solar-plexus kind of way.

The worst part though was Will's distance. Whatever moment we'd shared last night in his room had disappeared. Will was all business. Agent Redding had returned with a vengeance.

I tried everything I could think of to bring the real Will back. I asked him about being in LANCE. I tried talking about

118

the Conservatory he'd attended. I even told him stupid anecdotes from my life from back when superheroes and secret agents were just things you saw in headlines and movies.

In return I got one-word answers and another demonstration on the proper technique to break a choke hold.

The torture finally ended with a curt nod from Will. I dragged my sore body away from the full-floor home gym we'd been using. My first time out of the Keep's general living quarters, and it was to get my rear-end kicked in a gym. Super awesome.

Breakfast was a new form of torture. Will had been as gentle as possible, but I still had some impressive bruises. Sitting on my chair to shovel cereal in my mouth hurt. Will wasn't looking at me, so he missed the death glares I kept sending in his direction.

Ginny watched the two of us for a moment. "Training went well, I take it."

Will made some incoherent murmur, still not looking at me.

"I have sore muscles in places I didn't know had muscles," I griped.

Ginny grinned. "I haven't found you a school I like yet, so this afternoon, you'll code with me instead of more traditional academic subjects."

That perked me up. I could do coding sitting down. In a chair. With no one throwing me to the ground.

"Can we start now?" I asked her.

"Not yet, Princess." Arthur strolled into the room and grabbed an apple off the back wall's buffet. "You're mine until lunch." He flashed me a mischievous grin.

I groaned and dropped my head onto the table. "Why am I sure this will be even worse than training with Will?"

It was, and it wasn't. Arthur didn't share Will's reticence, so he talked non-stop from the moment we left the small breakfast room until the elevator reached the armory. This was another room that took up a whole floor, but instead of workout equipment and mats, robotic knights filled the space.

Like every other floor, the armory was a perfect circle. Niches lined the entire outer wall with robots standing in them like silent sentries. In the center of the room was another circle of niches filled with knights. We walked into the wide hallway formed by the two.

"Meet my Knights of the Round Table or at least my round tower," Arthur said with a small snort, amused by his joke. "I think you've met Gawain and his brothers Agravaine, Gaheris, and Gareth." He waved at various knights as we passed. They still all looked the same but engraved nameplates mounted above each niche named the knights inside.

At first I had thought every niche was full, but we passed empty ones as we made our way to a door set in the wall of inner niches. When I asked Arthur about it, he pulled up one of his mid-air screens. Even here in the armory the things were ubiquitous. The screen followed Arthur as we kept walking. "Yep," he said, confirming a thought he'd had. "Most are patrolling around Keep Tower, but a couple are escorting our guests."

Arthur, though, wouldn't tell me who the guests were. No amount of pestering would get him to ruin the surprise. By the time we reached the door, he was rubbing at his eyes as if my persistent questions and begging were giving him a migraine, so I stopped. Besides, he'd promised that the guests were on track, and I'd find out soon enough.

I forgot all about mysterious guests when we stepped into the inner room. I had thought the outer armory of knights was impressive, but this room took my breath away. Literally. I realized when I became light-headed that I'd been holding my breath as if the magnificence of the room had made my body forget how to breathe.

This room was a throne room, despite not having chairs. On one wall were six niches, only these were more ornate than the ones in the outer corridor. Those had been impressive feats of technology able to run diagnostics or charge the knights. But, compared to the niches in this room, those had been like the basic charging cable that came with every Keep smart phone.

These niches were works of art. It looked as if a medieval monk had hand illuminated each one. There were hand painted dragons around the niche holding Pendragon. Like outside, this niche had an engraved plate above with Pendragon's name. This plate though looked as if Arthur had made it out of solid gold.

Three of the niches were empty with no nameplates as if they weren't in use, but two knights flanked Pendragon. Both were smaller than Pendragon or the knights in the other room, but I was relieved to see that at least they were the same shape as all the other knights. No weird breastplates.

The knight Arthur had shown me the day before sat in a niche marked Morgause. The weird, pointy boobs were gone. Arthur tapped on a screen on the wall of the niche and a complete schematic with readouts appeared.

"Dame Morgause looks in good shape," he said. "Percival, let's get Elaine suited up and start her training."

Both Pendragon and my armor stepped out of their niches. Arthur handed me a headset. It looked like the ones telemarketers wore with a headband holding a single ear bud attached to a small arm with a microphone that sat on my cheek close to my mouth. The thing was form fitting and comfortable, and within seconds, I forgot it was there.

"Ready?" Arthur asked after checking his own headset.

I didn't answer. Instead, I pointed at the other knight still in its niche. It was golden like Pendragon's old armor. In fact it kind of looked like the match of the armor he used to wear, complete with a small crown. The plate above the niche said "Leodegrance," but that didn't tell me anything. "Whose armor is that?"

Arthur made a grumbling sound through his headset. It wasn't a sound he meant for me to hear, but the microphones in our headsets were that sensitive. Good to know.

"That is Ginny's armor," he said. "Not that I've ever gotten her to so much as try it on." He glared at the armor before turning his back to it in a supreme gesture of disinterest. Even I could take the hint he didn't want to talk about it.

"Ready?" he asked again.

"I guess." I sighed. Might as well get this over with.

My armor fell into a jillion pieces before reassembling

around me.

"Initializing," said Percival.

The screens lit up around my head, and I bent and flexed my arms, legs, and finger joints. Percival had taught me the basic voice commands to control a knight yesterday. Arthur now took me through more complicated physical instructions. Sensors throughout the inside of the armor monitored my every muscle. If I wanted to walk, I moved as if I wanted to walk. Percival and the armor did the rest.

However, there were physical commands that controlled less obvious motions. Wiggling my pinky fingers activated the lasers embedded in the armor just above my wrists. Various toe motions controlled flight. Arthur had me practice each movement even though we weren't flying around the throne room.

Within minutes, I had no trouble running, jumping, or even doing a high-kick in my armor. Remembering the other commands would take time, but Arthur called it "building unnatural reflexes." Controlling my borrowed knight yesterday hadn't been burdensome, but armor that fit had many advantages. It didn't feel like I was wearing the armor, more like I had gained a thicker skin.

When I'd convinced Arthur I could walk across the throne room without tripping or launching myself into flight on accident, he opened the room above us.

A small circular door, wide enough for three knights to fly side by side, opened in the ceiling. I waited but no ladder or staircase appeared.

Arthur ignited the rockets on his back, and he shot through the hole.

"Oh, of course. Flight. Duh." We'd just been practicing flight controls.

I'd been talking to myself, but Percival answered. "Boosters engaged," he said. Faster than I would have thought possible I shot straight up through the hole in the ceiling.

I was in a massive training room. Like the armory and the Keeps home gym, it took up the whole floor's footprint. Unlike those other spaces, it was four stories tall. This was a good thing because all of Arthur's careful training flew out of my head the same time my boosters engaged. The roof of the building approached faster than I would like. Any minute I would splat flatter than a bug on a windshield, and I didn't remember how to stop.

"Stop!" I shrieked at Percival and my suit. "Stop, stop, stop, stop, stop!" The words blurred together. Percival must have been able to figure out what I meant because I halted mid-air about six feet from the top of the room. Arthur flew up to where I hovered, staring at the ceiling.

"Not elegant, but effective," Arthur said. Pendragon's face didn't show emotions, but I could tell Arthur was grinning. Even over the comms his suppressed laughter filled his voice. "In a pinch you can always just yell commands at Percival, and he'll respond. It's faster though to do things the right way. In a fight you might not have time to think up the words, much less say them. Percival can respond faster if he reads your muscle movements rather than listens for commands. Let's go through all the flight motions again, shall we?"

The rest of training didn't go much better. I soon got to where I remembered most of the commands, but then Arthur decided I was ready to start combat training. If I had thought self-defense with Will was hard, doing the same maneuvers mid-air was impossible. I also had to worry about things not just coming at me from the front, back, and sides, but also from above and below. It was enough to make a girl cry. Which I did—although I swore Percival to secrecy. I didn't need Arthur feeling sorry for me. All of this might be miserable, but it was necessary. I had to learn to defend myself, to keep from being another potential victim again. So even though I cried again from frustration when another knight tossed me into the wall for the eighth time, I kept at it. The next time the Dreki came for me, I would toss them out the door, not hide behind a desk.

By the time we put our armor back in their niches and headed down for lunch, my bruises had bruises. I knew that if I hadn't been wearing the armor, I'd be suffering from broken bones or worse. It didn't help that Arthur informed me in a cheerful voice that he'd set all the knights to "crowd-control," the least lethal setting. He assured me we'd be working at their most lethal by the end of the month.

"I can't wait to see you dodging bomblets," he continued as he led me back into the breakfast room where we'd eat lunch. "You've got some real grace out there. It must be all that dance you've done."

At no point today had I done anything graceful. I'd spent

the entire day being tossed around. I assumed parental love was blinding Arthur to my many, many training failures.

"Our guests have arrived," Ginny said. She sat at the table, her ever-present notebooks and tablets spread around her plate. Will also sat, shoveling food in his mouth like he hadn't eaten in weeks. Unlike me, he'd gotten to shower, and he'd changed into one of his LANCE gray suits. I settled in for another uncomfortable meal with Agent Redding.

"Are they coming in for lunch?" asked Arthur. He gave Ginny a kiss on the cheek before dropping into his chair. Arthur couldn't seem to sit still though. He kept turning to stare at the doorway, wiggling in his seat like a toddler promised ice cream.

I missed Ginny's answer. I hovered behind my chair, unsure if my aching body could handle sitting down. Besides, I was pretty sure I'd guessed who these exciting mystery guests were. There were only two people I wanted to see right now. Considering how excited Arthur was and how pleased Ginny looked, I figured they'd managed to get them for me.

Some device beeped on Arthur's wrist. "At last," he said. He got up to welcome his guests. I got ready to throw myself in my parents' arms.

Our guests entered the room, but instead of running, I froze. It wasn't them.

My parents hadn't come.

WHERE I DRAW SOME UNWELCOME CONCLUSIONS

I TRIED TO APPEAR PLEASED TO SEE OUR GUESTS, BUT BASED ON THE look Will gave me, I failed. He was the only one looking at me. Arthur and Ginny had both gone to greet the visitors.

"Cassie, Patrick," Ginny said. "Welcome. We're so glad you could come." She kissed both guests on both cheeks.

Cassie smiled and glanced over at me. I tried to smile back. Normally, I would have been beyond excited to have Patrick Jennings in the room. I'd seen every one of his movies and almost every episode of *Danger Road*. Never mind he was also the Defender and Cassie was a famous clairvoyant I'd met yesterday. I couldn't gather up the enthusiasm though. As soon as I could leave without being glaringly rude, I fled to my room. I didn't even bother to eat lunch even though getting pummeled in my armor had worked up an appetite.

Will tried to follow me, but to my relief, Ginny called him back. Patrick and Arthur were deep in some discussion about training exercises. Cassie watched me go, but she said nothing.

She continued to eat enchiladas instead.

When I got to my room, I grabbed the prototype phone Arthur had given me yesterday. Other than grabbing it off the breakfast room table after dinner last night, I'd forgotten it. Between my new armor, the vision, and throwing myself off the terrace, a new phone hadn't been at the front of my mind. But now I stared at the special phone app. I scrolled through my email and texts, but there weren't any new messages from my folks. They had dropped off the face of the planet.

I don't know how long I laid on my bed staring at the home screen of my phone before someone knocked on my door. Before I could tell them to go away, one of the knights that now guarded the hall had opened the door. He gestured inside, and Cassie entered my room. She held a small tray with a plate of food and a drink. "I suspected you were hungry," she said.

I rolled over and sat up. "You Saw that?" I could not even imagine being that powerful of a Seer.

"No." Cassie shook her head and gave a small laugh. "Your stomach was growling the whole time you were in the room." She sat the tray on the small table in front of my room's sofa. She sat down and gestured. "You need to eat. I heard about the training Arthur and Will put you through this morning. You need calories."

"And vitamins and electrolytes." I was still a sweaty mess, but I hadn't bothered to shower, choosing to wallow in misery on my bed instead. I sat on the floor across from Cassie. Before I scooped the first bite in my mouth, I said, "You know what upset me though. I bet you Saw that."

Cassie nodded. "You'll tell me in a minute. I think you still should," she added when I opened my mouth to point out I didn't need to now. "Even though it's awkward, it'll help to get the words out."

I stuffed another bite of refried beans in my mouth so I wouldn't have to talk right that second. While I thought, I traced shapes in my food. One of them was an abstract conception of my mother's face.

"It's not that I'm upset to have you here." I said after a swallow of the lemonade Cassie had brought. "I mean, it's good to have another superhero here, and the gods know I need some kind of mentor. It's not like Arthur or Ginny can help me with this whole Seer stuff."

Cassie opened her mouth like she was about to say something. Instead, her eyes clouded over, and she left for a moment. Her eyes cleared, but whatever she had planned to say had gone.

"Does that happen a lot?" I asked. "You getting sucked into a vision?"

Cassie shook her head. "No, at this point, I can stop a vision or even cause one if I want. I didn't stop that one because it seemed relevant."

She didn't explain further, but I was a little relieved. I didn't want to spend the rest of my life with one foot in the present while the other skipped around in the future.

"You said you don't mind us being here," she prompted when I ate instead of talking.

"Yeah, that." I swallowed. "It's just, Arthur was vague about who was coming. He wanted it to be a surprise. And that's sweet," I added. I didn't want Cassie thinking I was mad at Arthur. I wasn't. This whole mess wasn't his fault, not really. He didn't make my mom hack the Illuminati. He didn't send LANCE and the Dreki after me when I showed signs of clairvoyance. For the first time it occurred to me that maybe Arthur was doing the best he could too.

"It's just …" I couldn't figure out a good way to say something so hard. I went with the blunt truth. "I thought he'd found my parents—that Mom and Dad were coming through the door. I mean," I rushed on, "I'm still glad you guys are here."

"You just wished they had been here instead," Cassie finished for me.

I nodded, not trusting myself to speak. I also looked down at my lap so Cassie wouldn't see my face.

"Then, I think we know what visions we'll work on first," Cassie said with a decisive nod. "It won't be quite the same. You won't be able to interact with them, but we're going to practice until you can call up visions of your parents."

"How?" I asked. "I thought touch triggers my visions. I can't touch them because they aren't here." The frustration leaked into my voice although I was trying to stay calm. "That's the whole problem."

"I knew I wasn't clear enough yesterday," Cassie said. She sat back against the sofa, her fingers tapping little rhythms on the cushions. "I was in a hurry though. After I Saw the Dreki and

Pendragon coming, I didn't want to be there for that."

I nodded and took another bite of food. Even though no one had gotten hurt, I wouldn't have wanted to stick around for a meeting between Vortigern and Arthur either.

"Yes, touch trigger your visions. Scents trigger mine, but a strong Seer can have visions independent of their triggers. After all, it sounds like you've been having pre-visions for years, and touch didn't trigger those. And you were practicing hand to hand combat today with Agent Redding. Were you using gloves?"

I shook my head.

"Did it trigger a vision?"

"No." Horrified, I imagined how much worse training with Will would have gone if I'd Seen a vision every single time I'd grabbed his wrists.

"Our visions are tied to our emotions and to our loved ones as well. My strongest visions involve Patrick, and they are most easily brought on by smelling his cologne. Visions tied to my love for him and triggered by his smell."

My strongest visions so far had both been while holding Will's hand. I did not even sort of want to contemplate what that might mean. Instead I tried to figure out Cassie's point. "So, you're saying that even though they aren't physically here, I should be able to See my parents since I'm tied to them?"

Cassie smiled, pleased I'd made the connection. "Exactly."

"But I still don't get how to trigger a vision without, you know, a trigger."

"It's a lot harder, but most Seers can do it. Only Ahmet, the

LANCE Seer, has to be in a deep trance state to See. The rest of us can call up a vision if we work hard at it."

"Us? How many Seers are there?"

"A fair few." Cassie dodged the question. She watched me eat for a few more minutes, and then she sat up straight. "If you're finished eating, we can try to channel a vision now." She glanced down at her watch. "Ginny doesn't expect you in her office for another twenty minutes."

Ginny and the coding lessons. I had completely forgotten about them. Pushing the tray of mostly eaten food further down the coffee table and out of the way, I decided to find my parents using my Sight. But if it didn't work, with Ginny I had another way. I would hack my way to them.

Cassie joined me on the floor, and we sat facing each other. I matched Cassie's cross-legged position.

"So, how do we do this?" I asked.

"We focus," Cassie said. "How much do you know about meditation?"

FROM THEN ON, MY DAYS SETTLED INTO A ROUTINE—A WEIRD ROUTINE, but it became more normal as the days went on. First thing every morning, Will taught me self-defense and hand-to-hand combat with everyday objects.

"Why don't we ever use guns or swords?" I asked him one day when he was showing me how to incapacitate someone with a spatula.

"Don't you get enough of that with Pendragon and the

Defender?" Will seemed surprised by the question. He let his guard down just enough I was able to kick him in the stomach. I ruined the triumphant moment by tripping on my feet and slamming into him. Will managed to keep us both upright, but I somehow elbowed him in the eye, giving him a nasty bruise. It did not mar his good looks in the least. Some things are just not fair.

While we were getting Will some ice for his eye, Will asked again why I was so eager for conventional weapons.

"I don't want them, not really," I explained. "It's just that armor that sprouts guns and electric-edged swords are all fine and good, but it's not like I'll ever face an enemy with those things."

Will winced, and I apologized again for the eye.

He waved me away. "It's not that. Arthur had a robot go rogue last year. LANCE had to help hunt it down. Trust me. It's a good thing to have lots of practice with electric-edged swords."

"Yeah, but assuming I'm ever allowed to leave Keep Tower again—without armor," I added when I could see Will about to point out I left every morning on a training flight with Pendragon or the Defender. "But if I ever get to go out again in normal clothes, the people I might fight then will attack me with more conventional weapons. I doubt the Dreki will come after me with a spatula."

Will didn't argue. Instead, he gave me a long thoughtful look before I left for the armory to get my Morgause armor on. The next day he taught me how to disarm a gunman and then turn the guy's weapon against him.

Training with Pendragon and the Defender wasn't as physically tiring, but it was more frustrating. Within a week I ducked and dodged with the best. What I could not seem to do was fight.

A week after Will started teaching me how to use normal weapons, the Defender hovered above me near a wall in Arthur's training room. Patrick didn't wear his Defender costume. Instead he was in regular workout gear, looking like he was sitting on an invisible chair suspended sixty feet above the ground. I had asked Cassie about him, but she'd given me some vague response about how Patrick wasn't "quite human." Since the not-human parts of him meant he could fly, had super-strength, could spit fire, and knock a person over with his movie-star good looks, I didn't think he'd suffered from his differences.

I was staring at him when one of Arthur's knights rammed me from behind. For the fourth time in as many days, I slammed into the wall upside down. My rockets kept me from sliding down three stories to the floor. My armor protected my body from cracking in two, but it still wasn't comfortable. I snapped the visor up on my helm to get some fresh air.

"Do I have to keep getting thrown like that?"

A light popped on in the control room where Arthur, augmented by Percival, sat controlling a baker's dozen of knights all at one time.

"I'll keep throwing you until you manage to fight back."

Above me, Patrick laughed, but he didn't comment.

I righted myself and flew down to sit on an overturned car I'd tossed in the corner after the knights and I had finished playing keep-away. "It's fourteen to one. I'd like to see you do better."

Arthur swung his feet down off the electronic control board, stood, and stretched his back. "You're on, Princess." He disappeared from the control room.

The Defender drifted down next to me. "I'm not sure you'll like this," he said. "I watched Arthur take out forty-two Dreki foot soldiers in six minutes once."

"Arthur is always saying that one knight is worth ten men," I said back in a prim voice. "I'd like to see him knock out fourteen knights in six minutes." I glared at the empty control room as if I could fry Arthur with my annoyance.

Patrick shrugged and shot up to the top of the room out of the way.

"And no helping him," I yelled up after the superhero.

Arthur strolled into the training area, headset on, his Pendragon armor wandering in behind him. If he heard my little talk with the Defender, he didn't mention it. "Watch the master at work," he said instead. "Percival, execute Elaine practice four, target me."

Before he even got into his suit, the fourteen knights gathered and attacked him. Arthur jumped back, and Pendragon opened and shut around him. Faster than I could familiarize myself with my armor's displays, Arthur took out the nearest knight with a laser shot to the eye slit. Spinning and jumping, flying when necessary, Arthur performed a virtual ballet across the floor incapacitating knights as he went. In less than four minutes, not a single robot remained standing. Pendragon didn't get thrown once.

Careful not to set off by accident the micro-rockets mounted on my knuckles, I clapped as slow as possible, infusing each clap with as much sarcasm as I could manage.

"Bravo," I said. "Very impressive. You realize it's kind of cheating to fight knights you programmed. You knew where they were going to be."

Arthur popped Pendragon's visor up so I saw his huge smile. "Who cares? I took out all fourteen in under four minutes. What's your personal best? Three in eighteen minutes before you get thrown?"

I bit my tongue before I said something I would regret.

"Percival execute Elaine practice two, target Elaine," said Arthur. He leaned back against the wall, still in his armor, to watch. Patrick floated down to join him.

I slammed my visor back down and shot into the air, aiming at the three knights already regaining their feet and headed for me. I took the first one out, but the second grabbed my legs, and the third grabbed the boosters on my back. They tossed me, but at least I flew away before I hit a wall. Down below, Arthur and Patrick were laughing so hard, I thought they might fall down. I would have shot a rocket at them if there had been even the slightest chance it would have had an effect.

THE BEST PARTS OF MY DAY, THOUGH, WERE IN THE EVENINGS. Normal kids got evenings for regular extracurricular activities. I got to code with Ginny when she was available and to work on my psychic powers with Cassie when Ginny had pressing Keep Consolidated business to deal with. The basic coding skills I'd learned at school might not be up to Ginny's or my mom's standards, but it surprised me how fast I picked up the more advanced stuff Ginny taught. Soon, she started using Percival's code to demonstrate different concepts including machine learning.

She gave me my own dummy copy of Percival to tinker with the neural network algorithms. Ginny seemed pleased with my work, but the real Percival was not. At random moments he would offer comments on the code for dummy Percival. It was disconcerting, like operating on a patient while the patient critiqued your methods.

My sessions with Cassie though were not as productive. We'd sit on the floor meditating, and I would get a big fat nothing. It even felt like the calmer my mind got, any visions I might have drifted further away. In this state I could still bring up a vision if I touched someone's bare skin, but the images were faint, less substantial than the pictures that used to form in my mind back before I manifested real psychic powers. I still Saw several embarrassing scenes involving Cassie and Patrick that way—even if they were dim and muted by something that resembled distance. After the third time, I glimpsed them locked in a passionate embrace, Cassie decided we needed another test subject. To my horror, Cassie decided Will would be the best candidate.

She shrugged when I objected. "You have the easiest time calling up a vision with him."

"I don't call up visions of Will. They slam me over the head. It wasn't like I was trying to See Will die that time." I got up and paced around Cassie and Patrick's room. Their room was bigger than mine or Will's. They had a two-room suite with an entire living room to themselves where Cassie and I worked.

"Exactly," Cassie said. "Calming your emotions doesn't seem to be working. Let's try stirring them up. And based on what I'm watching right now, Will stirs them up quite nicely."

I groaned at her smirk. Will and I had been getting along better. He'd been easing back out of his Agent Redding persona over the last few weeks, but we still weren't comfortable with one another. Meals were a never-ending minefield of awkward, punctuated with glares from Arthur anytime I so much as glanced at Will.

If I thought about it, it was weird Will and I hadn't bonded more. We were the only kids in a house full of adults—and robots. But then again, Will tended to out-adult the adults. He acted decades more mature than Arthur on most occasions.

Will didn't seem any more thrilled than me the first time he sat in with us. With visible reluctance he placed his hand in mine at Cassie's request. If I hadn't been feeling just as nervous, I might have been a little insulted by his reluctance. After all, it wasn't like I had sweaty palms. Well, they weren't very sweaty. I'd just wiped them off on my jeans.

With my heart pounding so hard, Will probably felt it through my hand, I focused on his hand resting lightly in mine. I Saw a vision almost the instant I shut my eyes and focused. It wasn't of Will dying, which was a relief. He had some massive bruises on his face though. This wasn't some happy future like the one where we'd been hanging out watching a movie. Someone had tied Will's legs to a metal chair, and his hands were zip-tied in front of him, resting in his lap.

I pulled my hand out of Will's before I Saw more.

"Easy, Elaine," said Cassie. "Will, go grab Elaine some water."

Will rushed from the room. He glanced back at me, but concern hurried his steps. He ran for the kitchens.

"That got rid of him," Cassie said. "Do you want to tell me what you Saw? You're paler than a ghost, so I assume it wasn't a happy vision."

"Will wasn't dead," I said.

Cassie gave a small smile. "Then that's an improvement over last time."

I described the vision, and Cassie had me draw it. By the time Will had made it all the way back from the kitchens, I had recovered.

"Oh, silly me," Cassie said. She pointed to a small fridge tucked behind a cabinet door in the entertainment center. "I had water here."

Will only looked a little put out. I don't think he wanted to hear about his future either.

He looked relieved though when I showed him the picture. "That's not a big deal," he said. "I could get myself out of something like that in minutes."

When I shot him a disbelieving look, he only nodded. "Four minutes tops. I'll show you how tomorrow."

After that night, though, Cassie insisted that Will join us every evening we practiced calling up visions. "There's always one person that visions center on. For me, it's Patrick. For you, it's Will."

I tried not to make any assumptions about what that meant for Will and me, but seeing as she was marrying Patrick, it was hard not to wonder.

Will, though, seemed pleased by Cassie's comment. "You mean, I'm almost like a trigger?"

Cassie laughed. "Not quite. It's more like she'll always have more visions about you than anyone else. Seeing you will always be easiest. And it will be easier for her to have visions of other things if you're around."

I frowned at that. The whole point of all this training was to make me less dependent on other people, more able to take care of myself. Visions wouldn't be all that useful if I had to touch people or keep Will around me like a good luck charm.

Will gave me a thoughtful look, and then he broke into one of his heartbreaking smiles. "Then it's a good thing I'm sticking around for now." A slight cloud passed over his face. "At least for now."

"What does that mean?" I might resent that Will was my Sight's crystal ball, but that didn't mean I wanted to lose access to him.

Will looked away, a sure sign he had bad news. "Stormfield is not pleased with my performance here."

"Ridiculous," Cassie said before I could sputter out some incoherent denial. "You've been doing a fine job. I'll have Patrick and Arthur speak to him on your behalf. I'm sure there's some misunderstanding. Elaine's fighting has shown marked improvement in the last few weeks."

I flushed at the praise, slight though it had been, but Will seemed skeptical. He gave a polite thanks, and we got back to working on pulling visions out of the future.

One week later I Saw my parents for the first time.

13

WHERE I SEE MORE
THAN I BARGAINED FOR

OF COURSE, WHEN I HAD A VISION OF MY PARENTS, I HADN'T BEEN
trying to have one at all. I'd spent a full week working with Cassie
while Will hung out with us in the same room. Cassie was right
that Will's presence made it easier to See. I had two more visions
of him without even having to hold his hand. I also Saw Arthur
talking to two other-worldly looking warriors. The next day we
encountered some Fae in Central Park attempting to recapture an
escaped Hell Hound. That was the day I finally used my trigger to
call up a vision on command when I slapped my hand on a Fae.
The future I saw showed us how to contain the beast.

So, although I was getting greater control over my powers,
visions of my parents still eluded me. Yes, I'd been able to See
Arthur, but he'd only been a few rooms away at the time. Proximity
seemed to still be a factor. I needed Will and the person whose future I was trying to See to be nearby.

For his part, Will took on being my lucky charm with a lot
more grace than I would have if the roles had been reversed. He

rearranged his schedule, so he was always nearby in case I needed to summon a vision. He filled out his reports in the control room while I trained with Arthur and Patrick, and he worked in my room while I did online school or practiced coding with Ginny.

I would have resented needing to be so aware of someone else all the time, but Will just laughed when I complained to him on his own behalf.

"This isn't exactly a burden," he said. "I get to hang out with someone I like. I mean this is so much better than when I used to have to follow Stormfield around everywhere." Will frowned. "Being Stormfield's personal secretary is supposed to be an honor, but all I did was trail behind him and occasionally get sent on some trivial errand on his behalf."

For half a second I wondered if evaluating me for clairvoyance had been one of those "trivial errands." I didn't interrupt though. It had been awhile since the real Will had shown up. Agent Redding seemed to have finally gone away again. The guy lounging on my sofa almost seemed like a normal guy, like a senior at my school, and not like a professional agent.

"Besides," Will gave me a half smile that somehow managed to be one of the most tragic faces I'd ever seen. "It's nice to be needed." He picked his tablet back up and went back to reading. I wondered if he was reading another romance novel. Will had mentioned yesterday that they were his favorite kinds of books. He liked the happily-ever-afters.

I stared at Will, ignoring the chemistry tutorial playing on my computer. Will never talked about his family, never mentioned friends, or even other LANCE agents other than Stormfield. I realized asking him was pointless. Will was an expert at dodging questions. The only thing I'd gotten out of him in the last three weeks was that his mom had died when he was a baby, and LANCE had taken him out of foster care and stuck him in their Conservatory spy school when he was six.

For the first time, I stopped thinking entirely of myself and how I felt about things, and I tried to look at life from Will's perspective. He had to be lonely, and I'd discovered that under that professional demeanor, Will had an affectionate nature. When he forgot to be Agent Redding, I could count on Will for things like comforting hugs. Now, I wondered if the hugs were for me or really for him.

I paused the chemistry video. I'd learn about isotopes some other time. I got up and crossed over to the sofa, hovering for a moment until Will glanced up. He gave me a funny look and scooted over so he didn't take up the whole couch anymore. I sat down next to him, my body as stiff as if I'd turned into my desk chair.

"You okay?" Will asked.

"Are you?"

"Sure?" Will had no idea what I was asking, which was fair, since I didn't know myself. I tried to figure out how to ask if he was happy here, if things were okay. Instead, I glanced down at his tablet.

"*The Desperate Duke's Broken Heart*?" I asked instead. "Book one of the *Wallflower Brides Series*? You read historical fiction?"

Will shrugged. "I read all kinds of romance novels. It has over eight-hundred five-star reviews. I figured that many readers can't be wrong. And look." He brought up his web browser so I could see the page about the series. "There are fourteen more novels in this series. If I like this one, I'll be set for like two weeks. Arthur gave me an account. He said I can buy as many books as I want, no budget at all. This is even better than a library pass. I've already downloaded a hundred and sixty-two books since I got here." He said the last bit at a whisper with a glance around the room like someone might be listening. Arthur may have said Will could buy unlimited books, but Will clearly didn't want to test him on that offer.

I grinned back. Will's excitement was contagious. "No wonder you like this better than working for Stormfield. You have way more time to read."

Will's smile faded, and I could have kicked myself for bringing up LANCE.

"I always work for Stormfield." Will looked down at his tablet though he didn't seem to see the webpage. "Don't forget that." He looked back up and took my hand. A vision, the same one with Will tied to a chair, tried to appear, but I forced it from my mind like Cassie had taught me to do. "Elaine, you can't forget I'm with LANCE."

I nodded, but I didn't get up from the sofa. We sat there on it in silence for a few minutes, both of us leaning back against one of the couch arms. There wasn't a ton of room so I was crammed up against Will. He still held my hand. After a while it seemed like the most natural thing in the world to lean my head on his shoulder. Will let go of my hand and put his arm around my shoulders drawing me in a little closer. A minute later his free hand tapped on his tablet, and I realized he'd gone back to reading his book, to running after the happy ever after, even if it was at the end of a novel and not real life.

I closed my eyes, and I tried to visualize a happy ever after for Will. I tried to visualize one for me. They didn't have to be the same. Will wouldn't always need to be within twenty feet for me to have a vision without a trigger. Cassie had loads of visions without Patrick around. My Sight would get stronger, and we wouldn't need to spend so much time together. But maybe we would want to.

I held onto that thought for a moment, and then I thought about my parents. All the usual homesickness I'd been trying to bury away welled up again. I swallowed hard. I didn't want to blubber all over Will's shoulder. He wouldn't mind—he seemed to take stuff like that in stride—but crying would embarrass me.

I kept my eyes tight shut and tried to picture my parents at home in our house. Dad would be at his desk balancing books or whatever, and Mom would be cutting out letters for her scrap-books. At least I tried to imagine that. I'd seen them doing those activities like a hundred thousand times. Instead, Dad looked like he had the one time they'd contacted me at Keep Tower. He sat in front of a computer like usual, but he still had his hipster Santa look. The desk was wrong too. It wasn't L-shaped like at home. It was a big desk he was sharing with Mom. Mom didn't have a single scrapbooking thing in sight. Instead, her half of the desk had at least six monitors. Code scrolled down the screens except for the monitor with some sort of tracking map. Her side of the room looked more like Ginny's office than my mom's scrapbooking paradise.

Mom wasn't paying attention to her screens though. She stood staring out the room's window, a cup of steaming coffee in her hand. Since my mom had hated coffee in the past, part of me wondered if she'd taken on a new persona—if the mom I'd known had been an act, and now she had a new role. I walked over to stare out the window too. The house was in a suburban neighborhood somewhere different. We'd lived in the suburbs in North Texas. Cacti were not normal landscaping at our old house.

About that moment, I realized that I was in a vision, not reliving a weird version of a memory. I opened my eyes, but the scene didn't change.

"Will?" I called, but there wasn't an answer. Will wasn't in the room with me. I was somewhere in the future, and I had left Will behind with my body.

"Mom?" I asked, but she didn't turn or acknowledge me. Of course not. I wasn't there. I was only Seeing a possible event.

Mom turned away from the window and looked back at Dad. "Any luck?"

Dad looked up and shook his head. "They've hidden their paper trails a lot better this time around. I'll need proprietary numbers to go much farther." He pointed to the dozens of spreadsheet tabs open on his computer and the printouts of financial documents on his side of the desk. He leaned back in his chair and ran a hand down his beard. "They're moving money in and out of so many accounts and corporations we'd need to take down half the publicly traded companies on every major exchange to make even a dent in their cash flow. I'm not sure how well the world economy would handle that."

Mom looked like she wanted to throw her coffee at the wall, but instead she sat it carefully on the window sill. "We have to do something."

Dad stood up and hugged Mom. "We will. But LANCE has been fighting this for over a hundred years. They've attacked Elaine's father continuously for almost a dozen. I don't think well-placed financial disruptions will be enough. We tried that twelve years ago, and you remember what happened."

Mom sighed. "I know. But if we destroy the Illuminati, we could come out of hiding."

I choked on the imaginary air of my vision. Mom and Dad were trying to hack the Illuminati? Again? Had they not learned anything?

"I've made some incursions into the Dreki mainframe," Mom said, "but I can't do enough from there to destabilize them. We need to cut the funding."

"Is that safe?" Dad pulled back to study Mom's face. He looked concerned.

Mom shrugged. "I was careful."

A beeping sound came from one of Mom's monitors. Both ran over.

"Incoming," said Mom.

"Is it one of Arthur's?" Dad sounded hopeful, but his face had lost most of its color.

Mom shook her head. "We need to get out of here." They scrambled for laptops, unplugging and shoving as many devices and external hard drives as they could reach into bags. "Forty-five seconds," Mom yelled, and they ran from the room.

Not moving from my spot, I stared at the monitor. I had no idea what an incoming AGM-114 Hellfire might be, but it didn't sound good. I repeated the name over and over, figuring it might be important.

A blinding white light threw me out of the vision.

I was laying flat on my back on the couch. Will hovered over me.

"Percival," he yelled again, a note of panic in his voice. I stared at him, surprised. I'd never seen Will panic. "Where is Cassie? Why aren't the Keeps here yet?"

"I'm okay," I said, but Will didn't hear me. He was yelling at Percival again.

Arthur and Cassie ran into the room. I tried to sit up, but Arthur pushed me back down. "Easy," he said.

Cassie was trying to calm an agitated Will. Apparently, I'd been so deep in the vision, I hadn't responded at all, and at some point I seemed to stop breathing. I guessed that happened when the incoming Hellfire whatever thing hit my parents' house.

"Hellfire," I said. I pushed Arthur's concerned arms away and shoved myself into a sitting position. "An AG, some letter, and a bunch of numbers Hellfire something was incoming to their house."

149

"That's a missile," said Patrick from the doorway. Ginny pushed past him into the room.

"I'm aware of that," snapped Arthur. His eyes never left my face. "Where was the missile headed, Princess? Here?"

I shook my head. "No. I finally Saw my parents."

Ginny gasped, and Arthur's eyes narrowed. He swung away from me to Ginny. "Did you find them yet?"

Ginny's hand shook as she pulled up a mid-air screen. "No. There's been no sign of Tori anywhere. She's got a distinct style I should have been able to trace if she'd been in any of the normal targets. The only sign I've seen is that night she hacked in here."

"She hacked in to talk to me," I said.

Ginny and Arthur nodded.

"But I don't think Mom's been doing much hacking. Dad seemed to be working off public information, and the only place Mom mentioned poking around was the Dreki mainframe."

Arthur swore, and Patrick ran from the room. Ginny and Arthur pulled up screen after screen and yelled orders at Percival. My room became an impromptu command center.

"We have to find them," Arthur muttered.

"I'm aware of that," Ginny said in a clipped voice. "I'm tracing from known Dreki IPs now."

Cassie had pulled me to the side and handed me a sketch book and pencils. "Start drawing. Anything you can remember that can help us pinpoint a location."

I stared at her. Helplessness seemed to roll through me. "I was inside a house. That doesn't have a lot of geographical markers."

"Try."

I sat down to sketch. Will came and stood behind me, probably trying to get out of the way. Screens had filled every free bit of space in my room as Arthur and Ginny ran programs and then discarded screens.

"Is LANCE going to be a problem for us?" Arthur suddenly called out from the other side of the room. "They still have warrants out for Tori and Raul, and the orders don't require them to be taken alive."

"No, sir," Will said, answering Arthur's question. He dropped his phone on the floor and kicked it under the couch. "I seem to have lost my phone."

Arthur gave Will a long look before nodding his head. "Good man." He turned back to his screens.

I didn't stop sketching the cactus looking plant I'd seen from my parents' window, but I did glance up at Will for a nanosecond. "I thought you worked for Stormfield."

Will sat his hand on my shoulder, and it was as if the memory of the vision strengthened. I noticed that the spines on the cactus were golden. I wrote that down.

"I still work for Stormfield," he said. "I'll be filing a report about all this. It's just terrible luck it all happened while I was in another part of the Rook, and I only heard about it after the fact."

I rested my cheek on his hand for a moment. "Thank you, Will."

Cassie came back over and looked at my drawing. "They're in California or the Baja in Mexico," she called over to Arthur and Ginny.

"Did you See them too?" I asked.

Cassie pointed at my cactus. "That's a Golden Snake Cactus. They're rare, but you can find them around San Diego and Southern California and parts of the Baja Peninsula."

"How do you know that?" I asked.

"I told you before. You have to use details to figure out where and when a vision is taking place. Plants make good markers. Once we get better control of your visions, you and I will start an exhaustive study of botany."

"Yay?" I said.

"Gotcha," said Ginny. She looked up from her latest screen. "Cassie's right. I found her. The short version is that they're here." She expanded one screen, so it took up most of the room. There was a map of San Diego with a small dot pinpointed on a suburb on the coast.

"I assume there's no keeping you here?" Arthur said to me.

"Not on your life." I had already started for the door, passing through the screens as if they weren't there.

"What about you?" Arthur asked Will.

"Where she goes I go," Will said. "This isn't a training flight around the city."

Arthur sighed. "Of course not." He followed both of us out of the room at a run. "Let's get suited up."

WHERE I LEARN THAT FAMILY IS MORE THAN GENETICS

PATRICK MET US IN THE ARMORY. HE'D CHANGED INTO HIS DEFENDER outfit—a brown leather jacket with a silver "D" on the back and brown leather pants with black military boots. When we ran into the room, Patrick was just pulling his silver mask over his head. I didn't look twice at him once we'd moved into the throne room since I was too busy staring at the knights housed there. I'd been here this morning for training, and the room had looked normal with the three suits of armor in their respective niches. Now there were four.

The new knight stood in the previously empty niche next to mine. It looked almost identical to mine except it was taller, the same height as Pendragon. At least it didn't have Pendragon's silly purple cape. I looked for the knight's name, but there wasn't one.

Arthur saw where I was looking. "I haven't gotten the name-plate up yet," he said. "This one is Galahad." He waved at Will. "Go on, and suit up. Let's see if Percival got the measurements right."

Will stared at Arthur for a moment. His mouth moved, but he

couldn't seem to get words out.

"You made Will his own armor?" I asked for him.

Arthur didn't look thrilled, but he nodded. "Even I could anticipate the day would come when your crystal ball would need to come out with us. Besides, he'll be less sulky if he can keep an eye on you. He takes your protection almost as seriously as me." Arthur gave Will a smile, probably the first one I'd ever seen him make in Will's direction.

"And you named it Galahad." At this point Will stood in front of the knight staring at it in open awe. He ran his hand down the front of the smooth armor.

"Yes, I did."

Will turned and looked at Arthur, and Arthur stared back with no expression on his face. The name Galahad meant nothing to me. I assumed it was another of the mythical Arthur's never-ending Knights of the Round Table. However, something of significance seemed to pass between Arthur and Will. Will gave a small bow of his head almost like a knight of old pledging his allegiance to the king. Little goosebumps broke out up and down my arms as if the atmosphere of the room was noting some kind of momentous change.

The Defender cleared his throat, breaking the mood. "Isn't this matter time-sensitive?" he asked.

"Yep," Arthur said, turning away to his own armor. He tossed me my headset and threw on his own. Will didn't have one yet, but the armor worked fine without it. The headsets were better for communication but not required.

I held out my arms, and my suit flowed around me. Next to me, Pendragon and Galahad were doing the same. As soon as Percival had initialized, I checked in with Will and Arthur. Will was listing out all the flight control movements to Arthur. Clearly, he'd been paying attention to my training. When the hole in the ceiling opened into the training room, Will shot up as if he'd been born in the suit. I muttered about the unfairness of natural born spies.

Arthur laughed at me. "You aren't so bad yourself," he said. "But Will has spent the last eleven years undergoing rigorous physical training. You spent it practicing ballet."

"Ballet is incredibly rigorous." I turned on my boosters and shot up after Will.

"True, but not when you only do it one hour a week."

Pendragon and the Defender followed me. Before we reached the top of the training room, Percival opened the door to outside. The four of us shot into the sky. Behind us, a troop of knights followed.

According to Percival, a commercial flight takes over six hours to get between New York City and San Diego. We did it in just over one hour. To my surprise, the Defender had no trouble keeping up with us. Super flying speeds must be another of his superpowers.

Arthur and I spent most of the flight arguing. He wanted me to stay a mile back in case we weren't in time.

"These are my parents," I finally shouted at him. "You can't keep me away."

"I know, Princess," Arthur's voice stayed calm, but the slight strain in his tone showed his patience was wearing thin. "The knights and I will bring them right to you as soon as we have them."

"You don't understand." I gritted my teeth trying to figure out how to get my point across to Arthur. He was a world-class genius. He had to know what I meant. "You don't know what it feels like to be this worried."

"Of course, I do, Princess." Arthur's voice sort of choked for a minute before coming back on as clear as ever. "You feel the way I feel right now when I think about you being in that house when the missile hits. It's an unbearable fear, almost paralyzing, but instead of freezing you up, it pushes you to act, sometimes without thinking."

That shut me up.

We were almost to the house on Ginny's map when alarms went off in all the knights. I could hear my alarms, but also the ones in Will's and Arthur's suits.

"Defender, we have incoming," Arthur said over the headsets.

"On it," said the Defender. He shot back the way we had come, outdistancing the seven knights that turned to follow him. I tried not to give him a second glance, but I hadn't realized that our supersonic flight had been slowing him down.

Arthur sent thirty knights on ahead so we would come at the house from all sides. They put on a small burst of speed, but at that rate, they could only hold that speed for ten seconds. After that, they would have to drop to regular, sonic speeds. They would be slow getting back to Keep Tower, but they disappeared across the horizon now.

"Got it." The Defender's voice came in over my headset, startling me. "It's a Hellfire all right, like in Elaine's vision. I'm sending it into space. Ginny calculated a nice little trajectory for me that will take out one of the Dreki's primary satellites. Since they were piggy-backing off a cable satellite, we might lose TV tonight."

Arthur groaned. "And I was looking forward to the new episode of *Danger Road*."

The Defender sounded surprised. "I can tell you what happens. We only filmed it four months ago. It's not like I've forgotten."

"No spoilers!" Arthur called out. "Ginny would kill me."

I didn't roll my eyes, but only because I worried Percival might think I wanted my knight to do something. "Can we please focus? Does that mean my parents are safe now?"

There was a pause as if Arthur was thinking or consulting his displays. "No. I wouldn't be surprised if the Dreki launch another kind of attack. The missile was just the easiest option."

At that moment, my parents' house came into view. Thirty knights hovered around it, high enough to be out of sight from someone on the ground, but low enough to swoop in and save the day. The street itself looked empty. Each house had a derelict look about it as if the neighborhood had been abandoned.

"According to Percival, the second housing crisis two years ago hit this neighborhood hard," Will said. "It doesn't seem to have recovered."

The one- and two-story houses all had the same basic fronts.

The house Ginny thought hid my mom and dad had the same look with the addition of a boarded-up window in the front.

Still, I knew we had the right place because my parents came tearing out of the house, like the place had caught on fire. Dad stuffed one last hard drive into his backpack before swinging it over his shoulders. They must have gotten the missile alert, but since Arthur's knights didn't register on anything, they didn't realize we were here.

I began to fly down toward them when a minivan turned onto their street. It was moving so fast, I couldn't believe it didn't topple over. It barely stayed up on two wheels taking the turn. As it came zooming down the street, the side door opened. Men with guns sprayed the sidewalk with bullets, but they were too far away still to hit my parents.

My parents dropped to the ground behind those special cacti, but that wouldn't offer much protection against bullets. Fortunately, the thirty knights hovering over their house dropped out of the sky to land in front of them. Half of them unsheathed their swords while the rest fired up the guns lining their arms.

I tried to join the knights defending my parents, but my knight seemed to have frozen in the sky. I hovered in mid-air, and nothing I did seemed to make the knight go.

"Percival!" I yelled. "Did you freeze up or something? Arthur, how do I reboot this thing?"

"I don't freeze, my lady," Percival said. "Lord Arthur has suspended all your flight controls."

"He did what?" I shouted. "Did he freeze all my weapons, too?

Because if not, aim a rocket at Pendragon's head." That would get his attention even though it wouldn't hurt him.

"Percival won't do that, Elaine," Arthur said. "But if you want to be useful, instead of throwing a tantrum, you should target that minivan. It seems to be evading our efforts."

I turned my attention back to the battle. The troops had spilled out of the car and were using anything around them as cover. A couple were squatting behind the community mailboxes, so I aimed a rocket at them. The mailboxes got blasted apart, and the goons were thrown from the fight.

"If it makes you feel any better, Arthur suspended my flight controls, too," Will said.

"That does not help." I continued to target Dreki, but from my distance, I couldn't do much more than shoot rockets. My cameras zoomed in so close I could see the stitching on the Dreki patches on each soldier's shoulder, but I couldn't throw a punch or slice with the electric dirks I'd been training to use. Feeling helpless and useless so far out of the way, it was like I was back in the school parking lot cowering under that truck with Will. I might be safer this time around, but I still had to wait while someone else saved the day.

Something flew between Will and me so fast they were nothing more than a brown blur. The sonic boom was so loud it reverberated through my armor, and the newcomer's wake pushed us aside. In the next second, the battle was over. Pendragon had incapacitated the three remaining Dreki, and the Defender held the minivan in such a way that the driver couldn't escape.

"Sorry I'm late," the Defender said. "It took me longer to reach the satellite than I thought."

My flight controls re-engaged, and I launched myself at the front of my parents' house. Like everything else, bullet holes and scorch marks riddled the place. I was relieved when Percival's scans showed no one else had been squatting in the other houses.

My parents' front yard was empty with no trace of them.

I had Percival drop me out of my armor, my running shoes crunching on spent bullets and glass. "Mom! Dad!" I called.

"Elaine, get back in your armor this moment," Pendragon boomed. "We don't know if the area is secured." There was some grumbling between Arthur and Percival since Arthur hadn't turned off his outer speakers. "Fine," Pendragon said again. "It is secure, but you still shouldn't be out of your armor. What if there was unexploded ordnance somewhere? Do you want to lose a foot?"

Will hovered in Galahad like he wanted to pick me up and swoop me out of there right that minute. I glared at him, just daring him to try. Will hung back.

The helm on the knight next to Pendragon swung up. "You should listen to your father, Elaine," Mom said. "He is the expert at this sort of thing."

I squealed and launched myself at my mom. Since carbon fiber titanium armor covered her, I sort of thudded into her chest, knocking the breath out of me.

"Oh my," Dad said from Pendragon's other side. That knight opened, and Raul stepped out. "These things take some getting used to. You wear this every day?"

"Yep." Pendragon flew into a bunch of little pieces and reassembled behind Arthur. "Elaine too, and our new protégé, Will, will start training tomorrow."

Galahad stood behind me and my mother. Will opened his helm, but he stayed in his armor. He seemed to be taking Arthur's warning more seriously than the rest of us.

"It's safe enough now," Arthur said, noticing Will's reluctance to step out. "Percival has scanned the area."

"If you let go, I can get out of this metal death trap. I don't know how you use them. I can see why Ginny has never approved."

I stepped back, and my mom stepped out of her armor.

"They're not so bad when custom-fitted," I said, realizing I spoke the truth. I didn't find my armor confining at all. In fact, I liked the flying around and the safety it provided. I wasn't so big on the fighting part, but armor had become part of my new normal. It would seem weird not to wear it at least once a day.

"I don't have as much experience with armor," said Will. Galahad dissolved from around him and reformed over by Pendragon. "The custom-fit though makes all the difference."

"Personalized armor too?" Mom said. She turned to Arthur. "Who is this beautiful young man hovering around our daughter? Don't tell me you and Ginny adopted without telling me."

Arthur snorted. "Wouldn't be any of your business if we did." He made a little motion at Will. "This is Agent Redding of LANCE. He's under my protection. Leave him alone."

Mom's eyebrows went up, and Dad took a step back. "Not

planning on taking us in, are you?" Raul said with a forced laugh.

Will studied the sky as if it contained the secrets of life written in the clouds. "Take who in? It is a shame I was busy sitting in my room writing up dull reports on Elaine's training while all this excitement was taking place on the other side of the country."

Arthur laughed, but Mom's eyes narrowed. She pulled me a little off to the side. "So, that's the LANCE handler." She eyed him up and down. "What unearthly beauty. Promise me you are using him for more than training exercises. Those lips are simply made for kissing."

My jaw about hit the ground. I didn't get to answer because Arthur must have heard her over the headset. "Tori," he yelled. He stomped over. "That's massively inappropriate."

Will and Raul glanced at him, and I thanked every deity from every pantheon that Will didn't have a headset. I would no longer have to worry about the Dreki getting me if I thought Will had overheard. I'd drop dead from mortification.

"What?" Mom turned back. "I'm sure that Elaine would enjoy some lovely kisses from that young man. Between you and me, Arthur, I suspect she needs the practice. According to a post on that account she blocked me from, you know the one, Elaine," Mom said to me. She turned back to a horrified Arthur. "Elaine had her first kiss a few years back, but she hasn't dated anyone since then. I doubt there has been a second kiss. She might as well practice on her LANCE handler. He has to be good for something."

My entire body caught on fire. I was wrong. I was going to spontaneously combust from embarrassment, and that would kill me. "Can we talk about me kissing people when we get home? Maybe in private? When I'm forty-five?"

Mom looked confused. "Home?" She glanced back at the damaged house. "I don't think this place is fit for humans anymore."

"Not here." I made a vague motion at the knights. "Keep Tower. Arthur's home. You're coming home with us, aren't you?"

Mom looked stricken, but she didn't answer.

"Of course, she is. Both of you are." Arthur turned to Raul, and beside him Will nodded. "The more the merrier at the Rook."

The Defender finished securing the last of the Dreki. He'd used his fire-breath to cauterize any wounds. "The Keep hospitality is unparalleled."

"So, you're there too?" Dad asked. He was looking more uncomfortable by the minute. I looked between my mom and my dad and my father. "So, many superheroes," Raul murmured, but I still heard.

"You have to come." I stared at Mom willing her to see how important this was, not just for their safety but for me.

"We can't." Mom looked at Will and Arthur. She glanced over her shoulder at the Defender.

Arthur came to stand behind me. He rested his hand on my shoulder. Will moved to stand next to him. He didn't put his hand on my other shoulder, but I could still feel his presence, like I'd developed a new sense that tracked him through a room.

"It would be for the best," Arthur said. His voice stayed calm and measured, not petulant, but there was still an undercurrent of steel beneath his words. I realized Arthur was angry. Very angry.

Livid. I also realized that Mom couldn't tell.

"It's not just for safety. It's best in every sense." His voice lowered in tone but not intensity. "Twelve years is too long to be cut off from family."

In that minute, I realized Arthur blamed Mom and Raul for missing all those years in my life. In that minute, I kind of blamed them too. They didn't have to disappear twelve years ago. Arthur would have protected them then, just like he would protect them now. They had made their choice then. I wished and wished they would make a different choice now.

Raul, though, was shaking his head, and Mom was staring at the ground. "Arthur …" Her voice petered out. She took a deep breath and looked up. Even though she said Arthur's name again, she was really talking to me. "Arthur, you have a LANCE agent and who knows how many superheroes living with you. And I love Ginny, and I love that the two of you found each other, but live with my best friend and my ex? No."

"But, Mom."

Mom shook her head, and Raul came and stood with her. "No, come with us, sweetie," he said. "It was good of Arthur to rescue you that day, and we couldn't think of a safe way for him to bring you back, but you're here now. Come with us. You'll enjoy not having to pretend to be a boring, perfect suburban family anymore."

Mom nodded. "We'll make a new life, maybe somewhere further North. We can pose as a family from the Midwest. I'll be your older sister this time. I think I can pass for older twenties, and you would enjoy being twenty-one a little early, don't you think? You're old enough you can pick out a new name this time around. You can finally dump that Elaine nonsense. I've always hated it. I can't imagine why I let Arthur talk me into it. We'll disappear, and the Dreki and LANCE will never find us."

Arthur's hand tightened on my shoulder, but otherwise, he didn't show any sign he objected to the discussion. He didn't tell me not to go. Even though I knew how important I was to him, he didn't yell and scream at my parents like he had with Stormfield. He didn't bring up the revised custody agreement Mom had signed. Arthur stood there in silence, and it had to be killing him. Arthur was letting me decide.

There wasn't a decision though. "I can't leave Arthur or Will. I'm not going another twelve years without my father." Behind me Arthur shifted closer. He literally would have had my back no matter what I had chosen. "I like being Elaine. It wasn't a pretend life before. It was my life." My throat choked up, and I had to take a deep breath before getting it to work again.

Mom and Raul looked at each other for a second. It was a look I'd never seen before and didn't know how to interpret.

"And you can't keep me safe," I added. "The Dreki found you just fine. You would have died now if I hadn't Seen that missile coming. And I can't See without Will, and I can't survive the constant Dreki attacks without Arthur and Pendragon and the armor. You can't go off and keep hacking the Dreki and think they won't respond. You need to come with us."

But my parents wouldn't budge. The Defender left to take the

Dreki into a LANCE detention center. He probably also left to give us some privacy. I was uncomfortable, and this was my family.

In the end, my parents agreed to go to Arthur's ranch in Montana. He could protect them there—it was even more secure than the Rook. Before they climbed into the knights that would fly them there, Arthur handed them phones. Each one was a duplicate of the prototype back home in my room.

"You will keep in touch," Arthur said, the steel in his voice again. "These phones are untraceable." He showed them the special app. "You can keep in secure contact with Ginny and your daughter." He stressed the last few words, but my parents only nodded. They each gave me a quick hug before climbing into a knight, but there weren't any long goodbyes. It felt perfunctory.

"We'll be in touch when we can," Raul called in that cheerful voice I'd heard my whole life. I felt like I was waving goodbye to a stranger. The knights with my parents and half the knights Arthur had brought with us took off and headed for Montana.

I stood on the street, watching them fly away, with Will and Arthur on either side of me.

"They won't stay," I said. The knights had long since disappeared, but I kept watching that piece of sky as if I thought Tori and Raul would come back and say they'd changed their minds. That they didn't mind staying with Arthur if it meant staying with me. The sky remained a cloudless blue.

"They won't stay in Montana." My voice cracked, and my throat clogged even though the tears were pooling way up in my eyes. "They'll disappear again. Hopefully they won't mess with the

Dreki, but they won't stay in contact with us either."

Arthur's arm wrapped around me and gently pulled me against his chest. "I know, Princess," he said into my hair. "I know."

Will's arms embraced me from behind so that his chest pressed against my back. My father's other arm wrapped around Will and me. The three of us stood there in a little knot while I cried, and the knights circled around us protecting us from physical danger.

15

WHERE I CORRUPT WILL FOR MY OWN ENDS

THE NEXT MORNING, I WAS WAITING BY THE DOOR WHEN WILL showed up to take me on our morning run. Most mornings he had to bang on the door for half a minute before I opened up. Today, I had it open before he even raised his hand to knock.

"You seem eager." The shock was written on his face.

"Not to run." I pulled him into my room, slamming the door behind us. "Percival, shut off every sensor and tracking device in this room. Get out of here and off my tablet too."

"Yes, my lady," Percival said. Small red and blue lights all over the room blinked off. I checked on the tablet I'd gotten from Ginny last night, but Percival wasn't running in the background.

The curious expression on Will's face had turned to alarm. "Look, I don't know how comfortable I am with randomly being used for kissing practice, or whatever it was your mom said."

At any other moment, I would have expired from embarrassment or died from the confirmation that Will wasn't attracted to me that way. I had more important topics to discuss, but I decided to put him at ease first. "Please, I'm the least attractive person ever born." I gestured at my unwashed hair. "No doubt you'll be able to keep your hands to yourself, and I have other stuff on my mind." I pulled him over to my desk. He couldn't possibly think I'd want to do anything scandalous somewhere as uncomfortable as my old-fashioned metal desk.

I propped up my tablet and pointed to the lines of code, scrolling up and down so Will got a glimpse of the scope. "That is the dummy code Ginny gave me so I could learn how Percival works. We're going to make this code not so dumb."

Will quirked one eyebrow at me because of course he would do something so sexy when I wanted to have a serious conversation. "We?"

"Oh, please. Don't pretend you don't have some kind of extensive coding and hacking experience. You're a super spy from super spy boarding school with the most secret of secret agencies. If you aren't spending half your day rooting around the Keep systems, then I'm pretty sure you aren't doing your job."

Will dropped into my desk chair like I'd somehow punched him in the gut, knocking all the air out of him. We'd been training for weeks now, and I'd never once seen him look even half this defeated after one of our training sessions.

"What did I say?" I asked.

Will put his head in his hands, covering his eyes the same way Arthur did when stressed. Arthur's mannerisms had rubbed off on all of us.

"I'm not doing my job."

"What?" I sat my tablet aside, my Percival Project forgotten. "What are you talking about? You've been invaluable here, and I'm not talking about the whole vision lodestone thing. No one could have predicted that."

"Ahmet the LANCE Seer should have Seen it," Will said with a small smile. He dropped his hands from his face, but he still looked ill.

"Seriously, you are an excellent agent." I struck a fighting stance. "Look at how good my form's gotten. Come on, try to throw me. I dare you."

Will's smile widened, but it was still only half-hearted. He knew as well as I did that he could still toss me over one shoulder if he wanted.

"I've been an excellent fight instructor and trainer," Will said. "Not a good agent."

I knelt on the floor and took Will's hands in mine. "Explain."

Will sighed, but he didn't let go of my hands. "Arthur was right to not want LANCE agents here. I am your handler, but my mission went well beyond keeping you safe and seeing you trained." He let go of one of my hands to pull his phone from his hoodie pocket and brought up his emails, loading a memo from Stormfield. He handed the phone over.

I skimmed the email, and my other hand fell out of Will's. He let me go, and I sank to the floor. "Complete inventory of Keep tech? Technical specifications for as many inventions as possible? Permanent backdoor into Keep systems? Neutralize Arthur Keep if necessary?" I looked up at Will. "Does neutralize mean what I think it does?" My voice dropped to a whisper, but Will still heard me. "Do you have a kill order for my father?"

Will didn't answer. His head dropped back into his hands before he gave a sharp nod.

"Well, clearly you haven't killed Arthur, but how much of the rest of this have you done?" My voice had a hard, brittle quality I didn't hide. I'd been more than half-crushing over this wyvern hiding in our home, and the whole time he'd been betraying us for his lousy secret organization. Will might say LANCE was the good guys, but I was having some serious doubts. I opened my mouth to tell him what I thought of him and his precious fellow agents.

"None of them," Will said before I could start. He reached for one of my hands again. "I swear I haven't been doing any of them. And I don't know how much longer Stormfield will tolerate my being here if I don't start. His communications are getting explicit."

The phone fell from my lifeless fingers. "None of them? But Will, doesn't that mean you aren't useful to LANCE. Doesn't that put you in danger of …"

"Retirement." Will finished the sentence when I couldn't. "Dangerously close. Despite starting me at the Conservatory at six, despite making me his personal secretary, despite my supposed abilities, it's always been clear that Stormfield doesn't trust me. That being his secretary was to keep me under direct supervision, not an earned accolade. The excuses I've been giving him have been wearing thin, and my report from yesterday seems to have raised even more red flags. From the texts I received last night, it's clear he doesn't believe I'm ignorant of Tori and Raul's current location. He flat out questioned my loyalty before going silent. I have one week to turn in a report of measurable value." Will's voice and head sank again, but his grip on my hand tightened.

I panicked. There was no other word for it. Gripping onto his hand, I threw myself at a vision, any vision, of Will's future.

I snapped into one at once with none of the strain or difficulty I normally had. The vision was as clear as the one I'd had of Vortigern shooting Will in the head. Only, the vision didn't show me if Will would survive Stormfield's wrath. Once again it showed the same image of Will tied to a chair.

I'd Seen this vision four different times now, and I'd drawn it twice as many. Will never found it upsetting. He maintained he could get out of a setup like this anytime, and he'd taught me how. The Will in my vision didn't try to get free. He sat in his chair radiating a calm I didn't share. Since I was fully immersed in this vision for the first time, I tried to take Cassie's advice and hunt for clues in the room. It was a boring institutional gray cube with no windows and a single door. There didn't seem to be a way to open it from the inside. Perhaps that was why Will was so patient. Other than the chair with Will, there was nothing else in the room.

I circled the chair and studied the knots holding his legs in place. The zip tie I ignored. For some reason, Will wore his gray suit again. Will hadn't worn it in weeks except for the one time he'd reported in person at the New York LANCE headquarters.

Most likely I wasn't Seeing a vision from today. I realized that if I angled myself just right, Will's phone stuck out of his jacket's pocket. Something had broken the screen, but the date and time still showed. The date was six days out. One week from Stormfield's ultimatum.

With a wrench, I pulled myself out of my vision. "It's a LANCE holding cell. That's why you're not trying to escape, Will. It's a LANCE holding cell."

"What?" It was a sign of how upset Will was. He hadn't noticed I'd gone into a vision.

"My vision. I pulled myself into that vision I keep having of you."

For a moment, life seemed to return to Will. "You called up a fully immersive vision at will? That's a fantastic leap in your abilities, Elaine."

I waved away his true, but irrelevant, statement. He wasn't getting the important parts. "You don't understand. I think you're tied up in a LANCE cell. It'll happen on the day of Stormfield's ultimatum."

Will looked skeptical. "I don't know. No, it's not that I don't believe you," he said, noticing my outraged expression. "I bet I will be tied up in six days. It's more that it doesn't sound like LANCE. If they retire me, they won't beat me up and then tie me up somewhere first. It'll be a lot faster than that. I won't realize it's happening."

"That is not comforting." I stood up and paced in front of him. "We need to tell Arthur and Ginny about this."

Will looked horrified. "You can't. They'll never believe I haven't been following my directive. I couldn't betray them like that. Your father barely tolerates me now. Can you imagine how he'll act if he finds this out?"

I fiddled with my hair while I marched up and down my room. Will had a point. Arthur and Will had some sort of turning point yesterday, but that might all go away with a revelation like this. "Ginny would understand," I tried, but Will shook his head.

"She'd tell Arthur."

I shrugged, but Will was right. They were the kind of couple that didn't hide stuff from one another. It made for a healthy relationship, but it wasn't useful for our current crisis.

"There must be something we can do," I said. "Can we fake an inventory list? Give LANCE bad plans?"

Will shook his head. "They already have a rough idea of what Arthur has developed. They'd know some of the things that should be on the list, and they'd notice if I left them off. And I don't have the engineering experience to fake technical drawings. Do you?"

I glared at Will. "Don't be ridiculous."

I sighed. My pacing had brought me back to Will, and I dropped myself down on his lap since he was sitting on my only desk chair. I hugged him tight, my chin digging into his shoulder. "We'll figure out something. You're not allowed to give up. Understand?" I pulled back so I could stare into his beautiful eyes. "Promise?"

Will nodded and stared back. His eyes seemed to search my face. For some reason, they settled on my mouth. I wrinkled my forehead at him, trying to figure out what was going on when the speakers in my room squawked.

"Why is Will in your room with the sensors off? Why did you need to kick Percival out?" Arthur hissed over the intercom. "Will, you can't let her pressure you into doing things that make you uncomfortable."

"What? Me pressure Will?" I sputtered. I stood up and told Percival to turn all the sensors back on. Lights blinked on all over my room, and I brought up a mid-room screen with my livid parent seething at me. "I'm the girl here. Will is the one who's supposed to be pressuring me."

Will now made sputtering noises from behind me, but both of us ignored him.

"Please. I can't imagine anyone can pressure you into anything." Arthur frowned at me and turned his attention to Will. "You can always tell her no. She won't like you any less for it. It won't change your place in this family."

Will didn't respond, but I didn't turn around to see if he'd gone into shock. "Why are you so convinced I'm in here trying to make out with Will? Is it because of what Mom said?"

"Make out with Will?" Arthur looked horrified. "Who said anything about kissing anyone?" He rubbed his eyes for a second. "But thank you for giving me something new to worry about. This parenting thing is hard," he said to an offscreen Ginny.

"Then what am I pressuring Will into doing?" I asked. I glanced around the room as if the answers had been written on the walls.

"I assumed you were trying to talk him into some bad idea. Just because you both have armor now, it doesn't mean you two can fly around anywhere you like." Arthur gave me a pointed stare. "Was I wrong?"

"Elaine isn't trying to pressure me into anything," Will said. I glanced back at him to find him giving me a considering look. "I don't think."

Ginny came wandering into view in an exquisite silk robe embroidered with poppies. She yawned and gave a small wave. "What are you two doing that requires such secrecy? You can see why we might have gotten the wrong impression."

I thought fast. Reaching over, I grabbed my tablet and showed Ginny the dummy Percival code. "I wanted to make a change and surprise you with Percival's code, but I need Will to help. But it occurred to me you might not be real thrilled if I showed it to a LANCE agent even if it was just Will. I mean, no one's forgotten Arthur complaining that any LANCE agent here would steal all his stuff."

I didn't look at Will again. It was hard not to turn my head, but I didn't want to draw more attention to him.

Arthur looked put out, but Ginny gave a small smile. "You may show Will, dear. We trust him. Besides that's an older version of Percival, about eight years out of date. LANCE has already seen much of that code, and they could see the rest with my blessing. LANCE's AI Dandrane is based on Percival's original code."

"Of course," Will said. "Dandrane is Percival's sister." I shot him a funny look, so he added, "In the Arthurian myths, I mean.

I read all of them—the Vulgate, Mallory, even Tennyson—when I first got here."

Ginny looked pleased that he'd caught the symbolism behind the AI's name. "So, feel free to help Elaine with her project. Like I said, we trust you."

Arthur didn't say anything, but Ginny nudged him in the back. His head sort of wobbled back and forth, but it was an agreeing sort of bobble. "We trust Will." He ran his fingers across his face, rubbing his eyes for a minute. When he brought his hand back down, he seemed surprised as if he'd had a revelation in the last second. He smiled and all of him seemed to relax. "We trust Will absolutely." Ginny smiled at us from behind him.

"Okay," I said. "Great then." I smiled, but my heart fell. There was no way we could tell Arthur about Will's problem with LANCE now.

Will came to stand beside me in front of the screen. "Thank you for the confidence, sir." He reached over and squeezed my hand. "You won't be let down."

Arthur frowned at our joined hands. Ginny poked Arthur in the back again. He managed a grimace that might have been intended as a smile. "Get training, you two. You can tinker with your practice Percival this evening."

We nodded, and I shut the screen down. We headed for the terrace and ran the first mile in silence.

"Why do we need our own working Percival?" Will asked me during our second mile.

I admired his clever timing. My groaning and wheezing made

it impossible for any of the mics on the terrace to pick up his words. I was in better shape than when we first started five weeks ago, but I still found running four miles all but impossible.

"Want armor Arthur can't lock us out of," I gasped out. Since I only managed one-word every ten steps, Will surprised me by figuring out my meaning. "You in?"

"I don't know, Elaine."

When we finished our run, I stood near the moat's decorative waterfall bent over gasping for air. Will bent down. On the cameras it would like he was tying his shoes, but really he had his head near mine. Between the noise of the waterfall and my continued coughs and choking sounds, it would be harder to hear what we were saying. Will wasn't the only one with some spy-craft skills.

"Look, I know you gave your undying loyalty or whatever to Arthur, but this is important, and I don't think I can jailbreak Percival on my own. Arthur can't lock me out of my armor again."

"It's for your safety."

I didn't stand up, but I shot Will a death glare that would have incinerated him on the spot if I had the superpowers of the Red Ranger. Instead, he waited in a patient silence.

"This is about more than just staying safe. Yes, the armor is for protection, but it's also to make sure others stay safe. The armor is more than a physical firewall for me to hide behind. It's for keeping the ones I love safe too. Arthur, Ginny, you, Tori, Raul. Even the world. Being a knight of Arthur's Round Table means something. Yes, it's Arthur's weird obsession, but it also stands for a lot of noble things. Being a knight might not have been my first choice. It wasn't yours, but we are ones now. And that means Arthur can't lock us out anytime things get dicey. We need our own Percivals outside Arthur's control." I'd gotten so into my little speech, I'd forgotten to stay crouched over or to cough. We now stood facing each other. At some point I'd reached up and grabbed Will's shoulders although I didn't remember moving. I hoped the waterfall was loud enough to mask my voice. "Are you in?" I asked Will again.

Will glanced at the sky as if the answer was there. He then looked deep into my eyes, like he was the Seer trying to pull out a vision. Finally, he took a deep breath. My heart sank. He was going to think I was pressuring him like Arthur had said, and he'd now say no. I didn't have the coding skills yet to hack my way into a new Percival. I hadn't been lying about that.

"Yes," Will said. "I'm in."

16

WHERE I FIND AN UPSIDE TO BEING A KEEP

WILL WAS EVEN BETTER AT CODING THAN I HAD SUSPECTED. HE WAS no Ginny, but he had our outdated Percival ready for my modifications in only two days.

"You could have totally put a LANCE backdoor into the Keep systems." I stared at his elegant additions. The Percival in front of us was now just as effective as the one running the Rook even if this version was years out of date. I turned to stare at Will's satisfied smirk. "Why didn't you? You could have done it the day you got here."

"That day was a little busy," Will said in a dry tone. "Someone jumped off a building if you remember."

"How could I forget? You and Arthur remind me at least once a week." I gave him a smile though so he'd know I wasn't actually annoyed. "And you jump off buildings now, too." Starting the day before yesterday, Will had joined Arthur and me in our training session. To my disgust, Will in his Galahad armor took out five knights this morning. After five and a half weeks my personal best was still two.

"I don't jump off buildings without armor on."

"Stop avoiding the question." I stuck my finger in Will's face. "Why isn't there a LANCE backdoor in the Keep Systems courtesy of Will's sneaky coding skills?"

Will crossed his arms over his chest almost as if he were hugging himself rather than being defiant. He half turned away. "How could you think I would betray Arthur like that? Betray Ginny after all they've done for me? Arthur promised to protect me, me, even from LANCE itself if he had too. I don't know if he meant it. He probably didn't, but he said it."

It was a good thing Will wasn't looking at me since my mouth was opening and closing like a floundering fish.

"Do you think so little of me?" Will added, his tone so low I almost didn't hear him. "Do you really think I would do something like that to them? Open their secrets up to LANCE to exploit?"

I didn't know what to say. I had thought Will had started drifting away from LANCE the day he got Galahad, but that was foolish of me. If Will had been a good little agent, he would have been following his orders, at least at the start. Will had never followed his directive. At least, he hadn't done any of the stuff that hadn't involved training and reporting on me.

No wonder he'd been so stiff those first couple of weeks. He'd been fighting an internal war between his agent training and his preference for Arthur's style of heroism. After all, Arthur hadn't promised to keep Will safe because Arthur liked him. I remembered that promise, made the first night Will spent here, just hours after I'd had my first horrible vision and had run away from home like a frightened child. Arthur hadn't even been polite to Will back then, resenting a LANCE agent in his home. Still, he'd offered Will his protection not because he was a superhero or even to be kind, but because Arthur was fundamentally a decent human being, and it was the right thing to do.

I had to wonder if fundamentally decent human beings ran LANCE. In theory, LANCE was dedicated to the greater good, but I wondered how often they actually did the right thing.

I stood to hug Will, but my door flew open, slamming against the wall with a bang. Will and I both jumped, and Will reached for the gun he kept in a holster on his thigh.

Arthur came bouncing into the room. "You have got to see …" he began, but his voice trailed off. He took in Will's strained face and my stricken one. "What's the matter? Has something happened?" His eyes narrowed at both of us. "Are you two fighting?" He nodded as if he'd decided on the answer already. "Because Ginny and I have this wonderful counselor woman we talk to whenever we get in the big fights. Course," he added, tapping his chin, "we also talk to her once a week for stress and stuff. Ginny sometimes finds dealing with the whole Pendragon issue a bit much and then Luciana, the counselor you know, has to help us mediate boundaries." Arthur made a sour expression. "The boundaries always seem to be mine," he complained. "No knights standing guard in the bedrooms. No playing in the labs after midnight. No sending a Percival controlled Pendragon in my place to social functions."

Arthur's babbling didn't seem like it would ever stop. I stared in disbelief at the words vomiting from his mouth until Will pushed past Arthur with a mumbled apology and a vague reference to reports to write. He fled the room.

Arthur shut up and stared after Will for a second before closing my bedroom door. With all of his original spontaneity gone, Arthur settled himself on my couch and raised his eyebrows at me. "Well?" he said when I didn't respond. "What's the matter with Will? Do I need to call the counselor for you two, or are you going to tell me what's really going on?"

"We're not fighting," I said.

"I didn't think you were." Arthur crossed his arms and stared at me. "What's wrong with Will?"

I shut the cover on my tablet so Arthur wouldn't see my Percival code. I sat down and swiveled in my chair and faced Arthur. "Why do you think it's Will? This could be about me."

Arthur gave me a look that screamed, "oh, please." Instead, he said, "Because Will just ran out of this room looking like he was on the verge of tears. Now, LANCE agents are carved from cold marble and wrapped in steel hardened in the forges of Vulcan's fiery pit. That cult they call a school beats any emotion they might possess out of them. It's nice to see that Will is human and not another Conservatory-created drone, but that young man is beyond upset if he's lost his conditioning to this extent."

I pulled on the hem of my T-shirt, not sure what I could say that wouldn't betray Will but might help him instead.

"You need to be nice to Will, Princess," Arthur said.

I looked up in surprise, but Arthur wasn't looking at me but at the door as if he could still see Will on the other side. He turned back and nodded. I'd never seen him so serious, not even when he'd been explaining how my armor worked. "Ginny and I did some extensive digging after that first night Will was here. Remember? That night you told me LANCE would have Will killed? It took us awhile to get all the records, but it turns out he wasn't exaggerating about retirement. Conservatory-trained agents have ridiculously short life-spans considering how much money LANCE spends training them." Arthur shook his head. "Such a waste." He rubbed his eyes for a moment before he seemed to remember what we were discussing.

"Then there's some mystery surrounding Will that LANCE or possibly Stormfield removed from the online files. They've never sent a kid to the Conservatory at six like Will, not before or since. Everyone else starts at eleven or twelve. And although it isn't stated explicitly, Stormfield seems to have done his best to isolate and monitor Will to an extent that goes beyond any other LANCE operative I've seen. Stormfield resents what he doesn't know and fears what he can't control. He seems to both resent and fear Will."

I stuck my hands between my knees so Arthur wouldn't see them shaking. "What does that mean?"

"It means I was much too hard on Will when he first got here. I was mad that LANCE had finally gotten a foothold in my house. I didn't trust Will because of well, stuff …" Arthur's voice trailed off, and he gave me a sheepish grin. "And, I was jealous I would need to share your time with someone else. Twelve years you were gone, Princess." Arthur looked away again. "I'm not proud, but I resent every minute you spend with Will or Cassie or Ginny. I know I can't cram twelve years of time into a few weeks." Arthur waved away the objections I wasn't making. "The gods know I've spent enough time in counseling on that subject, but that doesn't mean I don't want to try." Arthur gave me a small tentative smile.

The smile I returned was just as awkward.

Arthur's smile faded. "But beyond needing to be kind to the lonely boy I suspect is trapped in all that agent training, I'm worried about the threat presented by Stormfield, and to a lesser extent, the entire LANCE organization. I'm not sure how safe Will is with them."

"Exactly." I scrambled for my desk drawer where I kept my sketches. Yanking the drawer open so hard I nearly pulled it all the way out of the desk, I pawed through my drawings trying to find the ones I'd made of Will in captivity. I pulled them out and hurried across the room, dropping them in Arthur's lap. Here was my chance to help Will without having to tell Arthur about all the awful stuff Stormfield had wanted Will to do.

"Dad, look. It's a vision I've been having of Will." I pointed at the drawings when Arthur seemed focused on me and not them. He glanced down and sort of growled as he took in the bruises on Will's face.

"I think this happens at LANCE. I think Will's in a LANCE holding cell here. Will said something about Stormfield expecting some kind of report in four days." I swallowed to give myself a little time to think. Report sounded vague enough I decided. "It happens then."

Arthur glared at the page for another moment, but then he snatched the pictures up and stormed from my room. At first I thought he would confront Will, but instead he crossed the hall and hammered on Cassie and Patrick's door.

"Something the matter?" Cassie asked.

Before she'd even gotten the door all the way open, Arthur thrust my sketches in her face. "Were you planning on telling me about this?"

Cassie looked surprised and then put out. "You didn't know?"

"Is that Ginny in the picture? Elaine? Me?" Arthur didn't wait for Cassie to answer. "It is not, so no, I didn't know." He pushed past her into the room. "Cassie, we're supposed to help each other with this kind of stuff." His voice had calmed down, but Arthur still looked upset. "You know my limits." He kind of collapsed down onto her sofa with his head in his hands, his eyes covered. He sat there for a moment before looking back up. "They haven't changed."

Although Cassie seemed to understand, I didn't. "What is going on?" I asked, but Arthur and Cassie didn't seem to hear me. Patrick, who had just wandered into the room carrying two suitcases, answered instead.

"I've got to be back on the *Danger Road* set tomorrow, and Cassie's coming with me." Patrick sat the suitcases down near the door where I still hovered. I tried to nudge one aside, but the thing had to weigh at least a hundred pounds. Patrick had carried them like they were empty.

"I'd forgotten," Arthur said. He tried to give them one of his devil-may-care grins, but he couldn't quite keep the despair from his face. "Are you sure you have to go with him, Cassie? It's seems like we're being hemmed in on all sides. There's this LANCE threat to Will, the Dreki are still after Elaine, and we got six more death threats against Ginny and me this morning."

"Death threats," I squeaked, but Cassie waved them away. "You get dozens of death threats every day," she said.

"One of them was credible." Arthur gave her a meaningful look.

Cassie nodded, understanding what he meant. "And has it been dealt with?"

"Of course. LANCE arrested the Moral Menace this morning."

Cassie shrugged. "Then you don't need me here." She sat down next to Arthur and grabbed one of his hands. She patted it in a consoling manner, the way a mother calms a frightened child. "Arthur, I See visions. I don't fight battles. I can get visions on a beach in Fiji just as easily as I can here in your fortress against the world."

"Fiji? Is that where you're headed?" I turned to Arthur. "I want to go with Patrick too."

Like I had intended, that got a real smile out of Arthur. "Not a chance, Princess. You're not going anywhere without armor until this Dreki situation calms down." He leaned forward as if sharing a deep secret even though everyone in the room could hear him. "And you do not want to take your armor anywhere near a beach if you can help it. Sand gets everywhere, I mean everywhere. Do you know how hard it is to get sand out of an armored glove? And the blisters it rubs until it's gone?" Arthur shook his head in a solemn manner, but the gleam had returned to his eyes. He seemed to have rebounded from whatever horrors worried him. "Definitely no beaches for now."

I mock-sighed a huge exaggerated gust of air. "I guess I'll live."

Arthur stood up and herded me out of the room. "Let's give them some privacy. Besides, once all this is over, Ginny and I will take you and the boyfriend to the island we own in the Caribbean."

I ignored the boyfriend jab. I assumed he meant Will. Will and I might get along better and share secrets these days, but we were a far cry from being boyfriend and girlfriend. That wasn't something I even pretended could happen. It seemed too far-fetched.

"You own an island?" I said instead.

"Six," Arthur replied. "But the one in the Caribbean is my favorite."

"You own six islands." I didn't bother hiding my disbelief.

"We," Arthur corrected. "They're owned by the family although your large trust holds your portion."

Until now I had focused on all the disadvantages of being Arthur Keep's daughter: the archvillain nemesis, the tabloids' interest, and the omnipresent danger.

"I own part of an island." It didn't sound any more believable just because I had said it out loud.

"Six of them," Arthur called back. He headed for the great hall, but I went back to my room, shaking my head. Maybe being Arthur Keep's kid had some perks after all.

WHERE PERCIVAL GETS
A MAKEOVER

WILL DIDN'T COME OUT OF HIS ROOM FOR THE REST OF THE AFTERNOON, not even when I took him a tray for dinner. He was polite, but he didn't invite me in, and I didn't push. With Patrick and Cassie gone and Will hiding in his room, dinner was a quiet affair.

Ginny talked at Arthur about some upcoming meeting through most of dinner. Even though she'd stressed how important the meeting was, and how important it was that he attend, he didn't seem to hear a word she said. Although she never raised her voice, by the end of dinner she was making outrageous suggestions. Arthur didn't even notice when she informed him she was divorcing him to take up with the recently widowed Prince of Sweden. She winked at me so I'd know she was only messing with Arthur, but he didn't notice. Around a mouth full of food, he told her to do "whatever was best," and went back to staring into space.

"Creative geniuses," Ginny muttered. Then, she left the table and stalked off to her office to prepare for the meeting. Arthur stood to leave, but before he made it out of the room, I tried to get his attention. It took waving my arms in his face before he focused on me.

"Can I go to the armory by myself, or do you have to be with me?" I asked. "I want to go look at my armor, maybe run a diagnostic to see how it's done."

Arthur gave me a suspicious look, but whatever had distracted him through dinner was still taking up most of his mind now. "Fine," he said. "I'll be in the armaments lab if you need me, but Percival can walk you through most stuff."

"And if I decide to fly around the training room?" I called after him.

Arthur waved his permission without turning around. "Whatever. But don't leave this building, understand? Percival, secure all exterior walls, windows, and doors. Elaine is not to leave this building."

"Yes, my lord."

I rolled my eyes, but I didn't complain. I had no intentions of leaving the building anyway.

After taking Will that dinner tray, I trotted over to the elevator and rode up to the armory in silence. Once inside I headed for my armor in the throne room. Pendragon, Leodegrance, and Galahad stood in their niches, but I ignored them.

"All right, Morgause," I said to my armor. "Open the front. I don't need you in a million pieces." The front of my armor split down an invisible seam and opened wide like a doll house. The back of the interior of my armor wasn't all that fascinating. I studied the back of my helm and then bent down to get a better look at the torso. I found what I was looking for there.

"Bingo," I whispered. I pulled a small USB drive from the pocket of my leggings. I plugged my drive in to the port in the torso and then waited a moment.

"New software detected," Percival said.

"Great. Percival, bring up a screen that allows me to see all the software installed in Morgause and the software on the USB drive."

One of the small readouts on the wall of my niche appeared to expand until it took up all of a mid-air screen in front of my armor. It looked like an FTP interface with Morgause installed software on one side and my USB software on the other. I copied the new Percival software onto the drive in my Morgause armor.

"Warning," Percival said. "Existing file detected with that name. Completing this command will override existing software. Do you wish to continue?"

"No," I said. I went back and changed the name of my new Percival file, going super-original and naming it Percival2. I tried copying the file again.

"Copying," Percival said. "Twenty-two minutes remaining."

"Hey, Percival," I said. "Can you talk while this thing is downloading, or are you too busy?"

"I can execute many trillions of computations at once," Percival said. I detected a hint of offense in his voice. "I can both download and converse with you at the same time."

"Of course, you can," I said to soothe Percival's ruffled feelings. "I don't know if you noticed, but I'm downloading a second

Percival program into my suit."

"I noticed," said Percival. "Since you are downloading the full file, it will use a fair amount of memory."

"Right." All the knights, except Pendragon, were technically secondary devices responding to Percival's primary computer setup. Percival himself lived on some central computer somewhere with a complete copy on Pendragon's hard drive. Percival ran the knights from one of those two locations. He wasn't in any of the other suits although there was a program in all of them giving the AI control.

What I was doing was adding a complete copy of Percival to my suit. It would take up almost all the solid and working memory to run him. I would have limited diagnostic functioning whenever he was on. My weapons response time might be slower too. Of course, that's why I would test out the new program now instead of waiting for a battle.

"So, I need you to do me a favor, Percival. Can you keep these modifications I'm making to yourself? Do you understand? I don't want you to tell Arthur and Ginny about it."

"I'm afraid that's impossible," Percival began.

"Now, Percival," Will said from behind me. "That doesn't seem reasonable."

I spun around, nearly tripping over some of the cords running across the floor. Grabbing at my racing heart, it pounded away through my shirt and the layers of skin underneath.

"You're lucky I'm not Arthur," Will said with a frown. "Next time you start a covert activity, you might want to at least lock yourself in the room. It'll buy you some time while someone tries to get in."

"Tip noted," I said. "What are you doing here?"

"Helping. When Percival mentioned you were up here, I came to investigate." He held up a hand to stop my questions. "Percival reports anytime you deviate from your routines."

"That's creepy," I said.

"Probably, but it's the trade-off for staying safe." Will turned away from me, done with the conversation. Whatever mood he'd been in since this afternoon had not worn off. "Now, Percival," Will said turning his attention to the ceiling as if the AI were a ghost floating around up there. "What Elaine is asking is reasonable."

"Is it?" Percival sounded doubtful, but he didn't contradict Will.

"Yes," said Will. "I'm sure you noticed that the new program can deny you, and by extension, Arthur and Ginny from accessing Elaine's suit."

"I noticed," Percival said.

Will's voice took on an almost hypnotic quality. He kept talking with Percival, and even though most of what he said wasn't all that persuasive, I found myself nodding along.

"And that is why, you'll keep Elaine's modifications to yourself," finished Will. "And if I change my suit, you will also leave no record or mention of it to Arthur or Ginny."

"Yes, sir." The AI's voice droned in an odd monotone. Then in his more normal tone, Percival added, "Download complete."

That seemed to snap me out of whatever sort of trance I'd been in. I opened my eyes because at some point they had fallen shut.

Will was studying me, but he smiled when my eyes focused on him. "Percival agreed to keep our changes unrecorded and unreported."

"He did?" I'd heard Percival agree, but my brain still felt foggy. "Why?"

Will looked away. "I can be persuasive."

"You persuaded a computer program to go against its programming." Something about this seemed familiar, but I couldn't figure out what.

Will rubbed at the back of his neck and shrugged. "It happens. Sometimes if I focus hard on what I'm saying, I can convince someone to see things my way."

"But Percival isn't a someone."

"I heard that." The AI sounded more than a little peeved.

"Sorry. Percival isn't an organic someone. He's a machine."

Will shrugged. "Percival is the most advanced AI out there. I think he's more person than machine at this point."

I stared at Will for a moment, wondering if this was why Stormfield feared Will. For a second, I was a little scared of Will. It was like he could remove a person's free will, make them his own personal automaton. That was a pretty terrifying power.

Will stared back, probably waiting to see if I would run screaming from the room.

"Do you do this often?" I asked.

"No." Will shook his head emphatically. "And you would know if I had. You would feel fuzzy and a little confused, and you'd feel like you had to do what I said no matter how much you might want to ignore me. It's like I create a compulsion you have to obey. I only persuade when there is no other recourse, like now."

I didn't feel compelled to do anything, but Will hadn't been talking to me. "Like now," I repeated, trying to process everything. It was true that Percival's programming didn't allow for leisurely discourse and a slow convincing. I also realized that with a power like this, Will could have had me whisked to the Tool Shed my first night here. If he had whispered a little persuasion in my ear, I would have begged Arthur to let me go. Will could have flat out made Arthur take me there himself. He could make Arthur hand over every invention he had ever made to the LANCE scientists right now.

"This is only the third time I've tried to persuade someone since I stopped using my power when I was six," Will said as if he could tell I needed more information. "I tried when I was fourteen." He looked away again. "It didn't go well. I swore I'd never use it on another human again." He paused a moment and then turned back. "The other two times since then were with Percival. Once to get him to bring me to the Rook instead of a regional LANCE head-quarters and just now."

"And I'll know if you ever use it on me?"

"You'll know."

I nodded. "Then I trust you."

Will's face filled with relief. I hadn't realized how tense he had been, how scared he was that I would reject him. I wondered what had happened when he was six and again at fourteen to keep him from using this power he possessed. Now did not seem like the time to ask.

I nodded again and turned back to my armor and studied all the readout displays on the niche to make sure it was still working even with the new programming. Everything seemed to be fine, so I ejected the USB drive. Glancing over at Will, I asked him if he wanted to install Percival2 on Galahad or test it out on my armor first.

"I wish we had tested it on Galahad first," Will said with a frown, "but since it's already in your suit, let's boot it up. We should keep my suit normal."

"Good idea. It can act as a control." I told Percival to load and run the new program.

Will shook his head. "Galahad can act as a safety net. If our programming goes catastrophically wrong, I want to be able to catch you."

I knew Will meant literally that he wanted to catch my plummeting armor, but it still sounded kind of romantic, and my heart made a flippity-flop in my chest. I hadn't forgotten Arthur's boyfriend comment from earlier. Sure, Arthur was being facetious, but a girl could hope.

"Oh ye of little faith." I grabbed a headset and tossed another one to Will. "Modified Percival is going to work just fine. Let's suit up."

Since Percival was always listening in, our suits broke into pieces and reformed around our outstretched arms and bodies.

"Initializing," said Percival. I waited for all of my readouts to boot up.

"You okay in there?" Will asked.

I finished studying my last diagnostic. "All fine so far. Percival, execute Percival2 and then get out of my suit for now. I want to run exclusively on the new program."

"Yes, my lady. Rebooting now."

All the displays in my suit turned off. I stood in the pitch black of my suit feeling a little claustrophobic while I waited.

"Initializing," said Percival2. The screens on my suit lit up again. All the pre-flight displays loaded. Once again, all the screens showed everything to be running normal. Only the memory usage on my suit ran high.

"So far so good," I told Will.

"Percival is monitoring you using the external sensors in my suit," Will said. "Everything looks fine from here."

"Of course, it does," the Percival in my suit said. "I'm amazing at what I do."

"Okay," I said to my suit. "Let's get ready to engage the flight boosters. Will," I called over the headset, "can you get Percival to open the iris to the training room?"

"Any chance we can listen to some tunes while you train?" my new Percival asked. "This suit is so dead boring, and I don't want to listen to battle chit-chat all night."

"Uh."

Above me the door to the training room opened, and Galahad shot up. My armor stayed put even though I used my toes to signal my suit to take off.

"About those tunes?" my Percival asked.

197

"I mean, I guess?"

"Everything okay down there?" Will asked. Galahad peered down at me through the hole.

"New Percival seems to have an attitude."

"I prefer Percy," said my custom AI. "Percival is so stick in the mud stuck up, you know?"

I glared at the invisible AI running my suit. "Look, Percy. I need this suit to run just like Galahad is running up there." I tried to point, but Percy had my suit frozen in place. "All Will has to do is say the word and Percival will be back in control, and you'll be back on a USB drive running on my tablet. Is that what you want?"

"No." Percy sounded sulkier than Arthur on a bad day.

"Fine. Then you can listen to as many tunes as you want, but we've got to get this armor running better than normal. Agreed?"

"Agreed." The flight rockets on my back ignited, and I shot into the training room before I had time to blink. However, Percy responded to my flight controls, so I stopped and hovered in the middle of the room.

"Your playlist is lame," Percy said.

I narrowed my eyes. "Boy bands are an underappreciated national treasure."

"Please," said Percy. "Ginny has way better taste."

Ginny had more eclectic tastes. For the rest of the hour, Percy blared everything from French experimental pop to sitar music and classic rock.

Percy might be dead annoying, but he controlled the armor

as well as Percival. There were no noticeable lags or drags. And it turned out the music helped my fighting. I had been dancing since the age of five, and it was like music reminded my body how to be coordinated. For the first time, I took out five knights in six minutes. I even managed to tie Will.

Even Arthur noticed the next day. This time I kept Percival in my suit monitoring my readouts for Arthur, but Percy was the AI at the metaphorical wheel. Once again, Percy had insisted on music, and once again, my performance was way better than normal. I took out six knights. It was nowhere near the fourteen Arthur could take down in Pendragon, but it was a lot better than anything I had managed before.

"Is that music playing in your suit?" Arthur asked from the control room.

I nodded. "I'm trying something new."

"Keep it up," Arthur said. "It's working."

"Of course, it's working," Percy said. "I'm an unqualified genius."

"Shut up," Percival and I said at the same time.

Will made a snorting sound over his headset, but it might have been a grunt. He was fighting three knights all at once.

Fortunately, Arthur didn't hear. Percy had figured out how to keep the mic on my headset off unless Arthur said something that needed a response. I was still connected to Will and Percival at all times, but we'd shut Arthur out.

Each day my training got better, much to Will's and Arthur's glee. It was like everything was finally coming together. My visions weren't getting any easier to call up by myself, but I could call at least a glimpse of the future if Will was close enough when I tried. My combat skills in my armor were better than ever though. I wondered if all the upgrades Ginny had been giving Percival over the years had been for stuff other than running the knights.

On Sunday, I took down nine knights in twelve minutes. When we finished training, Arthur made Will and me celebrate with sparkling grape juice. He declared me ready to fight a small Dreki troop by myself if I had to.

"Not that you ever will, Princess. I would never let that happen." He clinked his glass against mine and then Will's. "But it's good to know you could do it if it was necessary."

I nodded in agreement.

WHERE WE ALL EXAMINE
OUR PRIORITIES

THAT SAME NIGHT ARTHUR AND GINNY HAD A BARE-KNUCKLES, ALL out screaming fight over the upcoming Keep Consolidated board meeting. At least Arthur ranted and screamed, but even Ginny raised her voice and clenched her fists as she paced the room. Despite Ginny reminding him about it daily for almost a week, Arthur was only now connecting that the date for my vision and for the meeting were the same. Naturally, Arthur didn't want to go to LA to meet with the Board, and not just because he hated those kinds of things.

"I can't leave Elaine here, and there's the whole vision with Will," he yelled. "If Elaine's right, something bad happens to him too. You can't expect me to leave them."

Will and I were hovering in the hallway just outside the living room. Will raised his eyebrows like Arthur caring about my vision surprised him.

"He promised," I whispered to Will although it was unlikely the screaming adults would hear us.

"The timing is terrible," Ginny yelled back. She wasn't as loud as Arthur, and she didn't storm around waving her arms, but I'd never seen her fists so tightly clenched. "I can't control that. We can't postpone this meeting because of a possible threat. There is *always* a possible threat. They never go away."

Arthur looked like he wanted to throw something, but he turned to stare at the illuminated rose window instead.

"Besides," Ginny added in a lower voice at his back, "LANCE isn't storming the Rook to take Will by force. They aren't the Dreki. He's safe enough as long as he stays here."

Arthur rubbed at his eyes, but he didn't disagree.

In the end, I was the one that broke the stalemate, not their fancy counselor, even though they conferenced her in.

With Will following behind me, I braved my raging father and stepmother. "Arthur, you need to go to this meeting." I didn't speak all that loud, but it was enough to stun both Arthur and Ginny into shutting up.

"What?" Ginny said into the new silence.

"I don't think I'm needed here anymore," the counselor said from her screen. "I'll be sending the usual bill."

Arthur waved and her screen disappeared, but he never took his eyes off of me.

"I said Arthur needs to go to this meeting." I took a seat on the couch. Will sat next to me. I couldn't decide if he was there for moral support or if this was the kind of side-of-the-road accident Will couldn't keep his eyes off.

Ginny sat with us, but Arthur continued to storm up and

down the room. At least he stayed in enough control to listen and not bite my head off.

"Ginny's right," I said. "Everyone realizes you don't do much for Keep Consolidated."

Arthur interrupted me. "I do plenty. Between the three dozen research teams I remotely supervise, and the stuff I outright invent on my own, Keep has more patents than any other tech company on the planet."

"Fine," I said, trying to keep my temper. "But you don't do any of the business stuff. Everyone knows Ginny does all her CEO stuff and most of your President of the Board stuff too. No one expects you to do all that much beyond play in your lab."

"So, I don't need to go," Arthur said. He gave Ginny a triumphant smile.

"I didn't say that." I rubbed my hand down my face in an unconscious imitation of Arthur. "They don't expect much, but they do expect you to show up at stuff like this Board meeting."

Arthur growled, but then he seemed to get himself back under control. He came and sat on my other side. He reached for Ginny's hand and then mine.

"Princess, I can't just leave you here. I don't think you get it. I can't let anything happen to you." Arthur turned to Ginny. "I only just got her back." Most of the time, not just tonight, Arthur blustered and shouted to get his way, but now it felt like he was almost begging Ginny.

Ginny looked as if her heart would break. She reached up with her free hand and rested it on Arthur's cheek. He turned his head into her palm. "I know, love," she said, "but I don't know what to do. We both have to be at the meeting, but it's closed door. Elaine can't come, and you can't stay here. They need to see you alive and well and in person."

"Why can't Elaine go?" Will asked. "I'm not trying to pry, but isn't she the heir to the Keep kingdom or something?"

Ginny sighed. Her attention shifted from Arthur to us, but she never let go of Arthur. "Legally, yes. We settled that years ago. The problem is that Arthur has never acknowledged Elaine in public. For all the world—and that includes the Board and the financial markets—for all they know, Arthur is childless.

"When Elaine was born, we didn't tell anyone to protect Tori and Raul's privacy. After they disappeared, it seemed unwise to mention that Arthur had another loved one for his enemies to target. Obviously, we can't keep her, you, a secret any longer. But before we introduce Elaine as the future of Keep Consolidated, we first have to introduce her as Elaine Keep. And a private board meeting between the Trustees is not the time." She looked past me to Will. "You have to trust me on this one."

I could feel Will nod behind me. I didn't turn to look, but I reached out and held my hand out toward him, and he took it. The same vision tried to press in on me, but I pushed it away. Now was not the time to worry about Will.

"Dad, this meeting is bigger than Will or me," I said to him.

Arthur whipped around to face me, breaking his connection with Ginny. He squeezed my hand tight. "It's not. It's just another meeting between a bunch of rich people discussing the status of the world's second most valuable company. Business will never be more important than you." He paused and glanced behind me. "Or Will."

Will's fingers stilled in mine, but I didn't reassure or comfort him. I stayed focused on Arthur. "I didn't say more important. I said bigger. What was it you said? The world's second most valuable company? How many depend on that company? How many other kids need Keep Consolidated to keep going so their parents can pay for food and books and other important stuff?"

Arthur raised his eyebrows at me, but he didn't interrupt.

"And that's not even counting all the pensions and retirement accounts invested in Keep stock. Do you really want to risk the company's valuation?"

At this point Arthur openly gaped at me, but Ginny had a smug smile.

"Good to know someone listens when I talk at dinner," Ginny said. "Elaine, would you like to be looped in? You're a little young, but we could introduce you to the workings of the company. It will be a good bridge for meeting the various executives. Perhaps an internship next semester. Should I modify your high school curriculum to add business classes?"

"Please." I gave a sniff. "I grew up with the world's foremost forensic accountant. I can read a balance sheet."

"My mistake." Ginny smiled to herself. She pulled up a mid-air screen and started taking notes.

"Arthur," I turned my attention to my father. He still looked rebellious, but he had stopped fighting back. "Yes, it's only money, but money pays for all the stuff that keeps us safe. And money pays the salaries of your employees and keeps them sort of safe." I stumbled on the last few words because that wasn't quite what I meant. I shrugged. It had sounded good. "I'll be fine here tomorrow," I said with a confidence I didn't possess. "I have Will, and he has Galahad. I have my armor and tons of knights. I'll be fine."

"You'd better be." Arthur crushed me to him in a giant hug. With a small shock, I realized he had reached around so he was hugging Will too. "You'd better both be."

I MEANDERED INTO THE SMALL BREAKFAST ROOM THE NEXT MORNING AT the leisurely hour of seven. Arthur and Will had suspended training for the day in honor of the meeting that afternoon at Keep Consolidated's West Coast Headquarters. I had tried to sleep in, but apparently getting up a little before five every morning meant that "sleeping in" now consisted of waking up at six.

When I got to the breakfast table, Arthur and Ginny already sat there like a Norman Rockwell painting, if the people in a Norman Rockwell read their news on tablets instead of newspapers. Ginny was her usual impeccable self, but even Arthur wore a tailored suit instead of his usual aging-surfer-chic.

There was no sign of Will.

Ginny greeted me with a smile. Arthur glared, refused to say a word, and sulked as if he was being dragged to an execution rather than going to gloat with a bunch of other rich people about how much richer they were making each other.

"Elaine and Will could wait in the outer office while we all meet," Arthur said, breaking into the middle of a conversation that Ginny and I were having about the earnings report the Board would discuss today and release next week. It was like he was still in the conversation from last night.

"Security is good, but it's nothing compared to the Rook. They'll be safer here, and you know it." Ginny turned back to me and pointed to the projections for Keep's stock price.

Arthur brooded for a few more minutes before interrupting us again. "I could teleconference in from a lab. Then I could fix the bugs in this while you all babble at each other." He tapped a small button on the lapel of his suit's jacket. I hadn't noticed it before. I might have gotten better about determining how many exits a room had, but my general observational skills still needed work.

"In person, Arthur," said Ginny. "There's no network, not even one of mine, that I'd risk broadcasting a closed board meeting over." She turned back. "If you think the Dreki are bad, try fighting industrial espionage."

I didn't even want to think about that. Instead, I turned back to my glaring father. "What is that?" I asked, waving at the little button thing on his jacket. "Some new kind of camera?"

Arthur perked up a little. He tapped the button and shook his head. "This is a personal protection system. It generates an energy shield about a foot out from your body. It works on the principle of kinetic energy so it can stop high energy weapons like bullets."

"What about low energy? Could I still punch you?"

Arthur looked pleased by my question. "That's my girl. You're right. It's only for high energy projectiles. A good kick or punch would get through."

"Why are you wearing it if you're still perfecting it?"

Arthur gave an evil smile. "Right now bullets explode instead of being absorbed by the shield. It would protect me, but the explosions might just kill off half the board of Keep Consolidated sparing me from future tedious meetings."

Without a word, an irritated Ginny yanked the button off Arthur's jacket and tossed it onto the center of the table.

Arthur resumed sulking in his chair, but he didn't put the button back on.

"My lady," said Percival. "The helicopter has arrived to take you to the airport."

"Excellent." Ginny wiped her mouth with the cloth napkin and stood. "Come on, Arthur."

"Is Pendragon ready, Percival?" Arthur asked.

Ginny didn't let the AI answer. "Absolutely not. The President of Keep Consolidated's Board of Trustees is not arriving in LA in a costume."

"It's hardly a costume," started Arthur.

"I said no, Arthur."

"Fine." Arthur tossed his napkin on the table and stood. "I will ride in my stupid helicopter and my boring subsonic jet. But I'm still bringing eight knights and Pendragon. We can't go unprotected. They can fly in formation behind us."

"I would expect nothing else." Ginny leaned over to kiss me on the cheek. "Have a good day, dear. Call if you need us."

"Don't even think about leaving this place," said Arthur, "not even with Will."

"No fear there." The thought of leaving the building without Arthur and Pendragon terrified me. It wasn't like I'd forgotten the Dreki attacks or the thing with the Hell Hound in Central Park with the Fae, or even Vortigern's reptilian demeanor the one time I'd tried to be on my own. Part of me was relieved I didn't need to leave the Rook to go to the board meeting in LA. At this rate, I was in danger of becoming agoraphobic.

About ten minutes after Arthur and Ginny left, I finished breakfast and went off to hunt up Will. When I stuck my head in his room, I found him out of bed, but still in his pajamas and a fitted sleeveless shirt.

"You okay?" I asked, not venturing past the doorway.

Will looked up from his phone. The color had drained out of his face, leaving him wan. In his half-dressed state, he looked like a convalescent that had tried to stumble out of bed too soon after an illness. "LANCE ordered me to come in today and report in person. Stormfield's in New York, and he wants to chew me out, I guess."

"What?" I tried to keep my tone level, uninterested even. I didn't want to panic Will further.

"If I don't come in, he's coming here, probably with a large security detail. We can't have him here without Arthur. You might end up in the Tool Shed." The color had returned to Will's cheeks, but he still looked like he might crumple at any moment. "I don't know what to do. I promised Arthur I'd stay here, but I can't stay here."

Pulling Will over to the couch, I made him sit. "This is easy," I said when my fussing over him got on Will's nerves. He pushed away my attempt to prop a pillow under his head. "Don't go."

Will looked horrified, like I'd just asked him to punch a little old lady in the face. "I have to go. Stormfield can't come here. I don't think you get what a risk that is."

Now I was the one worried I would be sick all over the floor. "Well, you can't be considering going. Are Arthur and I the only ones taking my vision seriously? Cassie thinks it's no big deal. Ginny thinks you're safe enough here. I mean, she's right, but still. You're willing to go waltzing into LANCE headquarters with no care in the world."

"I'd hardly call it waltzing." Will tried to sit up, but I shoved hard on his bare shoulders to keep him laying down. My hands on his bare skin didn't spark a vision right then, possibly because I realized I was touching something other than his hand. I snatched my hands away like his shoulders burned. My face caught on fire. If Will noticed, he was nice enough not to comment.

"You cannot go present yourself at LANCE so they can beat you up and toss you in a cell." My voice rose.

"I can't stay here." Will ran his fingers through his hair and then sat up, reaching for me. I'd been kneeling next to the couch, but I moved until I was curled up next to him, my face buried in his neck. "Ginny's right that they won't storm the Rook," he said, "but they won't leave. And I wouldn't put it past Stormfield to get in here even without Arthur's permission. The Dreki got past Percival once. LANCE might have figured out how to do it too."

"I think you underestimate Arthur and Ginny," I said, my voice muffled. I refused to sit up and look at Will and the bleakness I would find in his eyes.

"I think you underestimate Stormfield."

We sat there on the couch for several minutes, me hugging the life out of Will while Will hugged me back. At some point he ran his fingers through my hair like I was a small child in need of comfort.

At that moment, I realized that once again, Will was in crisis, but he was the one comforting me, not the other way around. It was Will who was in danger of losing his freedom—or worse. And what was I doing? Figuring out how to save Will? No. I was letting him help me feel better.

I leaned back, breaking our embrace. My front felt cold without the warmth from his chest. I realized with horror I had been snuggling with Will. With even more horror, I realized that I wanted to do it again. I wanted to curl back up in his arms with that illusion of safety and love.

My heart almost stopped beating, and the blood drained out of my face to pool somewhere in my stomach. I didn't just need Will because he was my visions' crystal ball. I didn't want to hang out with him because he was kind and considerate and sometimes funny. And although there was plenty of attraction there, my feelings for him went well beyond it. I wanted to save Will from LANCE not because I was fundamentally decent but because I was inherently selfish. I wanted Will for myself. I wanted that future where we were curled up on the couch watching TV. I wanted Arthur's boyfriend comment to be real. Deep down where the feelings I didn't want to examine lived, I knew this was more than simple friendship.

And I had no idea if he even liked me back.

19

WHERE I TURN OUT TO BE A TRUE KEEP

To my surprise, I discovered then just how much I was my father's daughter. When I couldn't sway Will from going into LANCE headquarters, the tantrum I threw made Arthur's efforts from the night before look like mild discontent.

I ranted. I raved. I stomped up and down Will's room while Will looked on in frank astonishment. It wasn't pretty. I also finally got why Arthur reacted that way. I understood how he felt when we went to rescue my parents, and he wouldn't let me join the battle. Sure, I had been scared for my parents that day, but there wasn't anything they could do about the danger. A rocket was heading for them, and it was a matter of whether we would get there on time.

With Will though, he was knowingly putting himself into danger. It terrified me, and I was furious he would be so cavalier. No wonder Arthur had locked me out of my armor.

Eventually, my emotions wore me out, and I flung myself down on Will's bed with my arm over my eyes. "Fine," I said. "You insist on sacrificing yourself to the altar of honor or whatever." I sat up to glare at Will again. Since I'd been glaring at him for ten minutes straight, he was immune at this point. He stared back with no expression. "Can you at least postpone this reckoning? The vision was for today not tomorrow. Surely, Stormfield can wait a day. Wait until Arthur's back and can go with you. He will, you know. Go with you. Arthur, I mean. And Stormfield can't chew you out for not stealing Arthur's tech if Arthur is sitting next to you."

"The summons was for today, Elaine," Will said. For some reason, Will seemed to get calmer the angrier I got, almost as if I was sucking the fear and turmoil out of him like some kind of emotion-eating vampire. "Stormfield will not rearrange his schedule for an underling. If he wants to see me today, he'll make sure I see him today."

I had a brilliant idea. "You explain that with Arthur and Ginny and Cassie and the Defender gone, you can't leave me today. It wouldn't be safe to leave me alone. The Dreki might attack and all. You have to stay here." Popping off the bed, I danced around the room. Will seemed taken aback like he was finding my rapid mood changes as dizzying to watch as they were to experience firsthand. "Best of all, it's the absolute truth."

Will considered this for a moment, but then he shook his head. "Do you really want Stormfield to know Arthur's gone?"

"LANCE wouldn't storm the Rook," I repeated. We all kept saying this, but were we right? "Would they?" I asked in a smaller voice.

Will didn't answer. He didn't need to. We'd been through this already. Several times.

While I paced trying to think of another way to keep Will home, he got up and went into his closet. He came back out holding one of his gray suits.

"Wear something else," I told him. "You're wearing a suit in my vision."

Will gave me a look like I'd suggested he go to LANCE naked. "I can't go to LANCE in jeans. It would be inappropriate."

I barely kept from screaming. Instead, I stormed out of his room and headed for the breakfast room. If I couldn't keep Will from throwing himself at LANCE, at least I could give him some form of aid. I grabbed the little personal protection shield button thing off the table where Ginny had tossed it. Maybe someone would shoot at Will, and the faulty device would blow LANCE headquarters up. Normally, I wasn't so bloodthirsty, but the clandestine organization had rubbed my last nerve raw by threatening the guy I liked.

With the button clutched in my hand, I'd been pacing the small breakfast room like a soldier patrolling the perimeter, but my last thought stopped me short. I hadn't processed this whole being into Will thing yet. Now that I wasn't watching Will courageously throw himself at LANCE in some misguided attempt to protect me, did I still have the same feelings? I paused for a moment for soul-searching. I decided I did. But was it more than liking?

I decided I needed air. After telling Percival to send my armor out to meet me, I walked around outside, my armor a metallic shadow. Neither Percy nor Percival were chatty, so I worried over Will's interest like a kid with a loose tooth.

I knew one sided relationships existed. I'd seen enough movies about it, and I knew unrequited love (with a healthy dose of delusion) was how stalkers were born. Did that apply to me? On the whole, if someone disliked me, I disliked them—a mutually satisfactory arrangement. Will liked me. I was sure of that much. He wouldn't be so considerate and consoling and always willing to be around if he hated my guts. That did not mean he *liked me* liked me. He liked that Arthur and Ginny treated him more or less like family now. It didn't sound like LANCE had ever done that before. I kicked at an ornamental stone in one of the flower beds. I was probably like the sister he never had. How depressing.

I decided I needed a distraction. "Hey, Percy," I said to my armor. "How's that hack of Arthur's personal files going?"

"I managed access this morning." Percy radiated smugness from the speaker on my armor. Over the terrace's speaker, Percival sighed.

I didn't have any particular desire to rifle through Arthur's electronic life, but Percy had been complaining about being bored. He was the whiniest AI I'd ever met. So, I asked him to try this hack. He never would have gotten through a firewall Ginny set up, but Arthur wasn't in her league when it came to coding. His brilliance lay in the hardware.

"Anything interesting?" I asked Percy. I settled down on my back on the drawbridge, with one foot dangling over the edge a few feet over the water. Above me many dozens of knights swooped and swirled in the sky like swallows. Arthur had almost the entire armory either standing guard on the terrace or flying above.

"There's a file named 'For Elaine,' but I don't know if you'd find that interesting."

I rolled my eyes, not that Percy would care if he'd annoyed me. "What do you think? What's in it?"

"Videos," Percy said. "Over three hundred."

"Grief." I sat up, but I didn't get up off the bridge. Instead, I stared at the armor as if its faceless helm would give me a clue. "Why in the world would he have saved three hundred videos for me?"

"No idea. Want to watch one?"

"Can we do that out here?" I had no desire to go back inside while I was still irritated with Will. I wanted to be able to see him without screeching at him like a nagging scold when I had to tell him goodbye.

"Sure. Here's the first one in the file. It's from six years ago."

The terrace didn't have mid-air screens like indoors, but Percy had a few tricks up his sleeve. Literally. My armor lifted her arm and held her palm straight at me. She was standing the way I had drawn Pendragon that day I'd had my first true vision. The palm split open at the center, and a small hologram projected out. It showed Arthur in the center of a room I didn't recognize.

"Hi, Princess," past Arthur said. He still looked basically the same as he did now although his hair had a little less gray in it. He wore board shorts and a Hawaiian shirt, so his lousy taste in fashion wasn't new. "You have no idea how excited I am that we finally found you again. When Ginny showed me your location and we brought you all up on the satellite, I thought we were both going to cry. I got to tell you, you've grown a lot since I last saw you." He gave the camera a smile, but his eyes looked kind of glassy like he might cry then too.

"Ginny and Tori have been talking, and we're trying to figure out how you can visit me or how we can visit you. Things aren't all too safe these days with the Dreki still looking for your folks and their never-ending hatred of me." He stopped as if brooding for a minute before focusing on the camera again with a smile. "But that's not something for you to worry about. We've figured out harder stuff than this before, and we'll figure out tougher stuff again. But until I can see you, I thought I'd send you this video. I love you so much, Princess, and I've got so much to show you." He waved and a child-sized suit of armor marched onto the screen. "I've made you a couple of different ones over the years," he said, "but I'm so excited that you'll be able to have this one." He frowned for a minute. "Your mom and Ginny probably won't let you ride in it, but little Morgause here is an excellent knight to protect my Princess." He waved at the camera. "I'll go now, but I'll see you very soon. If you want, send me a video back or even call. I can't wait to hear from you." Arthur waved again, and the video cut out.

I stared in shock. I tried to speak, but for a moment nothing would come out. "Percy, load the next video," I said.

I watched the next five videos in a row, but after that I skipped around. Arthur had made at least one video a week for six years. For the first few years, all of them ended in the same way as the first, asking me to communicate back. He was never pushy, never demanding. Arthur didn't beg or ask why I never did. He just gave the camera a smile that got a little sadder with each video and asked me to respond.

By the time I was fourteen, it was clear he didn't think I was watching the videos. I couldn't decide if he thought I didn't care or if I wasn't getting them. He probably couldn't decide which it was either. He still kept making them though—even if sometimes his cheerfulness was a little forced. None of the videos were long—most were under four minutes—but he'd catch me up on the week or tell me about something he'd invented or a battle Pendragon had fought.

In the next-to-last video, he'd rescued Will and some boy on the way to LANCE's Institute. Arthur actually mentioned Will by name. Something about taking this Darren kid to the Tool Shed seemed to upset Arthur. He had a lot of nasty things to say about LANCE, and Will seemed to get caught up in that dislike. In the video, Arthur worried about the boy and some other kids trapped at the Institute. "Trapped" was the word he used. No wonder he had fought so hard to keep me out of there. He seemed to be fighting equally hard to get those kids back out.

When Will came to say goodbye some time later, he found me staring blankly off into space while still sitting on the drawbridge, tears streaming down my face.

He knelt down beside me. His thumb wiped at the tears on

the left side of my face, his touch so gentle I thought at first I'd imagined it. "Don't cry," he said.

"He didn't abandon me," I said turning to Will. "All this time, deep down, I thought it was all just talk. I mean, Arthur Keep, the Arthur Keep, the powerful Pendragon, couldn't just lose someone like he and Ginny claimed. I figured he'd always known where I was, that it was just easier or safer or whatever to stay away."

Will continued to kneel next to me, silent. He didn't interrupt my babbling.

"Even when he was arguing with Stormfield about the Institute or insisting I stay, I figured it was just guilt from having been absent for so long. Every kid dreams their dead-beat parent is being kept away or something, but Arthur really was." I reached out my hands, and Will took them, helping me stand up. "He made a video a week for years because he wanted to stay connected. Years. How could Tori and Raul have kept him away that whole time? Why didn't they remind me, tell me about him when Arthur and Ginny found us six years ago?"

My question had been rhetorical, but Will half-nodded. "They'd built a whole new life, and you didn't remember the old. They probably didn't want you to, for how would they explain Arthur without admitting who they had been?"

"Who they were still being when I wasn't around." I glared at Will, but both of us knew my anger wasn't for him. "Mom mentioned hacking someone a few months before Arthur rescued me. I doubt they ever gave up their old life. They just invented an illusion they didn't want me to see through."

"Maybe."

We stood there for a minute, each trapped in our own thoughts.

"I don't know much about parents," Will said, breaking the silence. "LANCE took me out of foster care and placed me in the Conservatory when I was six. Until then, the longest I ever stayed in one place was three months. And the Conservatory isn't the kind of place where you find the nurturing, parental types."

Since LANCE agents ran it, I could only imagine.

Will turned me so I was facing him and had my back to the moat. "But I've known since the minute I saw Arthur with you, even before he told us he was your dad, that Arthur loved you. He looks at you and Ginny in the same way. It's a different love, but it's the same look. That man would die for either one of you."

I knew Will was right.

His phone buzzed. He pulled it out and made a face before stuffing it into the inside pocket of his jacket. "I'll be late. Another thing to irritate Stormfield."

"Oh." I pulled the little button out of my pocket. "This might offer some protection. It won't stop a punch, but it should deflect a bullet." I frowned down at the little piece of tech before putting it in Will's hand. "It might blow up everything around you when it does, but it should protect you."

Will's hand closed around it, but otherwise he didn't move. "It'll be okay, Elaine."

I looked away, feeling abandoned all over again. "You don't know that."

"Yes, I do."

He sounded so certain, I looked back up at him. And then I realized why he felt so confident, why he was so sure it would all work out. "You're going to use your power on Stormfield," I said. I wanted to collapse from relief. All the fear I'd been keeping bottled up inside seemed to drain out of me onto the drawbridge and into the moat. "You're going to persuade yourself into safety."

Will looked horrified. Not just horrified, disgusted. "I told you I never do that."

"But you said when there was no other choice …" My voice faded away. Surely, Will understood that he needed to use everything he had to save himself.

"There is always another choice," said Will. "I don't use it on humans, just irritating AIs."

"But then, how do you know this is all going to be okay?" The confusion in my voice had to match the confusion on my face.

"Because I know that if something happens, you'll come rescue me."

Will wasn't lying. He wasn't persuading me out of my fears. He seemed to believe what he was saying. I couldn't think why he would have so much faith in me.

Will reached up and brushed back the hair that had blown in front of my eyes. He looked at my eyes and then at my mouth and then at my eyes again.

"Elaine," said Will, but his voice sounded different, lower like he was going hoarse. He leaned toward me, and I froze. I wasn't sure what had changed in the last moment, but my heart beat in my chest so loud I could hear it, like the thump-thump of whirling helicopter blades.

"Elaine." Will no longer sounded weird. He sounded panicked. His eyes opened wide, and he no longer seemed to be looking at me, but at something behind me. I turned, but I didn't even make it an eighth of the way around.

"Percival," Will yelled, "get Elaine in armor. Now!" He shoved me hard in the chest. I went flying off the drawbridge into the moat.

WHERE WILL SACRIFICES HIMSELF FOR NO REASON AT ALL

TIME SEEMED TO STOP. EVEN THOUGH I KNEW IT WAS ADRENALINE OR something, the world around me shifted into slow motion. Off to the side, my armor fell into individual pieces headed for my body. Behind Will a helicopter rose up inch by inch past the crenellations. I wondered if Will had seen another helicopter over my shoulder. As my body hurtled toward the moat, I marveled that one or more helicopters had gotten this close to the Rook without Percival or any of the dozens of guarding knights sounding an alarm.

Before I hit the water, the parts of my knight's armor enveloped me. As they snapped into place around me, I snapped back out of my shock. Time resumed a normal pace, and I had one final glimpse of Will's determined face turning to meet the threat before my helm slid in place, locking me in darkness. I landed in the water wearing close to a hundred pounds of graphene armor and sank down to the bottom of the moat.

"Initializing," said Percy. The symbols for possible hostile forces lit up all over my viewscreen. My jaw dropped open. There had to be sixty troops swarming out of four helicopters that hovered on the edges of the parapets. Sixty bad guys against Will, all alone up there on the terrace.

"Percy, show me Will. Percival, get Arthur back here now." My viewscreen zoomed in on a cluster of dots. Will ducked behind a large stone planter at the back end of the drawbridge, shooting at a group of Dreki advancing on him. Of course, it was Dreki. I could see the dragon patches on the shoulders of their SWAT uniforms.

"Percy, we have to get to Will. Fire flight rockets."

"We can't right now."

"Why not? Are we damaged?" My eyes shot around taking in all the various readouts and gauges, but all systems were running within normal parameters.

"No. The Dreki have activated a directed electromagnetic pulse. All the electronics are being fried. I'm cut off from Percival and all the rest of the Keep systems." I panned out wider and watched as Arthur's knights dropped out of the sky. For a second, I forgot I was in my armor, and I tried to raise my hand to my mouth in shock. All I did was knock my glove into my helm. I switched my viewscreen back to Will. He still held off the Dreki, but they were coming closer.

"Percy, get Arthur."

"I told you. All the unshielded electronic stuff is toast." Percy sounded more fretful than usual. "I hope Percival's somewhere safe."

As touching as the AI's concern was, seeing as I had thought the two programs hated each other, now was not the time. "Percy,"

I said, trying to redirect the AI's thoughts back to our crisis. "We need Arthur. This isn't something we can do on our own."

Percy huffed. "What do you want me to do? All the usual communication stuff isn't fit for a salvage yard at this point."

"Then use an unusual way."

Little clicking sounds indicated Percy was thinking. The whole time we'd been arguing, I'd been following the track of the battle. Will still held them off on the drawbridge. He must have had spare clips of bullets for his gun, and it wasn't electronic, so it still worked. I wanted out of the moat, to at least fight alongside him, but Percy was right about the weapon. Some energy pulse was still beating against the Rook, dropping every knight in sight. The Dreki had us trapped until they turned their weapons off.

"Elaine? Elaine?" Arthur's voice came through the speakers in my helm.

"Arthur?" I almost cried. I hadn't realized just how scared I'd been until I heard his voice. "I don't know what to do. There so many of them and some sort of weapon has knocked out everything. All the knights except mine seem to be down, and I guess all the house defenses and everything else is too."

"I know. Percival is feeding me the data. How come you have an operational copy of him in your suit?"

I didn't have an answer and was too distracted to come up with one.

"My lord," said Percy sounding exactly like Percival, "Lady Elaine thought it prudent for Morgause to have a complete copy should she ever find herself cut off from the copies in the Rook or Pendragon."

"That's good," Arthur said. I couldn't tell if he sounded suspicious or not. "I've been trying to warn you for the last few minutes, ever since I realized something was wrong. Whatever they were jamming the signal with must have fried with the rest of the electronics. Are you safe in one of the labs? Those are all protected from this kind of pulse. I never dreamed the Dreki had a weapon like this. We're going to have to protect the whole building." Arthur's irritation showed in his voice, and it was oddly comforting. If he could worry about the building and not me, I couldn't be in that much danger.

"I'm in the moat."

There was a pause, and then Arthur laughed. "Brilliant. The water turned your suit into a Faraday cage protecting all the electronics inside."

Bullets pinged the surrounding water. A few hit my suit, but they did no damage.

"I don't know what you're talking about, but I think they've noticed me. I'm being shot at."

Arthur's laughter cut off like I'd lost his feed for a second. "Elaine," he said before I panicked, "I've got six knights with me, and we're only three minutes out. Patrick is on his way, but he was on the other side of the world, so it'll take him a few more minutes to reach you. Visions haven't been timely or useful this time around."

I snorted at that. Seeing Will tied to a chair had been all fine and good, but it would have been a lot more useful if I'd Seen this scene instead. I started to answer, but Arthur kept going. "You can

227

hold them off for three minutes, Princess. This is no harder than a training exercise."

I laughed, a crazy uncontrolled cackle that bordered on hysterics. In no reality was this like a training exercise. More bullets bounced on my armor, and I could no longer see Will's position. The Dreki shooting at me blocked my sight. "Are you joking?" I asked Arthur. "There's at least sixty up there. I've never taken on more than eighteen knights. And I have never won."

"Please," Arthur said. "Each of my knights is like ten of those Dreki fools. It's like you're only fighting six knights. And you can take down six knights. You can do this, Elaine." There was a pause as if he were checking a data feed or something. "I will be there in time. You will do this."

"Percival," I said, not able to use my AI's preferred name while Arthur listened in, "is it safe to get back up there?"

"The pulse is dissipating. I'll power us up the second the danger's gone."

"Then the moment we are clear of the water, target and fire the two big M84 rockets at the weapon that took out all the other knights. I don't want to fall out of the sky."

"Target acquired."

In the left-hand corner, my viewscreen showed Percy aiming both M84s at a box on one of the helicopters. That must have been the pulse generator.

"And then, Percival? We're going to save Will."

"You bet." Percy sounded skeptical, but I ignored his tone. I could do this.

I took a deep breath. A vision or two of the future would have been nice right about then, but I didn't have any exposed Dreki skin to grab onto. But this was what I had been training for. I had to believe Arthur was right, that I had the skills to survive. I didn't have a choice. "Percival, fire flight rockets when it's safe."

Four seconds later, I shot out of the water, like an avenging angel, ready to spew my righteous fire on the sinners spread out below me. The shock on the Dreki troops' faces meant they had thought my armor incapacitated like the rest. Dreki troops seemed to freeze, giving us a chance. The second we were above the fray, Percival sent the M84s at the helicopter with the pulse generator. It blew the weapon to smithereens, taking the helicopter with it.

I held my arms up and shot the laser cannons at the men around Will. The blast knocked the ones furthest from him off their feet, but the three that had already reached Will continued fighting him hand to hand. Will's gun sat on the ground where he must have tossed it aside when he ran out of bullets, and I did kind of wonder why the men were trying to subdue him instead of just shooting him. I didn't complain though.

I landed on the ground about ten feet away. Drekis showered me with bullets, but I didn't feel them although they sounded like hail from a major thunderstorm pinging off my sides. I sprayed my own bullets at the men, but their body armor protected them too. It drove them back, but no one fell.

I turned to help Will, but something slammed into my back. I stumbled and almost fell, but instead I caught myself and turned around. Another one of the Dreki raised a shoulder mounted rocket launcher thing. I had no idea what the thing was, but I did not want it hitting me again. Before the soldier aimed it, I shot into the air and circled behind. I landed behind the Dreki, ripping the launcher out of the soldier's hands and tossing it over the side of the building.

Landing had been a mistake. One of Arthur's knights might be better than one Dreki, but I had just landed in the middle of a whole mess of them. They dogpiled on top of me. Their weapons weren't able to penetrate my armor, but their sheer weight forced me down. My knight had superhuman strength, but even she couldn't stay standing with the weight of thirty grown adults bearing down on her.

"Percival, suggestions?"

"Flight rockets."

"Do it."

The rockets on my back ignited, burning those touching my back. The whole pile of bodies slid to the side until I had oriented myself better. Percy redirected all the available power to the rockets, and I pushed up and free of the crush.

One stubborn Dreki, though, hung onto my neck, forcing me to give the goon the piggyback ride of a lifetime. I shifted and turned, bucked and tossed, trying to get the rhinoceros sized soldier off, but he stayed just out of reach. I changed my flight path and slammed the back of the guy against one of the Rook's walls. The impact knocked the air out of him. The guy's hold loosened, and I tossed him down to the terrace below. The guy must have done something to my armor just before I slung him off because my flight control became erratic. I dropped back down to the ground before I crashed, but my landing wasn't pretty. Picking myself up, I readied my weapons, but the Drekis were once again surrounding me.

I aimed at the nearest group, but I never had to fire.

Pendragon slammed down in front of me, his sword already unsheathed. The sword's laser edges activated, allowing Pendragon to slice through the group trying to swarm us. Around me six of the other eight knights Arthur had taken with him to LA landed and fired on the Dreki forces, driving them back. Arthur hadn't been kidding. One knight was equal to about ten Dreki soldiers. If even two of the knights Arthur had left behind had survived the pulse weapon, I might have been able to handle the Dreki attack all by myself. With six functioning knights led by Pendragon, the Dreki were in full retreat within seconds.

From inside his armor Arthur called commands to his knights. He destroyed the remaining two helicopters and had the knights gather up the surviving Drekis.

By the time the Defender flew in, less than two minutes later, the battle was over.

I ran back to the spot where I'd last left Will, relieved when I didn't find his body slumped on the ground. "Will!" I yelled. "Will, you okay?"

When he didn't answer, I had Percy scan the area. My heart sank with the results.

"I'm sorry, Elaine. I really am," said Percy. "I can't find Will anywhere."

WHERE WILL'S PAST
CATCHES UP TO HIM

I TURNED AND RAN FOR **P**ENDRAGON. **A**RTHUR HAD ALREADY STEPPED out of his armor, his tailored business suit rumpled from fighting in Pendragon. Arthur directed the knights into security and clean-up details. Behind us, Patrick secured the Dreki prisoners, tying them up with such speed, I couldn't follow it with my eyes, not that I tried.

"Percival, I'm reading damage to Dame Morgause," Arthur said, staring down at a small screen projecting out of the glove of his left hand. The glove was the only part of his armor he still wore. "Get her up to a diagnostic chamber and begin repairs immediately. Prioritize over any other knight."

"I got this," said Percy. "Don't worry, he'll never suspect a thing."

I didn't have time to answer. My armor flew off of me in little parts as I ran, not even slowing me down. I ignored it, uninterested in where it headed.

Arthur frowned at me as I ran up. "Most of these things will have to be rebuilt from scratch." He kicked at a knight injured by the pulse weapon. "Are you okay?" He pointed the glove still on his hand at me and frowned at something that appeared on the little screen. "Percival says your heart rate is through the roof."

"No." I panted trying to catch my breath from the sprinting and the unspent adrenaline caused by the battle. "They got Will, Dad."

Arthur looked confused. "Impossible. I locked him in his room this morning before I left. I told Percival to keep him there to thwart your vision. If I'd known you'd be in danger too, I would have locked you in yours. Or maybe locked up the two of you to-gether." He rubbed at his eyes again. "Or maybe not."

I glared at him and his high-handed attempts to protect Will and me. That, though, would have to be an argument for later.

"No, the Dreki have him. Will's the one who pushed me in the moat, saving me and the armor by accident."

Arthur paled. "I didn't see him, but I didn't look. I assumed he was locked up safe." He ran his unarmored hand over his eyes for a second. He shook his head. "Percival, how did Will get out of his room?"

"He was quite persuasive, my lord."

I gasped, furious at Will. Not only wouldn't he use his power to get himself out of trouble, he had used it to send himself into danger. How dare he think protecting me from LANCE more im-portant than his own life? Especially when I'd made my views on the matter clear.

Arthur had frowned at Percival's statement, but he didn't

comment. He pulled data up on his small screen and turned for the house. "Pendragon, follow." He didn't quite run, but he walked fast enough I had to trot to keep up. Pendragon brought up the rear.

"He was determined to go into LANCE this afternoon. Nothing I said was going to stop him. Dad, we have to go after him."

"I know." Arthur skidded to a stop in front of the huge bank of built-in cabinets lining the rear of Ginny's office. He yanked open one of the wooden doors revealing a second metal door with an electronic keypad, thumbprint lock, and retinal identifier. "All fried." Arthur waved Pendragon over. "Get us in there, but don't damage anything. Ginny will kill us if we disturb a single processor or somehow damage a byte of data."

Using his remaining glove, Pendragon cut open the metal door.

I paced back and forth while Arthur played with his little screen. After about half a second, I'd had enough. "Arthur, this is taking too long. I don't know what's in there, but we have to go after Will now."

"What? No more Dad?"

"What?" Sometimes it was like Arthur's grip on reality was even more tenuous than I had thought. "What are you talking about?"

"Not important." Arthur turned back, but his shoulders slumped a little bit like I'd somehow hurt his feelings. I didn't have time to deal with his adolescent mood swings.

"We have to go now."

"Princess, we have no idea where Will has gone. The battle damaged your armor, and except for Galahad and the three knights I left charging in the armory, we've lost the entire complement here. The best thing we can do is regroup and notify LANCE of Will's abduction. He is one of them after all."

"Is he?" I stared at an envelope on Ginny's desk addressed to Arthur in Will's handwriting. "He had to go in today because he's in trouble. He hasn't been stealing your tech like Stormfield wants."

"Not stealing? What do you mean he isn't giving LANCE my tech?" Arthur gave me a humorless smile that didn't reach his eyes. "And after I've been going to all the trouble of leaving worthless pieces lying all over the place."

"What?"

Arthur shrugged. "Ginny and I read a memo Stormfield sent Will when your young man first got here. That charming idiot running LANCE authorized Will to kill me if needed." Arthur smiled as if it was the greatest joke in the world, but there was no frivolity in his voice. "It's not like anything in that email was a surprise. LANCE has been trying to get their hands on my tech for decades. I sort of doubted they would pass up this rather prime opportunity. Oh, finally." Pendragon had gotten through the metal casing.

Arthur grabbed a bunch of wires and connected Pendragon's glove to the bank of computer equipment hiding behind the shielded metal door. "Will wasn't one of my favorite people back then, but I don't want him disobeying direct orders. I told you before that Ginny and I looked into the whole LANCE retirement program." He grinned up at me, pausing for a moment from whatever tinkering he was doing with Pendragon's glove. "And by 'looked into' I mean downloaded half the LANCE database and created a permanent hack into the rest. I wanted Will to do a good job here, no matter what tech I had to sacrifice to Stormfield's greed and paranoia."

I must have looked as surprised as I felt.

Arthur stared at me for another moment before going back to adjusting the new set of screens that projected out of the glove. It wasn't as elegant as the usual mess of floating screens that populated Ginny's office, but it was more functional than the little screen he'd projected before. "Don't look so surprised," he said. "I don't trust LANCE, but I do trust Will. And even when I didn't, death seemed like a high price for a career he didn't choose."

I didn't know why I felt as surprised as I did. I'd realized that Arthur was sorry for Will, but I'd never realized that at some point, he'd started liking Will too.

"Besides, Will grew on me," Arthur said with a small smile as if he was reading my mind. "He's actually a good man, and he'll make a good …" Arthur paused as if he had planned on saying one thing but had changed his mind. "Boyfriend," he finished. He made a weird grimace and then gave me a small apologetic smile. "Ginny says I have to stop freaking out about you dating. I have to stop thinking about you as a preschooler. Did you know Ginny and I had been trying to get full custody from Tori for years, even before you all vanished?" Arthur didn't give me a chance to answer. "There's a good chance I'm having trouble reconciling the memory of the little girl with the almost adult daughter I actually have. Twelve years is a lot to miss even if Tori was right and it kept you alive."

I didn't have an answer for Arthur. I didn't tell him about finding his videos. I didn't say I suspected he'd been kept away, not to keep me alive, but so my other parents could keep their secrets. Their illusion of the perfect, average suburban life would have fallen apart the moment Arthur had shown back up.

We sat there in silence for a moment while I tried to process everything. Arthur worked on something with a small curse every now and then when the screens didn't tell him something he wanted. I couldn't take the silence anymore.

"Arthur, we still have to save Will. You promised."

Arthur looked confused for a moment. "I did?"

"You promised him that no one would kill him while he lived here."

"Oh, that." Arthur's face took on the rather pleased, but fierce, look he got before going after some bad guy. "That's a promise I plan to keep." A screen beeped. Arthur tapped an icon and a self-satisfied look replaced his fierce one. He looked like a cat that had just discovered an unattended plate of chicken. "Gotcha."

The screen changed into a map of the eastern seaboard and the western part of the Atlantic Ocean. A small orange dot inched across part of the ocean.

"There he is." Arthur tapped on the dot, bringing up a screen full of numbers. "His vital signs appear good. It doesn't look like he's suffering from shock, so if he is injured, it's not serious." Arthur gave a half snort. "He looks pretty annoyed though if that heart rate is any indication. I pity the Dreki if your boyfriend gets loose."

"You mean that's Will? You can track him?"

"I implanted a small micro-transmitter. It feeds the system a constant stream of biodata and location coordinates. How else am I supposed to keep an agent like Will safe if I don't know when he's in trouble or where?"

"You chipped Will? Like a dog?"

Arthur gave me a wide-eyed innocent stare, like he couldn't understand my surprise. "Not like a dog. Like a loved one." He zoomed the map out to show three more dots. A yellow one moved somewhere over the Midwest. Arthur pointed to it. "That's Ginny flying back." He pointed at a blue and a green dot clustered together. "And that's you and me."

"I'm chipped too?" I couldn't decide if I was relieved that Arthur really would always know where to find me or revolted that Arthur really would always know where to find me.

"Of course, Princess. I implanted one in your neck the night of that first Dreki attack here. How do you think I followed you that day you ran away from home? I would have had a hard time saving you from Vortigern if I hadn't been able to follow you with this." He waved his arm at his creepy tracking system.

Deciding the ethics of secret family tracking systems would have to wait, I couldn't deny a chipped Will would prove mighty convenient today.

"Then if we can track Will, let's get going."

"Slow down, Princess." Arthur grabbed my arm, physically keeping me from dashing from the room. He pulled up another screen with a schematic of my armor. "Your armor has at least another fifteen minutes of repairs, and we don't have enough knights here. Even with Patrick and all of his powers, this will be hard for us to pull off by ourselves." He pointed at Will's dot crawling across the screen. "At least one helicopter survived the attack, and it's headed back to some sort of base. Those things don't have ocean crossing capabilities. We need more fire power to storm a Dreki aircraft carrier or whatever that helicopter is aiming for." He frowned and loosened his grip on my arm. "I don't like it either, but our best option is still to alert LANCE. They can mobilize a retrieval force faster than we can."

I protested, but Arthur didn't listen. He typed a string of code on his screen, and another screen opened in Ginny's office. It showed Stormfield from the back. Arthur had hacked into Stormfield's office's chat program.

Arthur was not subtle at getting Stormfield's attention. "Stormfield!" he yelled out.

Stormfield turned around and gave Arthur the irritated glare you give a toddler you find pulling all the pots and pans out of the kitchen cabinet. "I see your wife has been playing in our system again. I suppose that means we need to up our security. Again."

"It'll take Ginny two, three minutes to get through the new firewall," said Arthur. "I don't know why you bother. That's not why I called."

"Indeed."

"As I'm sure you noticed, Keep Tower was the subject of a Dreki attack," said Arthur in a formal tone. He added, almost as a sarcastic aside, "Thanks for coming to help, by the way. The Dreki had some kind of EMP that knocked out every knight except hers. They almost got Elaine."

Stormfield shrugged, and I wanted to slap the disinterested look off his face. Fortunately, he was on the other side of a view screen, so I was spared the temptation.

"I've said from the beginning that our Institute was the safest place for her," Stormfield said. "If Elaine gets captured or killed, that's on your head not mine."

"Well, she wasn't, thanks for the concern. And you will never put her in your Tool Shed." Arthur's fists clenched so tight I thought he might snap the electronics he held. "The Dreki took Will, though."

For a moment Stormfield looked as though he didn't know who Arthur was talking about. Now, I really wanted to strangle the man.

"Agent Redding? He's due to report here in five minutes." Stormfield looked around his office as if he expected Will to materialize for their appointment.

"Well, he'll be really, really late," said Arthur. He rubbed his eyes again as if having trouble focusing them. "If ever. You need to send a retrieval team after him. I'm not in a position right now to mount a rescue operation with all my knights here out of commission."

I tuned out as Stormfield and Arthur argued the merits of

mounting a rescue operation. Stormfield was put out when he discovered Arthur had chipped one of his agents "like a dog."

I wandered over to Ginny's desk where Will's letter to Arthur sat. Picking up the letter, I wished it was Will's hand. I could get a vision from holding Will's hand, not from his letter.

Or at least, that had been my assumption. I'd been holding the letter for less than a minute when my eyes clouded over, the telltale warning I was entering a vision. I froze, clutching the letter. This wasn't a fully immersive vision yet, but it was enough I could still See Will sitting tied to the chair, his immaculate suit from earlier filthy with a rip at the right shoulder seam.

I pushed myself all the way into the familiar vision, hoping I would be able to glean something new.

Like every other time, Will sat calmly, staring straight in front of him. He made no effort to escape his bonds. Instead, he might have been a carved sculpture. Even mussed and bruised from the fighting, he was handsome enough to be one.

I sighed, but Will didn't hear me. It wasn't like I'd teleported myself into the room. Just like the time I'd Seen my parents attacked, I was still nothing more than an observer of this same uninformative scene.

So, I was both frustrated and relieved when the scene changed. For the first time since I'd had this vision, the single door to the room opened and a girl about Will's age or a little older entered.

The human mind is a fickle thing. Here I was worried out of my skull for Will and his safety, but I still couldn't help feeling jealous. If Will and this girl were anything to go by, secret agents were just as hot in real life as they were in movies. This girl wore the same SWAT uniform like every other Dreki goon I'd seen, but on her, the outfit was form fitting and accentuated every curve. She'd pulled her hair back into an efficient ponytail, but it still looked full and lustrous, like she'd just stepped from a photo shoot. My hair was in a ponytail, but in a greasy, lumpy mess that made me look like I hadn't bothered to shower in thirty-six hours. In other words, the Dreki girl looked like a model, and I looked like my real life. No wonder Will was looking at the girl with a wary mixture of fondness and contempt.

"Will, Will, Will. What have you gotten yourself into?" asked the girl. "Long time no see."

Will rolled his eyes. "I missed you too, Evie. You realize that LANCE has a shoot on sight order out for you with the shot preferably going in your head."

Evie shrugged without the slightest hint of concern. "I never was one of their favorite students at the Conservatory."

My head snapped back as if vision Evie had somehow smacked me. Did Will know this girl, not because she was a wanted Dreki terrorist, but because they had attended morally questionable spy school together?

"I think this has less to do with your poor grade in Diplomatic Relations," started Will.

"I always was more of a shoot now, talk later kind of girl," said Evie with a grin.

"And more to do with the whole traitor thing," finished Will as if Evie had never interrupted him.

Evie held up a finger to correct him. "Not a traitor. Double-agent. A traitor is someone who changes loyalties. I was never loyal to LANCE but to the Dreki and my father."

"How is Vortigern these days?" asked Will. "I hear Arthur Keep almost gave him a laser lobotomy."

The blood rushed from my head, and for an idle second, I wondered what would happen if I passed out during a vision. Would I pass out in real life? Then, my brain refocused on what Will had said. Vortigern was Evie's father? Her father was my father's archnemesis. Did that somehow make us archnemeses by association? I didn't feel up to having a true archnemesis. Constant Dreki "recruitment" was bad enough.

Clearly, my mind was spiraling out of control. I pulled my focus back to the conversation.

"I had heard you were protecting Pendragon's latest pet," Evie said with a sneer. Now that I was looking for it, the family resemblance was obvious. Evie might be prettier than a botanical garden in full bloom, but she had Vortigern's cold, dead, snake eyes.

Will's eyes narrowed. "She's as much of a pet to Pendragon as you are to Vortigern. She's Arthur's daughter."

"What?" For a moment Evie lost her mocking mask, and the real girl seemed to peek through.

"Did Daddy forget to mention it?" asked Will in a condescending voice that kind of made me want to slap him. He might be tied up and in need of rescuing, but it still annoyed me when guys talked to girls like we were mentally deficient.

Apparently, Evie shared my feelings. She walked up and

slapped Will hard enough on the cheek that his chair rocked for a moment. "I have my father's full trust."

Will shrugged as much as his trussed-up body would allow. "I'm sure Vortigern forgot to mention it."

"Father and his men are coming soon." Evie had regained control of both her temper and her mocking manner. "I wanted to see your pretty face one more time before Dimitri starts in on you."

Will didn't answer or appear to respond. I balled my fists, frustrated by my utter uselessness but also frustrated with Will. He had the power to end all of this. He could "persuade" Evie to help him escape. Instead he'd used his powers to break out of the safety of his bedroom.

Evie patted her lips as if thinking. Then she gave a small tight-lipped smile. She leaned down and kissed Will. The kiss was long and deep, and it seemed to surprise Will. His eyes shot wide open, and then he kissed her back like kissing her was something he'd done before.

I felt like they'd kicked me in the gut. I barely kept myself from doubling over and being ill on the floor. I suppose I shouldn't have been surprised that the two had some sort of past. After all, they had gone to the same school for years and had lots of the same interests like guns and whatever secret agents did for fun.

And it wasn't like I was Will's girlfriend, no matter what Arthur said.

Evie finally came up for air and glanced up at a corner of the room. I almost missed it, her eyes darted there and back so fast I wondered if I had imagined it. Turning to see what she was looking at, I found a camera monitoring the entire scene. I wondered who was watching this little performance. And then I wondered if this was a performance or something else. Maybe Evie mourned seeing her ex turned over to her father and his goons.

Evie stroked his cheek for a moment. "Remember that day under the Eiffel Tower in Paris."

I wanted to gag. I could only imagine what they had been up to under the tower. If that kiss was any indication, massive amounts of PDA had been the tasteful parts.

Will tried to remain impassive, but his left eye twitched like he was holding in a strong emotion. He said nothing.

With one last pat on his cheek that bordered on the edge of another slap, Evie turned to leave. Since Will just sat tied to his chair, as stoic as ever, I turned to follow Evie from the room.

She twisted and turned down a few hallways until she entered a large control room. Vortigern looked up from a radar screen. I rotated in a slow circle taking in the room and its familiar surroundings.

At that point, perhaps because I had wandered too far from Will, Evie and her father faded only to be replaced by my father as he cut the connection to Stormfield's office in the middle of a Stormfield rant.

"Idiotic paper-pushing politician puppeteer," muttered Arthur. He shut his eyes and took a deep breath as if trying to calm himself enough to keep from killing Stormfield through the screen. "I can't tell if he's sending a team after Will or not. I'm not sure

Stormfield knows."

"It doesn't matter," I said.

Arthur's eyes popped open. "So, you're back from your vision."

I gave Arthur a big smile, pleased he had noticed my clouded eyes even while arguing with Stormfield. "I'm more than back."

Turning, I ran to the file cabinet where Ginny had stored the drawings I had spent so much time creating my first week in the Rook. I pulled out one that looked almost like a floor plan and another of an elaborate control room.

"Dad, I Saw where they've taken Will." I pointed to a room in the flying fortress thing I had drawn all those weeks ago. "He's here, and I know how we'll get him."

WHERE I DEMONSTRATE THAT PLANNING MIGHT NOT BE ONE OF MY STRENGTHS

To his credit, Arthur listened to my idea, and he didn't try again to talk me out of going after Will. Even he admitted that LANCE was no longer Will's best option. He rubbed his eyes again, as if getting a massive migraine, and then sighed. He opened his eyes and gave me a small smile. "This isn't the worst plan ever, but it'll be close."

By that point Patrick had joined us in Ginny's office. He shook his head. "I don't like it."

"It's not brilliant, but do you have anything better?" I asked.

"I don't think it would matter if we did," Arthur said, not answering my question. "You're determined to be the one that rescues Will, no matter what. I don't like it either, but I can see it working."

Patrick opened his mouth to say something or to argue, but Arthur rubbed at his eyes again and cut The Defender off before he could speak. "I can see it working," he said again.

Patrick's mouth snapped shut, and he gave a sharp nod to

Arthur. He didn't look happy, but he would help.

Arthur tossed Pendragon back his glove, and then he turned to leave and waved for Pendragon and the rest of us to follow. "Let's go see if Dame Morgause has been fixed." Arthur turned and gave me a stern glare, the kind that wasn't half-joking but dead serious. "And you're not stepping a toe out of this place until we've got your armor repaired—even if I have to lock you in the labs to keep you there. Do you understand? My minuscule faith in your plan disappears if you don't have working armor. Are we clear?"

"Like a cloudless day," I said, following him out of the room toward the staircase hidden at the end of my hall. "I promise not to go anywhere without armor." I wanted to rescue Will, but I wasn't stupid. "But I doubt you've got so much as a working lock in this place. Isn't everything electronic?"

I couldn't see Arthur's face, but his hands clenched into fists. "Oh, the labs will be working. They have even more shielding than Ginny's servers, and those withstood the EMP just fine."

"You expected a pulse weapon?" I don't know why this surprised me. Arthur's paranoia knew no limits. "Why didn't you shield the whole place then?"

"A directed EMP pulse gun? No, I hadn't expected one of those. I have no idea how the Dreki got a hold of one without me even learning about a prototype." Arthur's already grim voice became even more pessimistic. "No, for some time now, I've expected a nuclear bomb."

"What?" I halted mid-step, tripping and stumbling up the stairs we climbed. "A nuke? Why?"

"Occupational hazard," Patrick said with a shrug, but Arthur and I ignored him.

Arthur turned to glance down at me, probably wondering why I had stopped. "I built the entire core of this building to withstand a small nuclear blast even if someone dropped the bomb on the roof. All bedrooms and the labs and the part of the armory that houses the family armor are in that core. All the apartments on the lower public floors of the Rook are in the core too. Since a nuclear explosion also causes an EMP, shielding from the pulse weapon turned out to be a happy side effect."

"Happy, indeed," I whispered.

Arthur shrugged and went back to taking the stairs two at a time. "But I didn't shield the entire building because I couldn't afford it. Even I have monetary constraints, Princess, and a nuclear bomb proof eighty-five story building in the middle of Manhattan is one of them."

I followed, my head reeling. Not for the first time, I wished I'd never been introduced to a world where Will worried about his employers trying to kill him off and Arthur had legitimate concerns that someone would try to blow his home up with a nuke. Life had been so much simpler when my biggest worry was a history test.

Patrick left us at the door to the labs muttering something about preliminary reconnaissance. Arthur didn't seem to notice he'd gone.

Arthur had been right about the shielding protecting labs from the blast. Everything in Arthur's personal workspace still hummed along as if the pulse weapon had never happened. I'd only ventured into this room once before, but the place seemed the same. Robotic arms fitted complicated electronics and circuits onto the various pieces that would become one of Arthur's knights. The place hummed with the background noise of whirling gears and the clicks of pieces being snapped into place. We passed knights in various states of assembly and Arthur's all-purpose work table. Twelve screens filled with schematics hovered around the table while the actual surface was so littered with miscellaneous amounts of junk, it was a miracle Arthur ever managed to invent anything at all.

What the room didn't seem to have was my armor.

I stopped next to Arthur's work table. "I don't see it."

Arthur paused and turned to me. "See what?"

"My armor." I crossed my arms and glared. "This had better not be a trick to get me down here so you can lock me away in your Keep Tower and go after Will without me."

Arthur held up his hands in mock surrender. "When I said I'd lock you in here if your armor wasn't ready, I meant I'd lock you in here with me. The thought of you alone in here and the amount of damage you could do?" Arthur shuddered. "You don't see your armor because it's in a diagnostic chamber. In another room." He gestured at the back wall lined with huge shelves filled with spare parts for the knights.

"You have to be kidding," I said. "There's no door. You want me to believe you have a secret room on the other side? That seems unlikely."

Arthur shrugged. He turned and walked over to one of the shelves. Shifting over a metal glove, he revealed a keypad underneath. He typed in a code, and half of the wall swung on silent hinges into the lab. "You don't have to believe, Princess. But if you want your armor, I would suggest taking a leap of faith into my unlikely secret room." Arthur gave me a smirk and stepped through the doorway.

I followed Arthur into a giant room, twice the size of the one we had just left. Pods filled with armor in various states of repair lined the far wall while weapons lined another wall. They looked like weapons from a gun enthusiast's magazine from the future.

"Those are a few prototypes," said Arthur when he caught me staring at them. "Those are definitely things I don't want LANCE getting their hands on."

"You have a secret lab. Will and I have secret tracking chips. Anything else you're keeping from me?"

Arthur gave me his most brilliant smile. "Oh, I'm sure I've still got one or two surprises up my sleeve. What fun would it be if I shared everything about me all at once?"

I glared unsure if my father was inspiring waves of exasperation or unmitigated hatred. I was having trouble distinguishing between the two feelings.

"Is there anyone you trust?"

There was a long pause. Arthur's face turned serious, his smile sliding away. "Ginny," he finally said. "I trust Ginny." He touched my arm. "But I'm trying with you and maybe someday Will. I think at this point you know more about me, the real me, than anyone other than Ginny. But it takes time, Princess. The counselor says I have trust issues."

I snorted. "That's an understatement."

Arthur grinned. "Yes, well. The constant attacks on my life have made me a little wary." He pointed to one of the diagnostic chambers on the wall. "Now, do you want to go save your boyfriend or not?"

I nodded and all but ran over to my armor not willing to waste another second of Will's captivity. The armor stepped out of the chamber and made an odd bow followed by shooting into the air and after a somersault landing in a curtsy.

"Percy," I hissed.

"Very funny, Percival," said Arthur from behind me. I turned to find him fiddling with one of the mid-air screens. Arthur rolled his eyes at me. "I believe Percival is trying to tell us that the robot is in full working order."

"Apologies, my lady," said Percy, doing his best to imitate Percival. "I had hoped to add a whimsical element to the proceedings."

"I'll have Ginny check his code, especially his ability to contextualize situations," said Arthur, sending her a quick email. "Some of the lines in here don't look right."

I held my breath, hoping Arthur wouldn't examine it too closely and realize that I wasn't running an authorized Percival.

"If the EMP has scrambled him," Arthur continued, "it would be nice to know before we're in the middle of a Dreki stronghold fighting for our lives."

"I'm sure Percival is fine, Dad. We don't have time for Ginny to debug him."

Arthur gave me a long look before shrugging. "There's no glaring cause for concern." He handed me two headsets. The first I stuck on my head before sliding the one for Will in a small storage compartment on my armor. Arthur's aesthetic taste when it came to female armor might be lacking, but at least he gave a girl pockets.

"Pendragon, Morgause," called Arthur. He snapped his fingers and the two knights dissolved into their individual pieces and reformed around us.

"Initializing," said Percy into the darkness. I'd never been happier to hear the AI in my life. The familiar screens around me lit up, and I scanned all the readouts to make sure everything was checking out. When it came to the knights, I trusted Arthur with my life, but it would have been beyond foolish not to have inspected the displays myself.

I muted my headset so Arthur wouldn't hear me. "How're we doing in here?" I asked.

"Peachy," said Percy. "Repairs are flawless since I supervised them myself."

I double-checked the readouts.

"I even hooked back up with our favorite uptight AI," Percy added in a smug voice.

"Indeed." The original Percival's tone made it clear he'd noticed the insult. "I once again can direct your activities."

"Percival, I want what's left of the knights from here in the air

253

in thirty seconds, converging on Will's tracker," Arthur said over the comms.

I unmuted mine. "Do we have any left?" I asked.

"The six I brought back with me and Galahad and Leodegrance," Arthur said, his voice grim. "The whole family's coming out to play. And Percival," he added, "except for the thirty joining Ginny and the jet, I want all reinforcements headed to Will too. The Rook will just have to stay undefended for now."

"Reinforcements?"

"You didn't think I kept every knight here at the Rook, did you, Princess?"

I had thought that very thing.

"I've got at least one knight stashed at every Keep property, facility, office, and storage space on the planet. And all those knights will now show that floating Dreki castle thing I mean business."

"Great. Let's get Will." I turned to head out the door back into Arthur's public lab and the nearest exit from the building.

"Not so fast, Princess." Arthur tapped on something and my knight froze mid-stride. I almost fell flat on my well-armored face.

I swore, but otherwise Percy and I didn't react. Right now was not the time to let Arthur know he didn't control my armor.

"We aren't igniting a single rocket pack on a single knight," Arthur continued, "until we go over this asinine plan one more time."

"Arthur, there's not a whole lot to it. You, Patrick, and the knights attack the flying fortress thing using the plans I gave you to make the most noise and create the biggest distraction possible.

I then sort of sneak in and go get Will. The tracker will tell me his precise location, and I'm going in a suit of armor."

"With Galahad and a three knight escort."

I rolled my eyes, but Arthur's tone didn't leave room for argument. "That'll be subtle," I muttered. "Fine," I said louder even though Arthur had heard me over our comms. "With four additional knights. We grab Will, I throw him in Galahad, and then he and I take off out of there. Once we're clear you and the knights mop up, or whatever it is you do, striking a fatal blow to the Dreki cause." I managed to not sound sarcastic on that last part.

Arthur nodded, satisfied with my answer.

I wasn't satisfied though. Muting my headset again, I also enacted the firewall that would keep Percival from being able to hear me. I didn't think for a minute that Arthur freezing my armor was anything other than a direct reminder that he could. If Arthur decided this was too dangerous, he'd shut me out in a heartbeat and put Percival in full control.

"Percy, are we good? If we need to kick Percival out, are you up for it?"

"Please. That little suck-up has nothing on me."

I had to hope that was the case. This maneuver would only work once. It wasn't something we could practice in advance.

"Elaine," Arthur's voice broke through. Percival must have gotten through the firewall I'd put up and reinstated communication. "What is going on over there?" he sounded exasperated.

"Nothing," I said almost like a reflex. I winced as the words flew from my mouth, sounding like the classic kid caught misbehaving. I wouldn't have believed me for a second. Arthur didn't.

Although Pendragon's impassive visage didn't move a micrometer, it felt like the knight narrowed his eyes at me. "Elaine." Arthur drew out the word. "You and your downloaded Percival are acting weird."

I shrugged, and my armor shrugged with me.

"Everything still seems to work out," Arthur said, almost like he was talking to himself. I heard the frown in his voice though. "You sure everything is working over there?"

"Yeah, everything seems fine."

Arthur headed for the door. He turned back when I still stood there. "You coming? I thought you were in a hurry to save your boyfriend."

"Right, yes." I stopped studying my displays one last time and turned to catch up to them.

"Then let's do this," Arthur said. Pendragon held out an arm and rested it lightly on my armor's shoulder. "And Princess, be careful."

"Don't worry. I won't do anything stupid," I said, worrying I planned to do something tremendously stupid. Kicking Percival out of my suit in the middle of a battle if Arthur threatened to sideline me wasn't one of my better plans.

"Our definition of stupid doesn't always match." Pendragon's arms crossed over his chest, and I felt Arthur's glare even through two different suits of armor.

"That's true," I said. "I don't take the risks you do."

Pendragon's arms dropped, and Arthur seemed to cheer right up. "That's true. You'll be fine." Pendragon slapped me on the back, almost knocking me over.

With that we turned and at a jog headed for the nearest way out of the building.

WHERE I DISCOVER THAT RESCUE MISSIONS ARE EVEN MORE EXCITING IN REAL LIFE

GALAHAD AND LEODEGRANCE MET US OUTSIDE THE BUILDING. WE FLEW toward the ocean and the Dreki's flying fortress at top speed. Even so, it would take us seven minutes to get there. The helicopter had a huge head start, but we would arrive right behind it. If I was lucky, that kiss between Evie and Will would never happen.

I frowned at myself. I shouldn't be jealous. It wasn't like the two of us were together. Sure, I'd thought he might kiss me on the drawbridge right before the Dreki attacked, but he'd probably been staring at something on my face. I shut my eyes, my face heating even though my armor was climate controlled to the perfect temperature. I couldn't believe I'd thought he was about to kiss me when I'd probably been wearing part of my breakfast. Would it kill me to use a mirror every once in a while?

I was about to have Percy scan my face for food when Arthur swore over the comms.

I checked all of my readouts, but nothing seemed to be coming for us. "What?" I asked. "Everything looks okay from here."

"LANCE isn't coming." Arthur swore again, this time in a language I didn't recognize. "They're supposed to be one of those 'leave no one behind' kind of groups."

"Really?" My surprise was genuine. "I kind of got the impression they were one of those 'we pretend we don't exist so we can't help you' kind of groups."

"There's that," Arthur said with a small chuckle, "but that's more for when governments of countries that aren't in the League of Nations catch a LANCE agent. For something like a Dreki capture, they're happy to storm the castle. You saw how Stormfield got when I turned my weapons on the LANCE task force that night Will tried to claim you for the Tool Shed."

"That might be the answer to why Stormfield doesn't want to help you anymore," I said in a dry tone.

"Well, this wasn't about helping me." Arthur sounded peeved, like I was missing the point. "This is about one of their own. I can't figure out what about Will rubs Stormfield the wrong way. On paper Will is their perfect agent. Recruited insanely young, successful at every mission he's sent on, popular with agents and civilians alike. That young man even charmed me, and I was more than predisposed to hate him. What do you think Stormfield's problem is?"

"Well, actually," I started. I paused not sure how to go on.

"That was rhetorical, Elaine."

"I realized that, Arthur," I said back, just as snide. The stress was getting to all of us, so I took a deep breath before continuing. "The thing is, Will has this power thing he can do, and I bet Stormfield doesn't like that Will won't use it." I thought for a second. "Or at least he doesn't like that Will won't use it to do what Stormfield wants—if he even knows about it that is."

"What do you mean?" Arthur asked.

"Yes, what do you mean?" Patrick echoed although I hadn't realized that Arthur had given him a headset. I didn't see him yet, but we had to be getting close if he was in range of the comms.

By that point we were well over the Atlantic Ocean. A pit the size of the Grand Canyon had opened in the middle of my stomach. Will was waiting for us to save him. I shook a little in the armor, my jittery nerves reminding me I might have survived the last Dreki battle, but I had needed the help of Dad, Patrick, and extra knights to do it.

"ETA three minutes," Arthur said from over the comms. "You okay, Princess? I think you need to tell us about Will's power. Something has changed, but everything still seems on track for a successful rescue."

"Right." I'd almost forgotten. "Will has this power to tell people what to do. And they do it. He calls it 'persuading,' but it's more like he hypnotizes with his voice."

"Has he made you do something you didn't want?" Arthur's voice had gone low and dangerous, and I shuddered again although this time I was scared for Will not myself.

"Grief, no." I rushed to reassure him. "Will's never used it on any of us. He said we'd know if he had. He says he hasn't tried his power on anyone since he was fourteen, and I'm pretty sure that's what upsets Stormfield. I bet Stormfield suspects Will is capable of something like this, and it annoys him he doesn't use it for LANCE."

Pendragon didn't stop flying, but Arthur seemed to have paused, taking all this in.

"So, you're saying that Will could talk himself out of Dreki custody?" Patrick asked. "Just tell them to let him go."

"Yeah, but he won't. As far as I can tell, he only uses this weird power on Percival," I told them. "Dad, it's how he got out of his room today. I bet he 'persuaded' Percival to let him out."

Arthur didn't answer at first. We were flying high and fast enough that a small dark blob had appeared floating just above the horizon. It had to be the floating fortress. "Percival, you and I are having a long talk when all this is over."

Percival didn't answer, but I imagined the AI gulped.

"Right now though, we don't have time to worry about Will's powers. If he won't use them …"

"He won't," I interrupted.

"Then, we stick to the plan. You remember it, Elaine?"

"Don't worry, Dad. I'll follow the plan."

"I know. Just checking." Arthur clicked off the comms and started organizing the various knights that had converged on us from all directions.

I had to admire Arthur's confidence. I didn't feel nearly as sure of our success.

The Defender swooped down to join us. "The place is bigger than Elaine's drawing would have led me to believe, but I found a weak spot we can use to penetrate the interior." He gave a humorless chuckle. "It seems Vortigern is even more obsessed with medieval decor than you, Arthur. I've never seen a more ridiculous design for a military craft. I have no idea how no one has noticed it before."

We didn't get to answer. Although most surface radar couldn't detect us, the Dreki had better caliber stuff. We were still a half-mile out when anti-aircraft flak exploded around us. We were far enough away the weapons couldn't get a precise target on us. No knights took any damage, and the Defender amused himself by blowing some of the flak up by exhaling bursts of flames. Arthur and I saved our ammunition, but we were close enough I could almost feel the heat of the explosions through my armor.

"So much for the element of surprise," Arthur grumbled. "We'll have to do this with brute force."

At that point we had forty knights with us. Arthur hadn't been kidding when he said he kept the things stashed all over the world. He sent a small force of about seven knights straight ahead to knock out as many of the Dreki's weapons as possible. I had assumed it was a virtual suicide mission, not that the suits died. They were all run by Percival, the real Percival, and Arthur had his main program stored safe in Pendragon.

To my surprise, the fortified weapons—the huge laser cannons, the sonar pulse weapons, even the old-fashioned gun turrets spitting out live ammunition—all of it seemed to have been designed to combat larger threats like F-16s or even another floating fortress. It was almost as if the Dreki's levitating base was an old-fashioned frigate being harried by Arthur's knightly men at war.

The different weapons tried to target the seven knights headed for them, but they didn't have the maneuverability of the smaller invading force. An elephant had a better chance of swatting a specific gnat with the tip of its tail than the Dreki weapons had of even nicking one of Arthur's knights. Firing lasers and pulses from their swords, the knights knocked out most of the Dreki weapons faster than I would have believed. The Dreki managed to scramble a couple of nimble jet fighters and even a helicopter into the air to stop us, but by then they were too late. Arthur's entire force of knights, including me, had made it to the deck of the fortress.

Patrick hadn't been kidding. Vortigern and the Dreki seemed to have taken "flying fortress" a little too literal. If Arthur had built a castle tower in mid-Manhattan, Vortigern had created a flying bailey keep to hover in the sky.

When we had been flying, the flying fortress had looked like a rectangular prism covered in weapons. Landing on the top of that thing, we discovered that the top deck was a glass enclosure for a giant courtyard surrounded on all sides by a crenellated wall. Gone were the super-engineered metal alloys and futuristic weapons. Below us sat an entire European keep.

"Huh," Arthur grunted. Pendragon swung his huge sword down into the glass beneath our feet. The laser field running up and down the sword's edge cut through the foot thick glass like a knife slicing through a piece of plastic wrap used to protect a day old casserole from spoiling.

While the Defender continued tossing fighter jets out of the sky, Arthur's other knights followed Pendragon's lead. My armor, Galahad, and the three knights that made up my entourage hung back. For one thing, we didn't have the same kinds of swords. I didn't have a sword at all, just the dirks I had been training with. The three knights with me had swords, but they were the kind that only shot lasers, not the ones with a laser edge. Arthur's sword did both, but the rest of us had to make do with less impressive technology.

While we waited for Arthur and his knights to cut a hole large enough for the group to drop through, I ran a visual analysis of the ground beneath us trying to match the layout to the drawings I'd doodled when I first came to Keep Tower.

None of my visions had been of this courtyard. I hadn't even suspected it existed. I cursed which got Percy's attention.

"What's up, buttercup?" he asked.

I muted my comms and stuck a second firewall up, blocking Percival. "I don't trust Arthur not to keep me out here under Percival's control. Are you ready to kick Percival out if needed?"

"Please," said Percy in the verbal equivalent of a shrug. "Percival is too busy to bother with running a diagnostic. He hasn't even noticed you're not under his direct control anymore. Of course, that might be because I've got you spoofed in his system."

My jaw fell open almost hitting the bottom of my helm. "You can do that?" That was so much better than kicking Percival out, something Arthur would have noticed. But it wasn't something we'd planned on doing. Will and I hadn't coded him to do that.

"Like, duh," said Percy. "I wouldn't be much good if I couldn't."

I swallowed hard and turned my attention back to the cutting happening around us. Arthur and the knights were almost through. The square piece they were cutting out of the glass began to sag on one side. It was enough that Arthur dropped what looked like a small grenade through the hole. I half ducked even though the weapon was thirty feet below, and I was in nearly indestructible armor.

Percy snickered at me. "That wasn't a weapon, well not a physical one. Arthur just dropped a wireless relay that will allow Percival to hack into this ship's systems. The knights aren't the only brute force attack Arthur has planned."

I didn't bother to respond. With a huge shriek the glass broke free and shattered into a jillion safety glass sized pieces on the flagstones below. Three at a time, the knights jumped into the hole after Pendragon. Arthur led the way with my three knights, Galahad, and me tagging along at the end.

"Vortigern, you dragon-spawned-beast," Arthur shouted. Either the Dreki's firewalls were a joke, or Percival was as good of a hacker as Ginny. Arthur already had control of the Dreki's sound system. His voice projected from every speaker in every reach of the ship. Even through my armor the sound was deafening. "How dare you invade my home, attempt to steal my daughter and actually steal my son. Get out here and face me yourself, wyrmling." Arthur stumbled over the last word, so I almost missed it. It didn't matter. My brain had short-circuited at the word son. If it turned out I had a major crush on my brother? Well, I didn't know what

I'd do. Possibly bathe my brain in hydrochloric acid when we got back to the labs in the Rook.

"His son?" Percy said. He whirred in the background as if he was checking every bit of data, every byte Percival had ever stored, to see if there was a mention of a biological relationship between Will and Arthur. "I'm not finding anything about Will being his son. There aren't any records, and their DNA doesn't match at all."

"Not literal son," Arthur snapped at us. "I meant figuratively. Your boyfriend is not a case of genetic attraction. Just the usual kind."

I hadn't realized our comms were back on. Flushing redder than the dirt on Mars, I hoped that Arthur didn't notice how weird Percival sounded.

"And what is going on with Percival?" Arthur asked. "Why does he sound weird?"

"My lord, there is nothing wrong with my programming," Percy started to say, in his best Percival voice, but he didn't have time to finish. An entire battalion of troops dashed out of the building into the courtyard, surrounding us on all sides. From that moment on, both Arthur and Percival were too busy fighting to worry about my suit's AI.

In some ways I was overcome with an odd sense of déjà vu. It was my high school parking lot all over again. Knights pummeled men in tactical gear. Bullets sprayed all over the place, and the knights fought back with their enhanced versions of medieval weapons. There was the same cacophony, the same dizzying visuals as a thrown Dreki foot soldier sailed in front of my helm.

There was one significant difference though.

Me.

I wasn't cowering under a car this time. I didn't need Will or Dad to rescue me. Not this time. I was in a fully functional suit with knights for backup. I shot into the thick of the fighting, slashing with my dirks and firing with the small laser cannons on my arms. When a Dreki got too close, I wasn't above punching the soldier in the jaw.

The whole time I fought, Percy was in the background piggy-backing off Percival's system hack.

"Got him," Percy said. My display shifted to a map of the courtyard where we fought. A big red dot covered one of the exits into the actual structure. "That's the closest door to Will's cell. He's still being held in the room you Saw in your vision."

"Got it," I said. "Arthur," I called through my comms. "We've got a location for Will. I'm heading for him."

"Take your entourage," Arthur reminded me. "We'll keep them good and distracted out here."

"Come on 4Gs," I said. "You're with me."

Sirs Galahad, Gawain, Gareth, and Gaheris moved with me toward the door. We had to be artful about it though. We didn't just plow through the Dreki forces blocking our way. Instead, Percy and Percival worked together to make it seem as if the flow of battle was pushing us in that direction.

That was the whole plan: that we would sneak away from the battle and find and rescue Will without the Dreki noticing we had left the main skirmish.

It seemed to take forever, but finally I was by the open doorway. A Dreki soldier decided at that moment to launch a shoulder mounted rocket at me. I didn't even have to fake diving after Galahad through the doorway to take cover. The rocket exploded just behind me, slamming into the fortress's stone wall.

There was a creaking sound and stone crumbled around the new hole in the masonry. I didn't bother to wait and see if the other knights were behind me. I turned and sprinted down the hallway after Galahad.

Percy had used a combination of the drawings I had from my vision and the schematics he'd downloaded from Percival's hack to make a kind of map for us to follow. We encountered a pair of Dreki troops running for the mess in the courtyard, but a few well-aimed shots from the lasers on my dirks knocked them out of commission.

Within minutes, we stood in front of the metal door. Of course, the door was sealed shut with a complicated magnetic lock. I placed my armor's palm on it so that Percy could interface. "Can you hack it open?" I asked him.

Percy made a humming noise. It had a sing-song quality to it, like Percy was trying to hum classic rock songs. The AI had no ear for music, but it distinctly sounded like he was channeling the melody to "Hotel California."

"Uh, Percy, are you humming?"

"Sorry, I got distracted. Unlike their overall systems, this lock is trickier to break through. No idea why. I would've spent more time hardening my overall systems' firewalls not worried about an individual door's lock."

"Please focus." I shut my eyes for a second. I had an overwhelming urge to rub them but didn't bother trying since I was wearing a helmet.

"Can you hack it or not?" I added.

"Well." Percy drew out the word like a preschooler trying to avoid telling a parent bad news. "I mean, yes, eventually. But it seems like we're in a hurry, and you won't want to wait that long."

"Oh, for all that is holy." During our run I had sheathed my dirks, but I pulled one out and activated the laser setting. This shot a small pinpoint accurate laser at the door. Unlike Pendragon's Excalibur sword, my dirks did not have laser edges. There would be no slicing through the door. Instead I aimed the laser at one hinge. Slowly, the laser melted its way through.

I kept the laser steady, but inside my armor I fumed. This was taking forever, and I wanted Will free now. I unsheathed my second dirk and tried aiming both weapons' lasers at the same spot on the hinge. According to the readout in my armor, this melted the hinge faster but still not fast enough.

"Is anyone coming?" I asked Percy. "Keep an eye out. I don't want anyone attacking me from behind while I focus on this."

"Only one around is Sir Galahad," said Percy.

"My lady," said the real Percival from Galahad's armor, "I believe we could render you some assistance."

"Go for it." I shut the lasers off and stepped back.

"We would be honored, my lady," Percival said. Galahad took my place at the door. "And if I may speak plainly, I am still not

269

impressed with the upgrades to your suit's systems."

"Tell, me something I don't know," I muttered.

"Hey," Percy said, the insult clear in his voice. "Who asked you, you stuck up piece of code?"

"Rescuing Will," I reminded the two AIs. "We can argue about upgrades back at home once we're all safe."

"Of course, my lady." Percival had Galahad give me a small bow. Then the knight dug his fingers into the metal door. Each digit poked a hole in the door like a worm through a rotten apple. Galahad then gave a huge heave and, with a metallic shriek, ripped the door out of its frame.

"Oh," I said, my voice only trembling a little bit. "I didn't realize the knights were quite that strong."

"Indeed." Even though I knew it was my imagination, Percival sounded smug. "Perhaps if your downgraded AI had not barred me from your suit, I would have assisted sooner."

I didn't answer. At least Percy kept his mouth shut too.

Galahad tossed the door into the corridor with a grating thud. The door slid halfway down the hallway with a screech, and I winced. "That's subtle. If there weren't any Dreki coming this way before, they're on their way now."

"I believe the alarm that knight set off when he ripped off the door alerted them," said Percy with a sniff.

"Working on deactivating the alarm now," Percival said.

I didn't bother to reply or referee their argument. I stepped into the room. "Hey, Will, your knight in shining armor has arrived," I called. "Will?" I said again when he didn't answer. I flipped up my helm, scanning the room with my own eyes, since I was having trouble taking in the image on my viewscreen.

The chair where I had Seen Will in my vision was empty. I looked all the way around me, but the entire room was empty. Will wasn't there.

WHERE MY LESS THAN SUCCESSFUL RESCUE GOES SIDEWAYS

I STEPPED FURTHER INTO THE ROOM, BUT **W**ILL DEFINITELY WASN'T there. It was the same room from my vision, down to the scuff mark left by Will's chair and a spidered crack in the room's stereo-typical interrogation-room-gray walls.

"For all that's holy, Percy," I all but yelled. "You said he was in here."

"I don't understand," Percy said. "His tracker shows him in this room."

"I must concur, my lady," added Percival, joining the competition for most unhelpful AI. "Master Will should be in here."

"Should be and is are two very different things. Anyone got any brilliant ideas what happened? Did the Dreki spoof Will's tracking chip in our system? Does that mean the Dreki are in our system?"

Galahad had been patrolling the perimeter of the room. He stopped by a small dark stain and knelt down. He picked a small item off the floor.

"I believe I may have an answer," Percival said.

"Does it have to do with whatever Galahad just found?"

"Indeed, it does. He appears to have found Master Will's tracking chip. Either the Dreki discovered it, or Master Will removed it for his own reasons."

Either option was chilling. We had to find Will, and we needed to find him fast. "The tracker hasn't been shattered. My guess is the Dreki didn't find it. If they had, they would have destroyed it to keep us from tracking him." I froze for a moment. "Or they used it as a trap." Percy scanned the surrounding area, but no one was coming for us even though we had set off an alarm when Galahad ripped off the cell's door. Not a trap then. Besides, they would have just left the tracker in Will for that. "Will must have removed his chip. So, we don't know where Will is, but neither do the Dreki. That's an advantage, I guess."

"I guess," Percy agreed, but he sounded doubtful. It was less than encouraging.

"Your reasoning sounds logical," Percival said.

"Any ideas how we find Will? If he somehow took his own tracking chip out, then he probably left the room on his own. The Dreki didn't transfer him somewhere." My body tried to shudder as I remembered Evie's comment about torture, but my suit held me in place. I had to hope that Will had left of his own volition. "How did he get out of here?"

Percival reported that the door Galahad had mauled only locked from the exterior hallway. There was no way for Will to access the electronic lock from inside the room. There weren't any panels or access points for him to use to override the door's locks.

I scanned the walls of the cell, but there weren't any secret tunnels hidden behind any of them. The cell didn't sit on an exterior wall, and besides, it wasn't like this place had windows. It was as solid and secure as a medieval fortress even if it hovered over the ocean.

Finally, I looked up—straight into Will's grinning face.

I screamed in shock. It was not one of my finer moments.

Will laughed and swung himself down to the ground. He'd been suspended between two pipes running across the ceiling. I had known for quite some time that Will's gray suits hid an impressive array of muscles. I hadn't seen them in action like that before. He'd been holding himself up there for who knew how long, but he hadn't even broken into a sweat. It was unbelievable. It was unrealistic. It was movie-level feats of strength. My eyes narrowed, and I wondered if there was more to Will than a persuasive power. I didn't have time to worry about that now. We'd wasted enough time in this room.

Will had been shaking his head at me while I stood in my shocked silence—at least the silence I'd fallen into after my undignified screech. "Took you long enough," he said. He brushed at some dirt on his gray suit and frowned when the scab in the center of his hand reopened leaving a bright red line on his pant leg. "No one ever looks up. Lesson number one in infiltrating an enemy stronghold: always look up."

"Are you kidding me?" I found my voice again, and it was high-pitched with indignation and laced with annoyance. "You didn't show yourself the second we came in this room because you think this is some kind of training exercise?" I huffed for a second before muttering under my breath, "Besides, Percy and Percival didn't think to look up either."

Will got this serious expression identical to the one my old science teacher used to get before she would deliver a diatribe on neat handwriting. I didn't need to be a powerful Seer to realize a lecture was coming. "Always be training, Elaine. Use every situation to learn. It'll help keep you alive in the next."

"Yeah, yeah. Always be learning." I cut Will off before he went full on teacher mode. "You can continue your after-school-special after we get off this flying hunk of metal. You realize we're working under some serious time constraints, right?"

Will shrugged. "I kind of figured if you were getting me yourself, there was a sizable LANCE operation going on. It's not like Arthur would let you in on something like this without significant backup."

"You are wrong on so many levels. LANCE didn't come. It's just Arthur and me and Patrick and whatever knights we could scrounge up after this afternoon's attack."

The color drained out of Will's face, leaving his complexion almost pasty.

"And you're right," I continued, "that Arthur wouldn't send me without an entourage, but you're looking at what's left." I waved at his knight still standing in the corner where he'd found Will's tracking chip. I was a petty enough person to get some satisfaction out of Will's growing concern. It was nice to see him finally take this whole rescue thing seriously. "So, if you're done with the whole Very-Special-Episode of this week's 'LANCE Loves Lecturing Elaine,' I'd like to get out of here before Arthur loses his temper and does something stupid like blow up whatever keeps this thing in the sky before we've managed to fly away to safety."

Will nodded but kept his mouth shut.

I sighed. I wasn't trying to come off as an over-bearing rescuer. No wonder people hated being a Damsel in Distress. I pulled the handset I'd brought for Will out of my knight's compartment and tossed it at him. "Just get in your armor."

Percival opened the front of Galahad, and Will backed inside. A minute later, his voice came on over the comms. "Percival has everything up and running in here. What's the plan?"

"Percy and Percival, please find us the fastest way out of this place and back over open ocean. Percival, update Arthur on our status. Tell him we've secured Will and are attempting to retreat. Percy, get calculating on those routes."

"Percy and Percival?" Will asked. "Does Arthur know about Percy now?"

"No, but he knows about your persuasive power. He's not real thrilled you used it to get Percival to unlock your door."

"Seems fair."

"Gotta admit I'm not real thrilled either."

Will didn't answer, and Galahad's blank helm didn't give me any clues to Will's thoughts.

"Got it," Percy said. "We need to run down this hallway." A floor plan popped up in front of me with a red line showing the way out. We would turn right out the door and then run straight until the next-to-last turn left. That would take us to an access shaft we could blow open.

"Got that, Will?" I asked.

"Roger," Will said. "Percival has shown me the same map."

"Let's get this show on the road!" Percy shouted in the most cheerleader-rah-rah kind of voice I'd ever heard from either a real or artificial intelligence.

Galahad's head shook in disbelief, but I wasn't sure if that was Will or Percival controlling the knight.

I led the way out of the room and down the hallway. We were running as fast as our knights could go, but we still had a long way before our turn. The flying fortress was huge. I wasn't great at judging distance, but Percy was. We still had six hundred yards to go.

We'd only made it another two hundred yards when a figure stepped out in front of us. It was the hot girl from my vision, Evie. She held some sort of large weapon in her arms she aimed at us. I'd never seen anything like it. The rectangular thing was too weird to shoot bullets, and the front was too wide for something like a laser. If anything, it looked like a sonic pulse weapon Arthur was developing.

"Going somewhere?" Evie asked, sounding like the villain in pretty much every spy movie I'd ever seen. "I don't think so," she said, answering herself. She aimed and fired.

"Evie, no," yelled Will, but it was too late. Evie looked shocked for a moment, but then she regained control with a smug look on her diabolically gorgeous face.

"Sorry, Will. Looks like you picked the wrong side."

I flinched waiting for the shock wave or whatever to happen. There was a rippling effect in the air as whatever the weapon fired came toward us. It was like the air in front of us had turned to water, allowing us to see the waves caused by the rock Evie had thrown in this pond.

The wave hit us and seemed to wash over us. I squenched my eyes shut, but I felt nothing. I opened them back up, but all my displays seemed the same. Nothing seemed to have happened.

"That was anticlimactic," Percy said, and then my armor fell off.

It all just crashed down from my body. One minute, Will and I were standing in a pair of technological knights outfitted with weaponry LANCE and every government in the world would kill to get their hands on. The next moment, we were standing in our normal clothes with pieces of our knights scattered on the floor. Yes, I was wearing leggings and a T-shirt, and Will had on his dirty gray suit, but I'd never felt more naked, more exposed, in my entire life.

"Not much to look at now," Evie sneered. She pulled out a pair of regular pistols. In our bulletproof knights, the guns would have been pointless. Now, we were sitting ducks.

"Percy," I screamed into the comms set still attached to my head as both Will and I dove for the open doorway to our left.

"Still here," Percy said. "That wasn't another EMP. Everything's still functioning down here. The pieces for the armor just can't maintain magnetic cohesion for now. Percival and I are working on how to counteract the effect if we can. I've notified Arthur of the problem, but he can't send any knights down here in case that she-devil uses that weapon on one of them too."

"Well, isn't that just awesome," I said.

I turned to Will sure he'd already taken stock of the room we'd lunged into. It was a big space, kind of like Arthur's lab. It had desks and tables, but it did not have a bunch of inventions lying around. In other words, there wasn't anything we could use as weapons. There was a large table at the back of the room. Will pulled himself off the floor and headed to it. I followed. When we were close enough, we pulled over the nearest table, spilling its computer and papers all over the floor. We stacked the table in front of the larger one, and then we ducked under the one still upright. This gave us a small amount of cover from the front and above, but without weapons, we were only slightly more protected than the targets in the shooting booth of a carnival midway.

At least Will hadn't had to tell me what to do. In fact, we had worked together as a team without saying a single word. It was a radical departure from that time I had cowered with him behind a desk in my old room back in the Rook.

"We have about six seconds before your girlfriend gets here," I told Will. She'd been far down the hallway when she shot her weird weapon at us, but it wouldn't take her much longer to reach our room. It wasn't like she had to look for us. She'd seen us dive through this doorway.

"Girlfriend?" Will looked confused for a second. "Evie's not my girlfriend." He made a sour face like I'd suggested he eat a chocolate covered dog turd. "She's more like a big sister. She helped me get through the Conservatory."

"Whatever." I turned away and peeked out from the side of the desk. The room was still empty, but Evie should have reached us by now. I hoped she wasn't gathering tons of reinforcements. Arthur would kill me if the Dreki ended up getting their hands on me after all. "If I had a brother, I sure wouldn't kiss him like you kiss her," I muttered.

"Kiss her?" The disgust in Will's voice had me turning back to him. He looked pretty revolted. "The only time I kissed her in my entire life was today when she slipped me the razor blade I needed to cut the plastic cuffs and to get the tracker Arthur implanted out of my hand." Will's eyes widened. "Wait, did you See that kiss? Like See see it? With your clairvoyance?"

I nodded.

"But how? I wasn't around."

I shrugged like it was no big deal. "I touched something you had touched. Apparently, that's now enough."

"Your powers are growing so much so fast," Will said with a shake of his head. "You know that, right? That you are just so amazing." He gave me the sweetest, most sincere smile I'd ever seen. "There's absolutely no one else like you."

My anger at Will and my insecurities I'd been feeling all melted away. In that moment, I could have kissed him. So, doing the craziest, most insane thing in my life—and that included the time I had jumped off the top of Keep Tower with no guarantee

I wouldn't end up an Elaine-pancake on the pavement below—I grabbed Will by the front of his gray suit jacket and kissed him.

Will probably thought I had lost my mind, but I didn't care. We were about to die or be captured by the Dreki, which might be worse. I would not have this moment go by and then regret it for the rest of my life. Holding onto Will's jacket like it was the only thing keeping us from being pulled apart by Dreki goons, I let myself enjoy the kiss.

I didn't get to enjoy it for long. Just as I had begun to appreciate how very good at kissing Will seemed to be, I Saw Evie and two Dreki troops dash into the room. Since I had my eyes closed and a thick table sat between me and the door, I realized I was having a vision. But instead of this being something happening in the distant future or even in a few hours, it had to be a vision of something happening any second now.

To my surprise, I also realized I was watching this vision like I was a fly on the wall, and that the Elaine and Will in the vision weren't making out behind a table when Evie and her goons burst in. We had pressed up against the wall on either side of the door, and the second they arrived, Will and I each took a goon out.

Disappointed that I had to end the kiss, I pulled back. To my intense satisfaction, Will looked as dazed as I felt.

I crawled out from under the table. "Come on," I said to him. "I Saw a better plan."

Will frowned. "You had a vision while we kissed?"

I ran for the front of the room and flattened myself against the wall by the door. "It will probably save our lives. You got a problem with it?"

When he went to stand next to me, I waved him to the other side of the door. "Evie and two Dreki troops will come in through here. We need to take out the troops."

Will's eyes narrowed. "You Saw that while we kissed," he said again, as if he was having trouble believing what I'd just said.

"Again, problem?" I asked.

Will shook his head. "It's just LANCE trained me to be a better kisser than that. You're not supposed to get distracted."

Now I was the one getting annoyed. "Visions aren't exactly distractions. It's not like I was looking over your shoulder to watch TV. And what do you mean trained?"

Will didn't answer. Evie and the two Dreki soldiers ran into the room. They were looking straight ahead, so they were a few feet ahead of us before Will and I attacked. Using one of the moves, Will had taught me, I scissor kicked my guard. He fell to the ground, and I wrenched his arm behind him, incapacitating him. If he moved more than an inch in any direction, his shoulder would dislocate.

Will though, had not only knocked his target unconscious, he had grabbed the Dreki's weapon. He and Evie were standing, pointing their guns at each other in a true standoff.

"Now what?" Will asked me.

WHERE I FINALLY UNDERSTAND
THE POWER OF A SUPERPOWER

"Yeah, Will. Now what?" Evie echoed. Her hand was steady, and like Will she didn't waver. Even though I knew from experience that those pistols got heavy after more than a few seconds, neither of them dropped their weapon even a millimeter.

"You know, I can't just let you go." Evie's eyes flicked to a point just over my head. It seemed like a deliberate gesture, a signal to Will. I glanced just long enough to confirm what I suspected I'd find in the upper corner of the room. Sure enough, a camera with a red recording light stared down at all of us.

Evie might have helped Will before by slipping him a razor blade, but she wouldn't help us now with Dreki personnel watching. I managed to not shudder as a worse thought hit me. Even if she was on our side, she couldn't help if her father was watching. I hoped with every molecule of my being that Arthur had Vortigern busy deflecting the all out attack happening outside. I hated the idea we might have Vortigern's personal attention.

Will nodded like he understood although his eyes never left

Evie's face. "You realize I can't let you have Elaine." He shifted until he was now aiming his weapon at my head.

"Are you kidding me?" Normally, a gun pointed at my head would have freaked me out, but for some reason, Will pointing a gun at me made me livid. "Arthur will love this. Are you telling me you also have a shoot to kill order on me?"

Will looked physically ill for a moment before giving me a curt nod. "In a situation like this? Controller Stormfield was explicit."

"He would be," Evie and I both muttered at the same time. I raised my eyebrows at her for a moment, and she gave me a small half-grin. "I take it you aren't a fan of LANCE's fearless leader?" Evie asked.

"Elaine," Will said. "Believe me. If we're getting captured again by the Dreki, it would be a favor."

I glared at him. "Mercy killing me without my express permission is not a favor. It's murder." The man beneath me moved again, and I wrenched his arm even tighter. "When I have finished rescuing you, we will sit down and have a very long talk about this topic. I am not at all comfortable with the idea you think you can decide for me when life is no longer worth living. That's a big assumption."

Will nodded, and I could almost see the LANCE training warring with his inherent good qualities. It was almost like he was battling the instincts of a decent human being with the ethics of LANCE. I was having a hard time distinguishing LANCE from the Dreki. Both seemed committed to vague causes with a shocking disregard for whatever body count might accrue. It was like they were the same beast coming at each other from different sides.

"What makes you think you'll rescue him, little girl?" Evie asked with a sneer.

At that I snapped. There was no other word for it. One minute I was hunched down with a knee in some random Dreki dude's back, and the next I had launched myself in the air at Evie. It was like whatever little self-control I'd kept despite all the stress of the day had been tested beyond my endurance by Will's clear intention to execute a kill order on me if things didn't go our way. If even my protectors proved to be a danger? It was like the little stable world I'd been trying to build since Arthur scooped me out of the firefight in my school's parking lot had begun to crumble away.

True, Evie's snide little comment didn't warrant a fist to the jaw, but her dad was the whole reason I was in this mess, and she wasn't the one pointing a gun at me.

I caught Evie completely off guard. It was the only way I landed that first punch on her. Despite my presence, her focus had been entirely on Will. That had made sense. After all, he was the trained agent holding a weapon. I was the weird Seer pinning a man down.

But I was the weird psychic—one who worked best if she touched someone she wanted to See. And although punching Evie wasn't the normal way to spark a vision, it proved to be just as effective.

My vision of Evie was super short, only about the length of

time my knuckles were in contact with her jaw. It was enough. Even as I watched the shock register on real-time Evie's face, I also Saw her try to counter with a left hook to my jaw. I ducked and landed another uppercut. This allowed me to See her attempt at a spin kick. I caught her leg mid-air, destabilizing her balance and knocking her to the floor. Evie wasn't down by any stretch. She popped back up, and the two of us went at it in a bare-knuckles, no holds barred, no trick too dirty match.

Evie didn't land a single punch or kick. She never even came close even though she was a much better fighter. She might have even been better than Will. With every punch I blocked, with every kick of mine that connected, I Saw the next few seconds. Evie never pulled ahead in the fight. For the first time, I had full control of the visions. I wasn't just along for the ride. I could over-lay them on the world around me and keep them from skipping ahead where they wouldn't be as useful. I now understood what it felt like to have a true superpower.

With a perfectly timed chop, thanks to knowing where Evie would be at that moment, I struck Evie's neck. She slumped to the floor, unconscious.

"Elaine, how did you?" Will started to ask. He grabbed my hand. I turned to him, but with his hand on mine, I Saw the next few seconds coming.

"Duck," I yelled at Will, and I tackled him to the ground. Less than a second later, a pair of backup Dreki goons entered the room spraying gunfire at chest level. My continuing vision showed me we only had seconds before they looked down and spotted us. Rolling across the floor, I kicked at the back of their knees. Neither went down, but it distracted them enough that both men stumbled and the spray of bullets stopped. This gave Will enough time to incapacitate them both.

Meanwhile, the man I had pinned down earlier decided to rejoin the fight. For some reason, he hadn't moved when I'd attacked Evie. Maybe he had been just as shocked as the rest of us when I had leapt up. Or perhaps, Will had been pointing a gun at him until the moment I knocked Will to the floor. Either way, the Dreki got up and assumed a fighter stance. However, I grabbed at Will connecting my hand with his neck. I Saw where the Dreki would punch and when. I kept him distracted long enough by dodging his feints until Will knocked him in the back of the head with the barrel of his riffle.

"Let's get out of here," Will said, grabbing my hand again. He seemed to have figured out what was going on.

I held up my free hand to block him from running out the door. "Wait," I said. I Saw Galahad followed by a small horde of Dreki soldiers chasing and firing weapons at him running past our doorway. Two seconds later it happened in real time.

"Now," I said. We bolted into the corridor, running after the Dreki troops. We were far enough back, they didn't hear us following them. A few seconds later, the whole group turned down a corridor, but we kept running straight ahead. "Percy," I panted into my comms, "we saw Galahad. Does that mean the armor is back together? I want our knights right now."

"Yours is already on her way," Percy said, "but I don't think

Percival's going to get Galahad free soon. And can I say that was some kick-ass moves back there? Percival and I were watching from the room's camera."

I smiled, but I didn't take the compliment. "Rescue now, congratulate later."

"On it," Percy said. "I have a little weapon destroying detour first. They are never disintegrating a knight I'm in again."

We got to the end of the hallway. There was no sign of a way out.

"You missed your turn." Percy sounded like he was trying to be helpful, so I tried not to snap at him even though my self-control was in danger of breaking again.

"Yeah, it was the next-to-last left, wasn't it? So, now second right?"

"You got it, babe."

I had never been a fan of Percival's "my lady," but "babe" would definitely have to go.

We turned and headed back. By this point, I'd lost my grip on Will's hand, and my visions had faded. I needed to recharge my sight somehow. I reached over and grabbed Will's hand.

"Jump," I yelled, and we avoided a Dreki drudge that came sliding out an open doorway on her back. She wasn't trying to attack us. Instead, she seemed to be trying to recover from being tossed out the room. A moment later my armor came striding out the door.

"Surprise," Percy said. "I brought you a present, and the demagnetizing weapon is now toast. No more worries there."

"Follow us," I told him.

We kept down the hall and turned right at the next corner.

We had already turned and started down the hall before my vision showed me what we would find there. I tried to stop, to pull us back, but all I managed was to slip on the floor and fall, pulling Will down with me.

The hallway wasn't a long one, so when a mutant dragon man stepped out of the room at the end, he wasn't far from us. He was also cutting us off from the exterior wall we needed to use to escape.

The man who stepped out wore the standard Dreki SWAT style uniform, complete with dragon patches on the shoulder, but it was like the person inside had swollen to twice the normal size—or wore augmented body armor. Instead of a commando-style helmet and goggles, a huge helmet in the shape of a dragon's head covered his entire face. Even though I had no proof, I knew Vortigern was in there. Who else would wear something like that? And the helmet somehow replicated his cold, dead eyes.

"How kind of you to join me," the figure said, confirming my guess. Vortigern didn't have the kind of voice you forgot.

"Percy," I whispered at my headset.

"On it," he murmured back. My armor started to break apart behind me.

"No," Vortigern said, the mouth on his helmet moved when he spoke giving the weird impression that Vortigern had transformed into an actual dragon. He raised one of his arms, and it sprouted a rocket just like one of Arthur's knights might do. "If a single atom of that armor touches either of you, Redding loses his head."

Will and I froze. I was still on the ground where I had slid to a stop. Will hovered mid-crouch, but he did nothing to inflame the situation.

The dead eyes of the dragon fixed on me. "I have wanted Redding for too long now. If I'm forced to sacrifice him, you will not enjoy the result."

I didn't have to say anything. Behind me Morgause reformed, but she made no other move.

"Well, this sucks," Percy said.

I didn't answer.

"It was nice of Pendragon to deliver you both," Vortigern continued. He didn't lower the weapon on his armor, but he seemed to relax a bit. "Although, I would have preferred it if he hadn't destroyed my favorite home in the process."

"Consider it payback for destroying one of his," I said. My voice came out strong and sure, to my surprise. My voice had a bravery I didn't possess. It didn't help I was still Seeing into the future, and the future wasn't looking good. We had about three minutes before Vortigern summoned reinforcements. They would destroy Morgause and cuff Will and I without any of us being able to do a thing about it.

I realized we had to delay Vortigern's call for backup. It was our only chance. Hopefully, Percy had called Arthur, or perhaps Percival was monitoring a security camera somewhere. If nothing else, stalling might give Will or me time to come up with an escape.

"Why Will?" I asked. "Do you normally capture LANCE

agents, or is Will special?"

Vortigern laughed, and I flinched. The sound echoed through the hallway becoming less human by the second as if Vortigern was morphing into the dragons he admired so much.

Will didn't so much as wince, but he tilted his head on one side as if considering Vortigern. "Sometimes the Dreki capture LANCE agents for interrogation, but I don't think this was one of those times. I got the impression in the helicopter that this was a retrieval. Vortigern wanted both of us brought back."

Vortigern gave a slight shrug. I tensed, hoping to make a move, but Vortigern still didn't lower his weapon. "You both have skills that would enhance the Dreki cause."

Will's eyebrows lifted, and I stared at Vortigern, appalled. "Your recruitment method leaves a lot to be desired," I said.

Vortigern laughed again, unaware or not caring that the sound shocked us back into silence. "The future of this world is the future of the Dreki," he said. "With the two of you, we could stop this useless warring with LANCE and misguided people like your father, Elaine. With your visions and Will's powers, we would rule before the so-called leaders mounted a response. Finally, the illuminated way will spark the world. After all, the Illuminati have always wanted to enlighten, to do what's best for people."

"The Illuminati and the Dreki want to do what's best for the Illuminati," Will spat back. He dropped my hand and stood. I stayed on the floor for another minute, trying to keep the vision of the immediate future. I Saw a few more seconds ahead, but it only showed Vortigern talking, and then the vision faded away. Standing and brushing the back of my hand against Will's, I pushed hard, but no vision appeared. The future had returned to an impenetrable haze.

"Spoken like a true brat of LANCE." Vortigern's dragon face sneered. "Tell me, what has LANCE done to end poverty in this or any other nation? Have they shared any of the life-saving technologies they develop in that Institute where they've hoarded the world's greatest minds? Do they do anything other than fight philanthropists like me and violate the human rights of people with unlikely powers like you and Elaine? Do they?"

I wouldn't call Vortigern a philanthropist, but I couldn't argue his points about LANCE. Will didn't even try. "What do you mean, like me?" he asked. He tensed next to me, but I didn't think he was about to spring at Vortigern or lunge himself back into my armor. Not that he would fit into it. He was too tall for Morgause.

"Still trying to keep it a secret?" Vortigern laughed again, and this time Will winced along with me. There was something about the laugh, like it was modified as it filtered through the dragon helmet. It seemed to suck a little more life out of me with each chuckle. "But unlike LANCE there are no secrets in the Dreki." Vortigern turned his dragon eyes on me, and I wanted to shrink inside myself, hide in my armor, or duck behind Will—anything to avoid the dragon's gaze. "Will isn't a typical LANCE agent. He's not an agent at all, just a well-guarded asset. No, he has powers beyond what he even knows. Don't you, little giant?"

"I'm not a giant." Will seemed confused. I certainly was. Will wasn't short, but he wasn't even as tall as Arthur. Still, Will's eyes darted around, searching for an escape. His hand next to mine shook as if afraid of what Vortigern would say next.

Vortigern's dragon helmet smiled, and I was grateful Arthur's knights had blank visages instead of creepy pseudo-expressions that made my skin crawl. "I know more about you than you will ever find in a LANCE archive. Wilma Redding stole you from us all those years ago, and Stormfield didn't even bother to give you an original name when he tried to hide you away."

Will's shaking had gotten worse, and he looked ill. He reached for the wall as if half supporting himself with it.

"You were meant to be our weapon," Vortigern said, "not some plaything for LANCE. We have the means to control you, to hone you, to bring peace to this world. Enough of this. Come here, son."

Will swayed on his feet, and I realized that it wasn't my imagination. There was something off with Vortigern's helmet. It was doing something to his voice, modulating it. It was like Will's persuasive power, but a pale imitation. But, even a pale imitation was compelling when it was focused directly on you, like it was on Will.

Will took a step forward. "I'm not your son," he ground out between his clenched teeth. He seemed to be trying to fight back, but his left foot lifted to take another step. "I will never be your son."

"Nope, I claimed Will," Arthur said over our headset. "Finders keepers. Princess, Will, you've done a magnificent job keeping that idiot distracted, but I'm here now. Brace yourself."

Before I could even blink, the exterior wall behind Vortigern blew up.

WHERE I REFUSE TO BE SIDELINED NO MATTER THE COST

WHEN THE WALL BEHIND HIM BLEW UP, THE SUDDEN CHANGE IN AIR pressure sucked Vortigern out through the hole. Will and I both flew forward too, but Morgause's arms shot out grabbing us. My armor tucked each of us under one arm, almost like she'd turned us into human footballs. She kept running straight forward and launched into the air.

The flying fortress was much lower than it had been when we'd begun our attack. Pendragon or the Defender or some of the knights must have gotten to the engines, and the fortress headed for a watery grave.

I didn't pay attention to the fortress for long. Above us, Vortigern and Pendragon circled one another. Apparently, Vortigern's suit had flight capabilities in the form of two dragon styled wings that had extended from his back. He swooped and dodged as Pendragon shot various lasers and ammunition at him.

"Percy, I need in my armor," I said. "Will needs Galahad. Where is he?"

"I apologize, my lady," Percival answered instead, "but Galahad is indisposed at the moment, and there are no knights to spare. If Lord Arthur is to continue his private quarrel with Vortigern, the Defender and all the knights must continue distracting the remaining Dreki forces."

Vortigern spit flames out of his dragon mouth. Pendragon's cape caught fire, but to my disappointment it didn't burn away. Pendragon ripped the burning area off, leaving a singed strip behind.

"He needs help," I started to say, but Arthur cut me off.

"No, Elaine, this is my battle. It always has been."

I tried to argue, but Arthur interrupted me again. "Princess, it would be good if you didn't distract me. Percival, get her to safety. Now."

Morgause started to fly away, but I yelled at Percy to go back.

Percy stopped my knight and turned around, but even he wouldn't fly me back no matter how much I begged and pleaded.

"Elaine," Will said. He reached across Morgause chest and grabbed my hand. "Arthur's right. This is his battle, not ours."

I stopped struggling against the armored arm that held me and instead watched.

"Vortigern, this ends today," Arthur shouted over Pendragon's external speakers.

"Yes," Vortigern shouted back between bursts of dragon fire. "I should have finished you that day in the tunnel twelve years ago when you first interfered with the Dreki's divine purpose."

"You aren't finishing me today, either," Arthur said back, this time in a conversational tone, like he was discussing sports or the weather. "I swear, Vortigern, for all that knowledge you're supposed to have, it's like you've never read a fairy tale."

"What?" Vortigern shot a rocket at Pendragon, but Pendragon dodged and the rocket exploded many yards behind him. Debris rained down on the ocean.

"Fairy tales. You've got a daughter. If you'd spent time reading to her instead of smuggling her into LANCE's school, you'd know how this battle will end."

Vortigern's response was a barrage of bullets that pinged harmlessly off Pendragon's breastplate.

Pendragon's face didn't change, but I could hear Arthur's smile in his voice. "The knight always slays the dragon." He reached over his shoulder and unsheathed Excalibur.

The sword glowed from the lasers lining its edge. Pendragon sliced at Vortigern, shearing part of his left wing. The bit hung down destabilizing Vortigern's flight for a moment before he ripped it off and tossed it away. Pendragon had flown in, Excalibur aiming for the kill, when a pair of swords shot out of the arms of Vortigern's suit into his hands. He blocked Pendragon's attack and parried with his own.

The two flew at each other, swords clanging off one another in deafening blows. My unprotected ears ached, and I dropped Will's hand to cover them. I tried shutting my eyes, but I couldn't look away for more than a moment at a time. I also realized that although I was being held around the waist by a robot, I was still that scared girl cowering with her eyes shut and her ears covered.

No. I tried to straighten up, but since I was dangling from a robot, I just sort of straightened my spine. No. This wasn't Arthur's battle, at least not his alone. It was all the Keeps—Arthur and Ginny and me and Will, even if Will didn't share the last name—against this monster, this man who had mechanically turned himself into one of the greedy, scrabbling dragons of European myths. And he would not win because Arthur wanted to keep the rest of us safe.

And he was winning. Arthur was holding his own, but he wasn't managing any offensive strikes. He was on the defensive and losing ground. Vortigern had pushed him lower and closer to the dropping flying fortress. The closer they got, the less maneuverability Pendragon had, giving the bigger dragon the advantage.

However, as much as I wanted to help, there was a limit to what I could do from under a robot's arm. Percy wouldn't fly over there with Morgause carrying us like sacks of potatoes, and I couldn't get into my armor without dropping Will. Since we were still at least several hundred feet above the Atlantic, dropping Will wasn't an option. My only option was to get a vision that might help.

I grabbed Will's hand again, but still nothing happened. We hovered beside the battle, the combatants almost level with us now. Soot from the flames Vortigern's dragon head kept spouting covered Pendragon. Vortigern's armor had nicks and slices where Pendragon had got past Vortigern's blocks and parries, but none of the blows had done much damage. They were both too well-armored.

I tried to block the battle and pull up a vision, but still there was nothing. I took a deep breath and tried to remember everything Cassie had ever taught me. Touch triggered my visions. Check, but holding Will's hand wasn't enough. Pendragon and Vortigern wouldn't let me slap a hand on them, so that was out. Proximity aided my visions. I could see Arthur, but Percy wouldn't fly Morgause any closer. Emotions powered my visions. The more stirred up I got, the easier the visions came.

I turned to Will. Like me his legs hung down, and his free hand gripped the arm Morgause had around his waist like he didn't trust the armor not to toss him into the water below. Cassie said nothing stirred me up like Will. Cassie said Will would always bring on visions faster and easier than anyone else. Time to put that theory to the test.

I dropped Will's hand and reached across my armor's chest for the front of his shirt. "Will, I need to borrow your lips."

Will turned, his raised eyebrows lifting even higher in shock when he realized what I was doing. I reached with my other hand for the back of Will's head, and I pulled him into a kiss.

At first nothing happened. We sort of stared at each other with our lips smushed together in the world's most awkward embrace. Then Will shrugged, closed his eyes, and kissed me.

The result was immediate. My Sight came roaring back with a vengeance. It was like nothing I had ever Seen before. I might have closed my eyes too, but it didn't matter. Will and the ocean and Pendragon and the battle disappeared. Instead, the future stretched out before me like a fanned-out deck of cards. I Saw the different branches where a single decision could push the future to change. The brightest paths were probably the most likely futures, yet even those seemed improbable. Was that Will with a little girl with clouded-over-eyes in that particular distant future?

I turned away since I didn't have time to explore the infinite possibilities before me. Focusing as hard as I could, the distant futures faded away until Arthur's immediate future snapped into focus. The battle still raged, but now Pendragon had a new slice down the front of his armor, bisecting the coat of arms on his chest at a diagonal. He had been pressing an attack, but all of a sudden he froze and then screamed, "No!" He turned away, but Vortigern caught him with a kick to the chest. Pendragon flew back and slammed against the side of the flying fortress in a weird parody of all the times the knights had thrown me against the Rook's walls during practice. Vortigern swooped back, his long dragon wings beating the air, gaining distance. Then, he dove at Pendragon, slamming both of his swords into my father, impaling him like a bug on a board.

In the vision, both Will and I screamed, but the real me didn't panic like I had when I watched Vortigern kill Will that time.

"No," I said instead in a soft voice just like Arthur used when he was beyond screaming his anger. "Over my freaking dead body."

I rewound the vision, something I hadn't even realized was possible, and I watched it again. There was a moment before Vortigern struck when I had a chance, but I would need to have perfect timing.

I yanked myself out of the future. At some point, probably when I had zoned out of my body, Will had stopped kissing me, but his forehead still leaned against mine.

I pulled back, and Will opened his eyes, giving me a wry look. "Got what you needed?" he asked.

I nodded and turned back to the battle gauging where it was at. Pendragon didn't have the cut on his breastplate yet.

"Not that I'm not happy to help," Will said, "but is there a reason we needed to kiss?"

"Stronger visions."

"Huh." Will didn't sound real thrilled. Maybe when all this was over, I'd think about how rude it was to check-out of a kiss to go watch the future, but for now I watched the battle through narrowed eyes. Vortigern struck and got past Pendragon's guard. The resulting long slash across the coat of arms on Pendragon's breastplate was what I'd been waiting for.

"Percy, on my mark I need you to throw me thirty degrees to the right."

"What?" Percy and Will both said at the same time.

Pendragon feinted and then pressed his attack.

"Trust me on this one, boys," I said. "Percy?"

"As my lady wishes," said my AI.

"No!" yelled Will.

In the battle, Pendragon froze for a moment, then turned for me. Arthur yelled, "No!" just like in the vision.

"Three," I said.

Pendragon moved in my direction.

"Two."

Vortigern kicked.

"One."

Pendragon slammed into the flying fortress.

"Mark."

Percy had Morgause throw me in the direction I wanted. Even though she held me like a football, I got lobbed like a softball, high but fast. It didn't matter, Vortigern backed up, just like I had Seen, and I slammed into his side just like I had planned.

I wasn't wearing armor, so it felt like every bone in my body tried to shatter. Morgause had quite an arm on her. The pain was a shock, but I managed to scrabble at Vortigern's wing and climb the trussing there onto Vortigern's back.

Vortigern hadn't been expecting an attack from the side, certainly not one from me. He froze for a moment, trying to figure out what had happened. I used that minute to scramble up to his neck and latch on.

I didn't have a whole lot of offensive fighting options without armor. I was unprotected and couldn't do much more than hang on. It wasn't like I was going to damage Vortigern's body armor with my fingernails.

I was an amazing distraction though. Back at the Rook I had discovered how annoying it was when someone hangs onto your back, and I put that lesson to use. I kicked with my legs, making it hard for Vortigern's dragon wings to flap. I lunged and pushed my right arm across the Dragon's right eye in case it affected Vortigern's vision. Vortigern tried to swat at me with one of his swords, but he only damaged one of his own wings. I hung on for dear life as he attempted to shake me off, but nothing dislodged me. I was more tenacious than a hungry tick.

My distraction served its purpose. Arthur got the moment he needed to recover. He did more than recover. With a feral scream, Pendragon launched off the fortress wall, headed for us. I realized where Excalibur was aiming and lunged for Vortigern's right wing. Grabbing for one of the struts, I managed to catch it like a kid jumping for the monkey bars on the playground. I swung from Vortigern's wing out of the way as Arthur plunged his sword all the way through Vortigern's heart.

WHERE ALL'S FAIR IN LOVE, WAR, AND DEEP OCEAN RESCUES

VORTIGERN LURCHED TO THE LEFT WITH A SCREAM, AND MY BODY swung with him, coming dangerously close to the exposed edge of Excalibur where it stuck out the dragon's back.

"How?" Vortigern whispered. His horrible dragon mouth still moved when he spoke, but the rest seemed to be shutting down. Dragon wings no longer flapped. The only thing keeping him in the air was Pendragon's grip on Excalibur.

"It seems I never had the right incentive before," Arthur said. "Princess, don't you ever pull a stunt like that again."

I didn't answer, not sure what to do next. Morgause was coming for me, a cheering Will still dangling from her other arm, but Arthur didn't wait.

"Get ready to jump," he said. With a grunt, Pendragon lifted a leg and kicked Vortigern's lifeless body off his sword, dropping it into the ocean hundreds of feet below.

I swung myself away and jumped free of the lifeless debris, but I was still plummeting toward the ocean. Will and Evie probably learned how to skydive at the Conservatory, but I flailed about like fighting the air would keep myself up.

Something grabbed my shirt, jerking me to a halt, and then I was being crushed to a slashed up metal chest.

"I've got you, baby. You're safe, little girl. I didn't lose you," Dad kept murmuring over and over, long after I had stopped struggling, almost as if he was comforting himself. His voice was sort of choked up like he might even be crying.

I was glad Arthur had me, but he was wearing enhanced armor. "Can't breathe," I muttered. "Hug too tight. Cracking ribs."

Arthur shifted until he was carrying me on one hip with one arm like a little kid. I was more than a decade too old to be carried that way, but I didn't care. I grabbed around his neck and hung on, waiting for Morgause to reach us.

"You lot are in for a serious lecture when we get home," Arthur said, his voice back to normal. "I don't think there's an iota of common sense between the two of you." Pendragon looked down at me. "You launch yourself into the middle of a battle with no armor?" He turned to Will. "And you use your mysterious powers not to stay out of trouble but to get in it?" Pendragon's head shook. "At this rate, I'll go full on gray hair before I'm fifty. How is that going to look in the tabloids?"

Will's mouth dropped open, and he looked at me as if I should know what to say. I didn't bother answering. I laughed instead. If hysteria tinged my laughter, I'd earned it. My dad wasn't dead, pinned to the side of Vortigern's fortress. That was all that mattered. He could try to distract us by whining about trivial things all he wanted.

I hugged Pendragon's armor one more time before I let him pass me back to Morgause. "Take them straight home," Arthur told my armor. "No stopping, and Elaine?" Pendragon turned back to me. "What exactly is this Percy thing running your armor?"

"Oh, that." I looked away.

"Percival's opinion is low."

"Percival isn't alone," I admitted, "but Percy grows on you."

"I resemble that," Percy muttered.

"You do," I told him.

"Ginny will be running a full diagnostic before he gets to run your armor again." Pendragon glared at us even though the helm's expression hadn't changed. "I trust his judgment even less than yours. 'Throw my unarmored body into the center of a mid-air battle,'" Arthur said in a high-pitched voice I assumed was meant to be me. "'Sure, my lady, why not?'" Arthur now imitated Percy. "'Seems fine to me. What could go wrong?'" Arthur's voice then went back to normal. "I swear. And Ginny thinks I'm the risk-taker."

My armor started to fly away, back toward what I assumed was Manhattan. Arthur turned for the fortress. "I'll be right behind you, but Patrick is pinned down and needs help. As soon as the LANCE troops get here, I'll join you at home. Apparently Stormfield has deigned to join us now that we've done all the work." Pendragon turned and flew up, but we got to listen to Arthur grumble about LANCE the entire time we were still in range.

305

I closed my eyes and leaned against Morgause's body while the wind from flying pulled my hair from my face. I could not believe this was over. That we had won. That Vortigern was gone for good.

My eyes popped open when something wet drenched my feet. Instead of being several hundred feet above the ocean, we were now low enough to brush the tops of the bigger waves.

"Percy?" I asked.

He didn't answer, but we managed to climb a few dozen feet. Will and I both still got soaked from the waist down when a giant wave passed underneath.

"I think the fortress just hit the ocean," Will said, but I didn't answer. We'd dropped again.

"Percy," I said, "what's wrong?"

"Low," Percy said as if even that word was difficult for him to get out over the comms. "Battery must be damaged. Should have told Arthur."

"You think?" I scanned the horizon, but we were miles from anything. Once again, we were flying so low that the waves were lapping our feet with little brushes of mind-numbing cold.

"Deep breath," Percy said, and then Morgause dropped us.

We were only about four feet high, but it still hurt when I hit. I kicked myself to the surface, gasping. The Atlantic Ocean was cold. My family never spent much time at the beach when I was a kid, but we'd gone twice to a place on the Gulf of Mexico. I was used to refreshing dips in mild waves after roasting in the sun building sandcastles.

The temperature in the Atlantic was the bone crushing chill that had me wondering how soon we would succumb to hypothermia. After all, I'd learned all about the Titanic and how lots of people survived the ship's sinking only to freeze to death in the water.

Will was swimming over to me and reaching for me when my armor fell out of the sky. One moment it was hovering a little to our left, and the next it had plunked into the ocean next to us.

"Thank you, Percy," I said to the vanished armor. "You got us out safe." I had a copy of his program stored on my tablet back home, but I would miss this copy of my outrageous AI.

"So much for a comfortable ride home," I tried to say, turning to Will, but my teeth were chattering too hard to speak. I had no idea how Will seemed unaffected by the cold. He patiently treaded water next to me as if we were hanging out at a year-end pool party. I was trying to float, but I kept getting slapped in the face with waves and accidentally swallowing salt water. I would probably pickle from the inside out.

There was a noise behind us. Turning, I found my armor bobbing next to us. I had assumed the thing would sink like a rock to become another piece of deep ocean debris. I had never dreamed the knights could float. It hadn't floated while I was in it at the bottom of Arthur's moat. However, I now realized that might have been something Percy had done on purpose.

Will and I swam for the armor, and I grabbed on. Will climbed onto the armor's chest. It was weird and awkward, and he nearly flipped off it trying to get on.

"You can do this," he said once he was up there. "It's not much harder than getting on a surfboard after falling off in deep water."

I'd never been on a surfboard in my life, but I also didn't want to stay in the ocean. It felt like my life was leaching away into the water to mingle with the salts. I somehow managed to clamber over my knight's legs and then sort of pull myself onto the torso. I almost capsized us twice, and I used a lot of words that would have gotten me instant detentions if I had muttered them in school. When I finally got on, I somehow sort of leveraged myself forward so I fell flat on my face onto Will. I sat up so fast I nearly dumped us into the water again, and my face was now so red, my cheeks could single-handedly dry us off.

When I could bring myself to glance at Will's face, he was grinning. Mercifully, he chose not to comment in the face of my obvious discomfort.

Instead, he pulled off his jacket and peeled at his dripping wet shirt so that I got a glimpse of his abs. Little drops of water glistened on his six pack. To my horror, I stared as if my eyes had lost the ability to look away. He wrung at his shirt squeezing out some of the water.

"Like the view?" Will asked. "You're staring hard enough."

I snapped my eyes back up to his face. Will's grin before was nothing compared to the satisfaction oozing from him now.

"You're doing this on purpose," I said, narrowing my eyes. "You're trying to distract me from that conversation we need to have." For a second, he had also distracted me from how cold I was. It was a lot warmer sitting on my armor than it had been in the water, but I still shivered.

Will shrugged, but he didn't deny it.

I looked away at the horizon. I had no idea which direction led to the—hopefully sinking—flying fortress and the knights that would fly from there to rescue us. Everything looked the same from the surface of the water.

"Would you have really killed me?" I finally asked. I didn't turn back around because I didn't want to see Will's face when he admitted that he would have.

"What, no?" Will sounded horrified. When I didn't look back over, Will nudged my chin in his direction with his finger. His touch was so light, I could have resisted if I wanted, but I turned to him. Will frowned, his eyes not quite meeting mine. I couldn't tell if he was upset because he had scared me back at the Dreki base or because I believed him capable of shooting me in the head if those were his orders.

"Elaine, it was a bluff. I was trying to distract Evie while I figured out what to do. The Dreki, possibly her father, were watching through those cameras. She couldn't help, and I needed to think of a plausible way for it to appear like we escaped her. Pretending I'd kill you would buy us some time. I was hoping whoever was watching would tell Evie to stand down."

"So, there's no standing kill order?" I asked just to make sure.

Will shook his head. "LANCE hasn't given me one."

"That's reassuring."

"That doesn't mean there isn't one somewhere," Will added with the sense he was just being honest.

"Less reassuring."

Will reached over and pulled me up against his side. "Part of what made it a good bluff was that it was so believable," he said. "No one doubted for a minute that the controller had ordered something like that."

I shook my head, thwapping Will in the back with my wet ponytail. "I hate to say this, because I hate to think there's anything Vortigern is right about, but I think he may be right about LANCE. They seem like terrible people."

"The aims are good," Will said. He took a few deep breaths for a moment. "The goals, the mission, the ends are all for the greater good."

"But the means, Will."

Will's forehead creased for a second before he got what I meant. "Yeah, I'm also beginning to think the ends might not always justify the means." Then in a voice so quiet I almost didn't hear him over the waves, Will added, "But they're all I have."

In an equally quiet voice, I said, "You have us now. Arthur and Ginny and me."

I wasn't sure he heard me at first, but then his arm around me tightened, pulling me closer. We sat there for a few minutes, bobbing on my armor while the sun dried us and took away the worst of the chill.

"Do you think Vortigern was lying?" he asked at last. I realized this was what worried Will the most. "Do you think LANCE stole me from the Dreki?"

I shrugged, my T-shirt squishing against his side. "I'm not

sure it matters. LANCE, Dreki, they both want to use you for their own ends."

"I don't know what to do. How to be a good agent and not use this horrible curse I've got. As long as I have it, Controller Stormfield, Vortigern, people like the Dreki will want me as a weapon."

"We don't want you like that." I took my head off his shoulder so I could see him better even though my cheek missed the warmth. "Will, quit. Leave LANCE." My voice wasn't much above a whisper, but from the way he froze, he'd heard. I'd mentioned quitting to him before but never in such a direct manner.

Will gave a small laugh that wasn't funny. "LANCE isn't the kind of place you quit no matter how much you want to leave."

"LANCE isn't the kind of place most people quit," I corrected. "But most people don't live with Arthur Keep, with Pendragon and the Knights of the Round Table. Most people aren't under his protection." I took a deep breath, and then I did the bravest thing I'd ever done. Braver than kissing Will when I thought we'd die, braver than leaping up and punching a vastly superior, trained secret agent in the face, braver than jumping on Vortigern's back with no armor. That had just been my life at stake. This was putting my heart on the line. I said, "Most people aren't dating his daughter." I held my breath, waiting for Will's reaction and hoping against hope.

Will turned until we were facing each other. He cupped my cheek with one hand and stared at me. It was probably my imagination, but his eyes seemed to have turned a shade darker, like his pupil had dilated even though we sat in full sunlight. "No," he said after studying my face for an agonizing amount of time. "Most LANCE agents are not dating Keep's daughter. Thank God for that," he added. Then he leaned over and kissed me.

This kiss was different from the ones before. For one thing, we weren't worried about being interrupted by a hail of bullets. That kiss had been hurried with a touch of frantic. We weren't dangling at the edge of a battle, me desperate for a vision. That kiss had been brief and businesslike with no passion at all.

This kiss was slow and gentle and sweet—the kind that could go on for hours, maybe even days, if we didn't bother to breathe. This kiss was about us.

I had shut my eyes the moment our lips met, and that same moment, the future stretched out before me again in various strands. I shut that nonsense down before I so much as glimpsed a possibility. I didn't want to See what would happen in the next two seconds or what might come about in twenty years. For now, I preferred to wrap myself up in the kiss and in Will's arms. Nothing would distract me from this earth-shattering experience.

It might have only been a minute, it might have been closer to three hours before I realized that someone was clearing their throats behind us. Loudly. Insistently. Over a loudspeaker projected from a knight in a burnt—so even more hideous—purple cape.

Will and I broke apart, with a great deal of reluctance on my part.

"Lovely," Arthur said. "Is this what I have to look forward to every time I walk into a room? I'll have to get Percival to start delivering me warnings so I don't have to throw up a little bit in my mouth twenty times a day."

Will grinned at me. "He seems to be coming around to the idea of us being together. He didn't threaten to kill me this time."

I wrinkled my nose at Will before turning around and facing my father. "Dad," I said in a chipper voice, "we saved Will."

"I noticed."

"Yes, well, we're dating now. I thought you should know," I added in that same bright tone. I clutched Will's hand wondering if now was when Arthur made threats.

Pendragon's helm shot up so we could see Arthur's face, probably so we wouldn't miss him rolling his eyes at us. "I'd gotten the impression that might be the case. Ginny told me this was coming, and I could either accept it or be a baby about it. She told me to accept it." Arthur looked like he would start a grand sulk over accepting, so I decided to distract him with our other news.

"And, Dad," I added. "Will thinks he might want to quit LANCE, and I was hoping you'd make it so they didn't kill him for leaving."

Arthur shut his eyes, a pained expression crossing his face for a moment. He shook his head, but this wasn't about our dating. Arthur knew what a Herculean task it would be keeping not just me but Will out of LANCE's clutches.

"Princess, Will," Arthur said, and he opened his eyes back up. His voice was serious. There was no yelling but also no smile. "I'll do everything I can from lawyers to fighting LANCE soldiers myself to see that both of you stay safe. You have my word." His right hand made a fist over his heart, and he gave us a small bow.

I gave him an equally courtly nod and then smiled. Arthur might be ragingly immature and a real pain sometimes, but he was honest. He was good for his word. Arthur protected his own, and Will and I were both family. Even if I missed my old boring life, I now appreciated being a part of the circus act that came with being a Keep. I was glad Will was being folded into the show.

Pendragon's helm snapped back down hiding his face. I pretended it was because Arthur was too overcome with emotions he didn't want us to see, but I figured he was getting ready to take off. A trio of knights had just flown up and hovered around us.

"Vortigern's daughter and a small group of Dreki got away, but the Destroyer and the LANCE contingency Stormfield sent secured what's left of the sinking fortress." Arthur's irritated tone became tinged with sarcasm. "LANCE is picking over the tech in there like carrion birds. Fortunately, Morgause destroyed that knight-killing weapon, and Percival erased all records of its existence. Not a tech I would want in LANCE hands. Young man," Pendragon said, turning to Will, "you have no idea how pleased I am you want a new career."

The three extra knights flew down until they were within feet of where Will and I bobbed in the ocean.

"Your rides await." Pendragon gave us another mid-air bow. He reached over and took the hand I offered him. I had assumed he would help me stand so a knight could come together around me, but Arthur had a different idea. Pendragon tossed me straight up into the sky. Unlike the first time that had happened all those weeks ago, I didn't scream. Instead I laughed and aimed myself at the clouds, pretending I was flying for real, like the Defender did, with no armor. I knew the armor would form around me, and if for some reason it didn't, Pendragon—Arthur, my dad—was down below waiting to catch me.

EPILOGUE
THAT NIGHT

GINNY FROWNED AT THE SCREEN OF SECURITY FOOTAGE FROM THE Montana ranch. She backed up the video three seconds and played it again. Squinting and leaning closer to the screen, Ginny froze the image. There. The video looped there.

Ginny swore and pulled up the security logs for the ranch. It took her a minute, but she found the patch Tori had inserted to fool the system into believing she and Raul were still there. The timestamp marked the hack occurring just before the Dreki attacked the Rook and took Will. Ginny slammed her hand on the desk. The metal surface began to heat and glow until Ginny reined her fury back. She concentrated and siphoned the heat back into her body away from the table until the surface was once again cool to the touch. It had to be a coincidence that Tori and Raul had left the ranch just as Elaine and Will were put in danger. Surely, they hadn't sold their daughter out, cut some kind of deal, with the wannabe dragons.

Arthur rushed into the room, his face pale, his fingers making agitated motions as he reached for her. Ginny half rose from her chair, swiping shut her screen. She'd tell Arthur they'd lost Tori and Raul later.

Arthur got to Ginny before she could stand, pulling her the rest of the way up into a giant hug.

"What is it?" she asked although she suspected. Few things made Arthur this upset.

He shook his head for a second against her neck, but then he pulled away until he only held her hands. "I Saw the future shift. It's bad, Ginny. It's bad."

"You, me, or Elaine?" Ginny kept her voice calm, her posture relaxed, the way she outwardly reacted to all of his visions, but inside her heart began to race. It was always bad now. Except for the glimpses he'd gotten of Elaine and Will's daughter, it had been a long time since Arthur's visions had portended anything good.

"Will."

Ginny hid her surprise that Arthur now sensed Will's future too. Arthur had never once Seen Tori, despite her connection to both Arthur and Elaine. Will really was family.

Ginny turned, freeing her hands from Arthur's grasp and brought up the screen she kept tied to her hack into the LANCE system. She scanned the files for anything new concerning Will.

Her eyes widened when she found the memo with Will's name. Her hands shook slightly as she scrolled through to see if the request had been approved or was still pending. Her heart dropped.

"We have to do something," she said. "Stormfield's formal

request for termination was approved four minutes ago." She kept her voice controlled, but her mind flew to the two oblivious children tucked up in their beds. This would break Elaine's heart.

Arthur ran his fingers through his hair, but then dropped his hands to his side. "I know." His eyes clouded over. With only Ginny present, he didn't bother to hide the telltale evidence of his clairvoyance. When he had finished Seeing, he shook his head, his eyes clearing again. "If we don't act, LANCE retires Will in Stormfield's office in two weeks."

PROLOGUE

For my brothers and sisters:
Marie, Nancy, Amy,
David, Stephen, and Tony

First paperback edition 2008

Library of Congress Cataloging-in-Publication
Data is available.

Library of Congress Catalog Card Number
2006049575

ISBN 978-0-7636-3054-6 (hardcover)

ISBN 978-0-7636-3567-1 (paperback)

13 14 15 TWPS 10 9 8 7 6

Printed in Singapore

This book was typeset in Badger and Providence Sans.
The illustrations were done in watercolor and ink.

Candlewick Press
99 Dover Street
Somerville, Massachusetts 02144

visit us at www.candlewick.com

STICKY BURR

BURR

ADVENTURES IN
BURRWOOD FOREST

BURR: (n) the rough, prickly seedcase of certain plants

STICKY: (adj) tending to cling to things; difficult to deal with

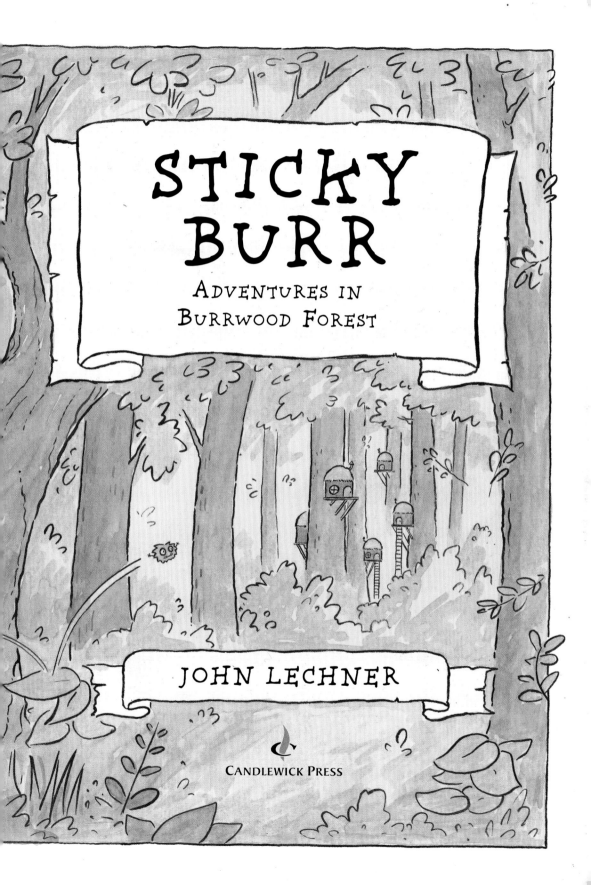

WELCOME TO BURRWOOD FOREST!
This is my village, where I live with all the other burrs. We spend our days gathering food and building houses out of sticks.

We gather berries in the summer and store them for the long winter.

We also plant gardens with wild daisies, chives, string beans, and sweet potatoes. It's a busy life, but we all pitch in.

~ ALL ABOUT BURRS ~

Me →

My Journal ↗

Let me tell you a little more about burrs. We are very small and covered with tiny hooks, so we stick to things. Sometimes this can be very inconvenient!

Me ↑
getting →
stuck

We tend to argue a lot, even when there is nothing to argue about.

No, we don't!

Yes, we do!

I'm hungry!

Our houses are built high off the ground, on stilts. Here is a picture of my house—I built a special elevator to get up and down fast.

And here is the inside—nice and cozy!

SCURVY BURR

Scurvy Burr is always up to no good. You might say he's a bad seed.

He is only having fun when he is making someone else NOT have fun.

He chases crickets.

He tramples flowers.

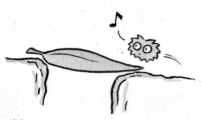

He sets traps.

He even takes candy from baby burrs!

His sidekick is called Spiny Burr—he's nasty, too!

YEAH!

The life of a burr can be very unpredictable! I hung on as tight as I could, but then . . .

INSECTS I HAVE KNOWN

Draffle is a dragonfly, and my best friend. There are lots of insects in Burrwood Forest, and you'll see all of them if you look carefully enough.

Ladybug

Cricket

Ant

Beetle

Wasp
(DANGEROUS!)

Caterpillar

Stinkbug

Mayfly

Grasshoppers are nimble and strong. Mossy Burr takes karate lessons from a grasshopper.

You have done well.

Thank you, Grasshopper!

Butterflies are like royalty. They don't talk much—just flutter around looking grand. Some folks say they can grant wishes.

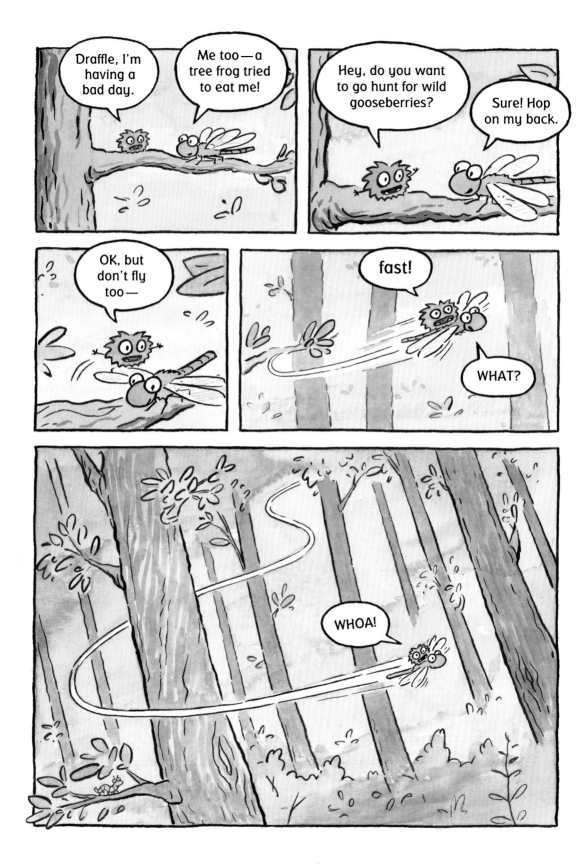

DANGERS IN THE FOREST

Wasps are the most dangerous insects in Burrwood Forest. Mossy Burr says to just be still and they will leave you alone. She is much braver than me.

Here are more creatures to avoid:

Wild Dogs

Snakes

Snapping Turtles

There are also dangerous places in the forest, like Gravel Gorge and Craggy Cave. If you ever visit Burrwood Forest, try to avoid them.

I couldn't believe my eyes. Growing right out of the swamp was the legendary Maze Tree!

THE MAZE TREE

My friend Walking Stick had told me about the Maze Tree, the most unusual tree in Burrwood Forest. It is filled with winding tunnels, and if you get lost in one, it is nearly impossible to find your way out!

Yum!

Walking Stick is an expert on trees—how they look, how they grow, how they taste. He even looks like a tree himself!

There are many other interesting trees in the forest, but none as strange or mysterious as the Maze Tree.

STICKY SITUATIONS

Life in Burrwood Forest can be dangerous,
and I've been in many sticky situations.
One time I got trapped on a branch during
the spring floods.

Hang on!

Another time, I got stuck
on the tail of a wild dog.

Finally he fell asleep, but it
took five burrs to pull me off!

Pull!

Once, I went into the forest to practice my ukulele and got stuck on a mossy tree. I called for help, but nobody heard me. I started to worry.

I made up a song to pass the time. It went like this:

Stuck on a tree,
Stuck on a tree,
Won't somebody help me?
Life can be funny,
Strange as can be,
When you're stuck on a tree,
Like me!

Finally Draffle came along and pulled me off.

Thanks!

We flew back through the forest.

Look!

But when we finally reached the village, we were greeted by a shocking sight. . . .

Later, we climbed the tallest tree and looked at the stars. It was a beautiful night.

Mossy Burr says stars are like burrs, and I think she's right. Each of us tries to shine out in the darkness and be seen. And every once in a while, we are.

EPILOGUE

THE BURRWOOD GAZETTE

WILD DOGS WRECK VILLAGE

The Burr Village was recently destroyed by a pack of wild dogs. Luckily, Sticky Burr led the dogs away with the help of some friendly lightning bugs. The wild dogs often roam the forest during the summer and are known for their fierce appetites. However, it is not true that they eat burrs for supper. "That's just a myth," said local dog expert Fluffy Burr.

MAZE TREE DISCOVERED

A rare tree was discovered in Dragonfly Swamp by Sticky Burr and Draffle. According to tree expert Walking Stick, the Maze Tree is filled with winding tunnels, which are quite easy to get lost in. Sticky Burr and Draffle not only escaped from the tree; they also helped rescue a group of lightning bugs who

had lost their way. This autumn, the Explorers Club plans an expedition to visit the tree and study it more closely.

HARVEST SEASON APPROACHES

It has been a busy summer for our local gardeners. Crops of sunflowers, beans, and potatoes have been better than ever, according to Tansy Burr of the Burrwood Garden Club. "The flowers are growing like weeds!" she said. "Even the weeds are growing like weeds!" There will be a harvest fair this fall, with prizes for the best vegetables and flowers.

ART EXHIBIT PLANNED

The first Burrwood art exhibit will be held this summer. All burrs are invited to submit a drawing, painting, or sculpture. "I'm making a squirrel out of pinecones!" said Balsam Burr, who lives in a pine tree. Other burrs are planning to make leaf prints, wood carvings, and bark paintings. If you are interested in participating, contact Sticky Burr.

LETTERS TO THE EDITOR

Dear Editor,

I am sick of all these cheerful and unprickly activities in our village. Please stop writing about them!

Signed, **Scurvy Burr**

Dear Editor,

Someone has been trampling the daisies in my garden. I wish that someone would stop doing it. Thank you.

Signed, **Thistle Burr**

Dear Editor,

Thank you to everyone who helped put the village back together after the wild dogs trampled it. Well done!

Signed, **Elder Burr**

NATURE NOTES by Sticky Burr

Trees are good for climbing and shade.

Trees are home to many creatures.

Trees give us clean air to breathe.

I love trees! (Except when I'm stuck to one!)

EVENTS

SUMMER SPORTS

The annual Burrwood Summer Games will be held next week. Events will include acorn throwing, rock climbing, leaf jumping, and the oak tree marathon, in which burrs run around the big oak tree five times. Sign up at the Burrwood Town Hall.

EXPLORERS CLUB TO MEET

The Burrwood Explorers Club, led by Mossy Burr, will have its first meeting at sunrise on Midsummer's Day by the hollow log. Any burrs interested in exploring the vast and wonderful expanse of Burrwood Forest, please come and join in. (Bring a bag lunch.)

ADVERTISEMENTS

THE BURRWOOD GAZETTE IS PUBLISHED SEVERAL TIMES A YEAR BY BURRWOOD PRESS. EDITOR IN CHIEF: STICKY BURR   REPORTER: MOSSY BURR   EVENTS: NETTLE BURR BRING YOUR NEWS ARTICLES TO OUR OFFICE IN THE SYCAMORE TREE.

Stuck on a Tree
a song by Sticky Burr

Bouncy

Stuck on a tree, stuck on a tree,

Won't some - body help me? _____

Life can be funny, strange as can be, When you're

stuck on a tree, like me! _____

(Try singing in a two-part round)